HAPPENSTANCE

HAPPENSTANCE

The Husband's Story

CAROL SHIELDS

Vintage Books
A Division of Random House of Canada
Toronto

For Anne

Copyright © Carol Shields, 1980, 1982

All rights reserved under International and Pan-American Copyright Conventions. Published in 1994 by Vintage Books, a division of Random House of Canada Limited, Toronto.

Canadian Cataloguing in Publication Data

Shields, Carol, 1935–
Happenstance

ISBN 0-394-22359-4

I. Title.

PS8587.H66H36 1993   C813´.54   C93-093838-0
PR9199.3.85H36 1993

Happenstance, The Husband's Story was first published as *Happenstance* in Canada by McGraw-Hill Ryerson in 1980. *Happenstance, The Wife's Story* was first published as *A Fairly Conventional Woman* in Canada by Macmillan of Canada 1982. This volume first published in Great Britain by Fourth Estate Limited 1991.

Printed in the United States of America

3   5   7   9   10   8   6   4   2

Chapter One

A T THE RESTAURANT JACK WANTED TO TELL BERNIE ABOUT
Harriet Post, a girl he had once been in love with. He
wanted to put his head down on the table and moan aloud with
rage. Instead he placed his fork into a square of ravioli and said
in a moderate tone, 'History consists of endings.'

Bernie was not really listening; he was removed today,
empty-eyed and vague, pulling at a dry wedge of bread and
looking out the window on to the street, where a cold rain was
falling. For almost a year now the topic of their Friday lunches
had been the defining of history; what was it? What was it for?
It occurred to Jack that perhaps Bernie had had enough of
history. Enough is enough, as Brenda, his wife, would say.

'History is eschatological,' Jack said. He stabbed into his small
side salad of lettuce, onions, celery, and radishes. 'History is not
the mere unrolling of a story. And it's not the story itself. It's the
end of the story.'

'Uhuh.' Bernie's eyes turned again toward the curtainless
square of window, made doubly opaque by the streaming
rainwater and by the inner coating of cooking grease. 'And
when,' he asked, chewing on a wad of bread, 'did you decide all
this?'

'Yesterday. Last night. About midnight. It came to me, the
final meaning of history. I've finally stumbled on what it's all
about. Endings.'

'Endings?'

'Yes, endings.'

'A bolt out of the blue?' Bernie said.

'You might say that. Or you could call it an empirical thrust.'

Bernie smirked openly.

'Go ahead,' Jack said. 'Laugh if you want to. I'm serious for a
change.'

'For a change.'

'History is no more than the human recognition of endings.
History – now listen, Bernie – history is putting a thumbprint on

1

a glass wall so you can see the wall. The conclusion of an era which defines and invents the era.'

'I get the feeling you've rehearsed this. While you were shaving this morning, maybe.'

'Let me ask you this, Bernie. What do we remember about history? No, never mind *us* – what does the man on the street remember about the past?'

'I *am* a man on the street. You tell me.'

'We remember the treaties, but not the wars. Am I right? Admit it. We remember the beheadings, but not the rebellions. It's that final cataclysmic act that we instinctively select and store away. You might say, ' he paused, 'that the ends of all stories are contained in their beginnings.'

'It's already been said, I think. Didn't Eliot – ?'

'But the ending *is* the story. Not just the signature. Take the French Revolution – '

'We've taken that. A number of times.' Bernie sat back, groggy after his veal and noodles. 'We took the French Revolution last week. And the week before that. Remember that session you gave me about the French Revolution two weeks ago? About the great libertine infusion? Rammed into Europe's flabby old buttocks?'

'Not true.' Jack pushed his plate away, belching silently; a gas pain shot across his heart. After twenty years the food at Roberto's was worse, not better – it was a miracle they'd managed to stay in business – and the old neighbourhood around the Institute, with its knocked-apart streets and boarded-up shirt laundries and hustling porn shops, was shifting from the decent shade of decay that had prevailed during the sixties to something more menacing. These days violence threatened, even in the daytime; and disease, too – someone or other had told him at a party the weekend before that you could get hepatitis from eating off cracked plates, and God knows what else. Furthermore, Jack had grown to dread the starchy monotony of Italian food; everything about it now, its wet weak uniformity of texture and its casual, moist presentation – the sight and smell of it made his heart plunge and squeeze. Was there really a time, he asked himself – of course there had been – when Italian food, even the fake Chicago variety, had seemed a passport to worldliness? Worldliness, ha! When the mere words – cannelloni, gnocchi, lasagna – had brimmed with rich, steamy eroticism? All you had to do was plunge your fork through the waiting, melting mozzarella and you were there, ah!

In 1958, Jack Bowman had eaten his first pizza at Roberto's, probably at this very table. Mushroom and green pepper. Bernie Koltz had been with him; it was the first pizza of their lives; neither of them could understand how this had happened. Jack was twenty-two years old, about to be married to Brenda Pulaski. The pizza – it was called *pizza pie* on the menu – arrived on a circle of pulpy cardboard, a glistening crimson pinwheel flecked with gold and green. Were they supposed to eat it with a fork? Neither knew. They had pondered the point, mock philosophically, until a comic courage seized them, and they had picked it up like a sandwich in young, decent, untrembling WASP fingers. The taste was a disappointment, catsup on piecrust, viscoid and undercooked, although neither of them remarked on it at the time.

In all probability, Jack thought, Bernie was fed up with Roberto's too. There was his ulcer to consider; these days Bernie automatically ordered the mildest dish on the menu and made at least a tentative effort to cut down on the wine. For some time Jack had wanted to announce, boldly, that they could both afford more than $6.25 for lunch these days; Bernie had tenure now (although Jack assumed, from Bernie's silence on the subject, that his promotion to full professor was not to be, not this year, anyway); Jack was slated to be Curator of Explorations at the Institute – it could happen any day now. They deserved better than these greasy menus and this lousy New York State wine, served in sticky glass carafes with bubbled sides; they should be kinder to themselves, move up a notch – nostalgia wasn't everything – and find a place where the tablecloths got washed and where the waiters looked less like hit men. There was food colouring, probably carcinogenic, in the spaghetti sauce – Jack could tell by the indelible pink swirls impregnated on the smooth moon surfaces of Roberto's lunch plates. On Fridays the place swarmed with wide-bottomed secretaries and sorrowing, introspective student lovers; it pained Jack to see how readily these lovers accepted the illuminated mural of the Po Valley on the back wall. It was time for a change, Jack had been on the point of saying to him. But he hadn't done it.

3

Something always stopped him. Bernie might balk; he could be difficult; he had always been somewhat prickly, and just beneath his pale, neutral, abstract freckledness lay an unpredictable populism. *So you're too good for the old proletarian hangout*, Bernie might think (but never say). *So now that you and Brenda and the kids have entrenched yourselves out there in Elm Park, you're hankering for something a little more country-clubby, huh*? Bernie's moods of grouchy unreasonableness had simmered and sputtered along for years, beginning, Jack thought, about the time Bernie's wife Sue decided to go back to medical school. But lately these moods had become more frequent – Jack wasn't the only one who'd noticed. Bernie preened his pessimism now. Brenda thought he'd behaved erratically when she saw him late in the summer; something he'd said or done, she hadn't been able to put her finger on it, but something was wrong. There didn't seem to be any single cause, although it might be any of the half-dozen phantoms that flickered at the back of Bernie's life – his stalled career, his wife Sue, his retarded daughter at Charleston Hospital. (Jack, who had his own set of free-swimming phantoms – who didn't? – could understand that.)

Whatever the root of Bernie's malaise, it was beginning to erode the old Friday spirit; the lunches – and Jack found the fact painful to face – were losing their old intensity. Sometimes, after summing up a crucial point, he had had the sick, dizzy sensation that the same point had been covered back in '75 or '68 or even '59. In mid-phrase his mouth stopped moving, frozen solid and self-conscious, stuck on a multiple memory track, gone gummy with overuse. Or worse, he heard his voice plumping up with an over-ripened, artificial passion that might have been seemly at twenty-two, but that at forty-three lacked moderation and civility and the *au point* Johnsonian balance he vaguely aspired to. And hadn't the old analytical machinery been more cleanly classical, more firmly grasped and more fruitful in the past? The year he and Bernie had discussed entropy, they'd managed to carve it up, beautifully, without all this rhetoric and false claiming of territory; it had fallen open for them with an open-throated, almost Grecian grace, slowly, mathematically, like a flower; he had *loved* entropy. *Bernie* had loved entropy, leaping in with the razzle-dazzle of a gymnast, a magician, glittering as he sprang from point to point. Demo-

4

cracy had prospered, too – they'd spent a year on democracy, June to June, 1965? – and the death of God, which started off slowly, but eventually led to scattered moments of near clarity – at least they'd gone into it bravely enough, unbothered by the chilly prevailing shadow of so-called experts, Tillich, Barth. But Watergate and the attendant moral compromises of America had occupied them a mere six moths, and now, with the concept of history – and Jack recalled that the topic had been Bernie's suggestion, not his – they seemed to have lost their way, making do with old arguments, retreaded, weary, occasionally corrupt. Sometimes Jack felt that they were simply reciting, and not very accurately, from under-graduate text-books: *A Survey Course in Fundamental Philosophy*. Clearly the Friday lunches had arrived at a shaky period, a critical period, and what worried Jack was that a change of venue at this moment might just signal the end – and that was one thing he didn't want to think about.

'Look,' he said to Bernie, enriching his voice with fervour, cringing to hear the squeaky tenor he struck, 'historians in the past have thought of history as a continuum. And we haven't been able to see what was patently obvious.'

'We?' Bernie knocked his head back, a cord of defence plinked.

'Universal we. Us. All of us, not just historians. It's our curse to overlook beginnings. Beginnings just don't register because we're locked into our vision of the status quo. We can't even be bothered to acknowledge the feeble stirrings – '

'You're not suggesting,' Bernie said, for a moment flashing his old Friday tone of false scorning, 'that no one acknowledged the storming of the Bastille?'

'Let's just say they didn't know what it signified.' Jack paused, shifting his legs under the table. 'It wasn't until a few heads dropped on the floor that anyone saw where it was all leading. And that,' he cut the air deftly with the side of his hand, a gesture he'd learned from long association with Dr. Middleton, 'that was history.'

'Hmmmm.'

'Maybe the French Revolution isn't such a good example, though. Too episodic. Take the steam engine – '

'Again?'

'When the steam engine was first demonstrated, no one

5

stood up and yelled out the big news that the Industrial Revolution had commenced – '

'Please, Jack. Please don't give me the Industrial Revolution today.'

'What's eating you, Bernie?'

'Didn't we agree not to call the Industrial Revolution a revolution?'

'Did we?' Jack asked.

'We agreed, remember, it was too poetic. Too cute, too much bottled-history stink to it. And it's a lousy example, anyway. It's too undefined. Just for once, give me something with edges.'

'All right,' Jack said. 'All right. I will. Remember I said this all came to me last night, about history consisting of endings?'

'So what happened last night?' Bernie asked.

'Well, let me go back a minute. Do you by any chance remember someone called Harriet Post?'

'Harriet. I haven't heard you talk about Harriet for years.'

'You *do* remember Harriet Post then?'

'Of course I remember Harriet Post. How could I forget Harriet Post?' A glutinous softening touched the sides of Bernie's face, his first smile of the day.

'It's been twenty-one years,' Jack said. 'I thought you'd have forgotten who Harriet was.'

'What about her? Isn't she in New York somewhere?'

'Rochester.'

'University of?'

'I don't think so. I don't know.'

'Well,' Bernie waited, showing impatience, 'you were saying – ?'

'She's written a book.'

'A book? I'll be damned. Good old Harriet. I'll bet there's lots of sex in it. I remember she had the thinnest little backside on any woman I've ever seen. I wonder if time's been kind to poor old Harriet's backside – '

'It's not a novel. And it isn't actually out yet. But it's been announced. In the new issue of the *Journal*. Which came in the mail yesterday.'

'*The Historical Journal*?'

'In the back. Where they have the forthcoming books section.'

'What do you know,' Bernie said with rising, almost subcutaneous excitement. 'Harriet also had very very strange tits. Very.

Ball bearings swinging around inside. Wasn't she in history, too?'

'I'm coming to that. The title of the book – of Harriet's book – are you listening? – is *Indian Trading Practices Prior to Colonization*.'

'Christ!' Bernie jerked upright and sucked for air. 'I don't believe it.'

There was a short silence, during which Jack drummed his fingers on the stained tablecloth and regarded Bernie's face. Outside on the street a car honked. In Roberto's back kitchen there was a minor crash of silverware.

Bernie swirled his crust of bread rapidly around his plate. 'Christ,' he moaned softly, his mouth loosening into a soft raspberry of helplessness. 'Christ.' He had a pale, witty, triangular face; there was a folded precision about his eyes, and his mouth was awkward in a sometimes touching way; women found him appealing, perhaps because of an inner ungainliness, the psychic equivalent of buck teeth or bowleggedness. A swamp of shyness dragged at him. 'All short men are like that,' Brenda once told Jack, 'especially short men with red hair.'

'You know,' Bernie said at last, working to get the words past his lips, 'it could be,' he paused again, 'that Harriet took a completely different tack than you.'

'But two books in one year, Bernie? In the same general – ' Jack stopped; a sigh sliced his breath in two.

'You never know these days, everything is so much more specialized than it used to be – '

'I did think of contacting her.' Jack fixed his eyes on Bernie. 'You know, phone her at Rochester. Out of the blue?'

'Well, why not?'

'No.' He shook his head. 'Well, maybe. But I don't think so.'

'The bitch. To tell you the truth, I never could see what you saw in Harriet Post. Those little tin tits –'

'Six hundred pages, it said in the announcement. Also maps, charts, and rare woodcuts. Rare woodcuts *never before published*.' Jack reached for the carafe and refilled Bernie's glass; pouring wine, even at Roberto's, never failed to give him stirrings of power and pleasure.

'When's it coming out?' Bernie demanded. He was alert now, intense.

'All it said was "summer publication".'

'Well, Christ, it's only January. Couldn't you, if you really stepped on it – ?'

'Not a hope. I mean, let's not kid ourselves, it's taken me years to get this far. It'll be another eight months just to get to proof stage. That's if I'm lucky. And I sure as hell don't have any rare woodcuts – '

'But it's possible.' Bernie's eyes gleamed golden under his fuzzed cinnamon halo. 'You have to admit it's within the realm of possibility.'

'Even if I could manage it – '

'We used to call her Sex Kit,' Bernie remembered. (Jack saw this diversion for what it was, a kindness.) 'After Eartha Kitt, I suppose. Though, if you want the truth, Jack,' his eyes narrowed, 'I never believed she was as sexy as she was cracked up to be.'

'She was.'

'That was before Brenda?'

'Just before.'

'It all comes back,' Bernie said.

'Like a bad dream. It wasn't, though, as a matter of fact. A bad dream, that is.'

Bernie nodded and chewed his lip; his fingers, lean but with wide pads, massaged the stem of his glass, and his eyes softened perceptively. 'About history – ' he prompted.

'Right,' Jack said, straightening, 'back to history. Where was I? When I saw that notice about Harriet's book, it came to me.'

'What?'

'That this is where it's ended. The whole thing with Harriet Post. Here she was, my first – well – lay. And now the ending.'

'Ending? I don't follow.'

'The ending is Harriet jumping me to a book twenty long years later.'

'I still don't see exactly – '

'It's an ending. A nice clean fatalistic conclusion. Lifted from the matrix – if you want to call it that – of what we can now recognize as the beginning and the middle.'

'I'm afraid I just can't see any cause-effect relationship between some ancient college screwing and the publication of a book on Indian trading practices twenty years – '

'Aha! But who said anything about cause and effect?'

'If there's no direct relationship, Jack, then what's the point?'

'There are other relationships,' he heard his voice ringing coolly, 'besides cause and effect.'

'My God, you're not going to be mystical and religious, are you, Jack?'

'Look. It's simple really. Here I've been grinding away at this Indian thing for years. And all the time she's been up to the same thing. Do you call that coincidence? Or do you call it historical destiny?'

'Destiny! Do you know something, Jack? That's a word I never thought I'd hear from you.'

' – and now the visible result. The ending. History.'

Bernie polished off his wine, licking the rim of his glass with the tip of his tongue. 'As a theory, isn't this a little on the surreal side? I mean, there are no real beginnings and endings. Mathematically speaking.'

'Maybe.' Jack eyed the drizzle of rain on the window.

'Anyway, it's lousy luck.'

'And if there's one thing I know it's that you don't pick a quarrel with history. You can't fight history.'

'Do you really believe that?' Bernie said, his head to one side and his hands spread in a lopsided Y. 'Or is that something you just this minute thought up?'

'I don't know. In a way I think I do believe it.'

'Well, do you know what I think?' Bernie said. 'I think your theory is a pile of horse shit.' But he spoke slowly, with compassion, bringing his fist down on the table so hard that the plates jumped.

Chapter Two

IT WAS JACK'S BELIEF THAT MEN SPEND WHOLE LIFETIMES preparing answers to certain questions that will never be asked of them. They long, passionately, to hear these questions, not wanting their careful preparation wasted. It was not judgment or redemption that was hoped for, but the experience of showing another human being that private and serious part of the mind that ticked away in obscurity. A wish to be *known*. And what they most desire is the moment when the stranger at the cocktail party (or the woman in the elevator or the man behind the bar) turns to them and asks, are you a happy man?

Happy? Happiness? Happiness is relative, Jack was ready to say (with an agreeable shrug); within the framework of relativity, he is a happy, or at least a fortunate, man. Pure happenstance had made him into a man without serious impairment or unspeakable losses. Evidence? There was a shelf full of evidence. He was healthy and solvent – solvency in the year 1978 was not to be despised. He was married to Brenda; how many marriages had lasted as long as theirs? He had only to look around him to see how rare that was. His children were reasonably normal. *Reasonably*: so far at least they'd remained untouched by drugs, shoplifting, truancy, and the other adolescent ills he read about every day in the paper. He loved his father and mother, who lived only a few miles away, and they loved him, although Jack acknowledged that their love, like all parental love, was composed of a number of darker feelings. He had one good friend, Bernie Koltz. His life had its particular rhythms and satisfactions. He owned his own house in Elm Park, which was now valued at an astronomical eighty thousand dollars, and worked on the staff at the Great Lakes Research Institute, the Chicago branch.

Certainly, as far as work went, there were worse lives, thousands of them. There was a neighbour of his, Bud Lewis, who worked in chemical sales and received a monthly rating from his firm. Sometimes he was number one; sometimes twenty-seven. There was his own father: forty years of standing all day in rubber-soled shoes, sorting letters into little wooden slots; retirement at sixty had been a deliverance. And occasionally when Jack was driving back and forth to the Institute he saw work gangs tearing up the streets; they worked right through the winter, these short, dark-faced, thick-chested men in their hard hats and padded jackets, hands reddened by wind, and feet heavy and inhuman in laced boots – where did such boots come from, he wondered? The bodies of these men under their stiff mud-caked workclothes seemed to Jack to be both wretched and nameless. But, of course, they weren't nameless; this was America, each of them carried a Social Security card, it was the law. Why then could he not imagine the streets and rooms where these men returned at the end of their working day? (He taunted himself with his lack of knowing.) He wondered if there would be food waiting for them, what sort of food? Would there be furniture of a familiar and accommodating sort? music of some kind? an ease of language that allowed greetings and disclosures? children? Of course – these things *must* exist. It was only some perceptual failure of his own that kept him from knowing. There must be women, too (what manner of women?) who stroked these men's bodies into forgetfulness and ecstasy before they rose to another day – 6 AM, darkness. Over and over again, Holy Christ. There would be a revolution – Jack felt sure of it – if even one of these chilled roughened workmen were to discover how he, Jack Bowman, put in his days. The softness, the security, the comfort, it was incredible, they would be goggle-eyed, they would chop him to pieces with their picks and shovels, the French Revolution all over again, and he wouldn't blame them. Sometimes, driving to work and catching glimpses of these men, he heard himself murmuring into the warm interior of the car, thank God, thank God. It had to be some kind of joke.

Here in his small corner office, the smooth walls hung with framed prints and diplomas and a photograph of Brenda and the children, he was allowed to pass entire mornings grazing on sets of footnotes or collating the latest journals, fulfilling the first commandment of the Institute, which was: Do not produce, but keep up in your field. This place was no less than a bloody sanctuary. Walk through the plate glass door downstairs and you were in another world; even Dr. Middleton, with his thickly planted, lushly growing civility, admitted it. Here there was a premium placed on lassitude, an assumption that leisure, far from being shameful, constituted the primary condition for inquiry. No five-year plans around here, and no questions asked. An occasional low-key exhibition, with the public invited; the *public* – that was another joke. Monthly meetings in the boardroom where a few items of business were disposed of. Jack could not imagine how it had happened to him – this privacy, this privilege; no clocks to punch; no timesheets to fill out – somehow, by some accident of fate, he had fallen into a job that matched almost exactly his temperament; let others scramble and scratch and change the shape of the world – all that was required of him was that he record and chart the flow of events.

Not that it was a particularly luxurious life. He'd known from the beginning that he would never be rich, not even wealthy. The low-lined sportscars he dreamed of – a particular dark red Ferrari swam into view – would in fact never materialize. Even the sixty-dollar suede vest he'd bought recently had been an extravagance. There was a ceiling now on the salaries of non-Ph.D. men. Non-Ph.D. men, in fact, were no longer considered for permanent appointments. When Jack travelled to Detroit or Milwaukee or Cleveland on behalf of the Institute to attend conferences or present papers, he was obliged to travel tourist class and, later, to hand over to Moira Burke the stapled receipts for his meals and taxis. (An endowment committee, Chicago meat-packing money mostly, examined Institute expenses twice a year.) He shared a secretary, away now on vacation in Colorado, with two other staff members, Calvin White in Geology and Brian Petrie in Cultural Anthropology. His office was small and modest, really more of a cubicle in a line of cubicles: industrial carpeting in medium grey, and a metal desk (only Dr. Middleton had a desk of distinction – mahogany, antique, immense.) The lighting at the Institute was blinding: a universalized whiteness that seemed to have no source. Jack's desk chair was standard issue, although comfortable enough; occasionally, returning from Roberto's on Friday afternoons, he had actually fallen asleep in that chair. There was only one window, curtainless, but with a neat Venetian blind; it overlooked Keeley Avenue, which was wide, ugly, and busy with traffic.

Dr. Middleton's office, which had an outer reception area for Moira Burke, was larger than Jack's or Calvin White's or Brian

Petrie's, larger and better located, positioned at the far north end of the building overlooking a tiny, soot-green park. If you craned your neck you could see a slice of Lake Michigan floating on the horizon. The grey carpeting ended at Dr. Middleton's threshold, giving way to a width of polished wood and a rich busy Indian carpet in tones of rose and blue. Jack stared down at this carpet, breathing in the cleanly filtered air, waiting for Dr. Middleton to get back from lunch.

'He should be here any minute.' Moira Burke told him. 'Why don't you sit down and wait.'

He looked at her closely, still a little wobbly from the wine. She smiled back cheerfully, and he remembered that Monday would be her last day; she and her husband were retiring to Arizona. 'The last lap,' Jack said to her conversationally. 'How does it feel?'

'Half and half,' she answered. She was polishing Dr. Middleton's oak bookshelves with an oiled cloth.

Jack looked at her quizzically. Moira had a good figure, a firm behind. Thick dark hair. In fact, she was a fairly good-looking woman. For her age. Fifty-five? In twelve years *he'd* be fifty-five.

'Half-glad, half-sad,' Moira said. 'I'm going to miss this – ' she stopped and gestured comically with her cloth, 'this joint.'

'But half-glad, too?'

'Oh, sure. Bradley's ready for a change. I guess we all need a change. I've been here so long I feel like part of the furniture.'

Was this a cue? It was said by Brian Petrie and others that Moira could be touchy. 'I'm sure no one here ever thinks of you as part of the furniture,' he told her.

'Hmm.' She straightened a book, glanced at her watch. 'I don't know what's keeping him. He's usually back by two. Must've got held up. This crummy rain.'

'Well, that's one thing you won't have to worry about in Phoenix.'

'Tucson.'

'That's right. I forgot.'

'That's what I mean.' She turned to face him. 'About being a part of the furniture around here.'

Jack was shocked into silence. What exactly had he said? 'Moira. I'm sorry. I remember now it was Tucson.'

Moira's eyes filmed over, and she shook her head violently.

The gold chains around her throat flashed. 'Just nerves,' she told Jack apologetically, managing a smile. 'Getting Mel trained for the job. It's taken a helluva lot out of me.'

Jack nodded. Moira's job was being filled by a young man with with shoulder-length golden hair. Dr. Middleton had announced the appointment at the last staff meeting. Male secretaries were coming back, he told them, an example of history repeating itself, back to the eighteenth century.

'I've been on edge lately. Putting the house on the market, you know what it's like.'

'Of course.' He hadn't realized Moira owned a house.

'Just my nutty nervous system.' She dabbed at her eyes.

'Can I get you something, Moira? Some coffee from the machine?'

'I'm fine. Fine.' She looked at her watch. 'I'm sure he'll be along in a minute. Any minute now.'

'I could leave it for Monday morning. I've got an appointment with him for ten-thirty on Monday. About the new chapter I'm working on.'

'I can give him a message when he comes in. Was it something urgent?'

Jack had brought along the new issue of the *Journal*. He wanted to point out to Dr. Middleton the note at the back about Harriet Post's book. Have you seen this, he had intended to ask, waiting for Dr. Middleton's calm, philosophical, transforming response, longing to hear him brush this catastrophe aside, to tell him how inconsequential this Harriet Post undoubtedly was. A housewife dissertation – he had once heard Dr. Middleton use that very phrase. But Dr. Middleton was still out for lunch; he might be another hour or two. Fridays at the Institute were traditionally relaxed.

'Well?' Moira said.

'It's nothing that can't wait.'

'By the way, your wife called this morning.'

'Brenda?'

'I left a memo on your desk. I guess you missed it.'

'I was out for lunch. I just got back.'

'That's right, you go out Fridays, don't you? Your wife just wanted to remind you to pick up some tickets. She said you'd know about it.'

'The tickets, yes, well, thanks, Moira.'

'Have a good weekend.'

'You too. I mean it.'

Chapter Three

TICKETS: DESPITE BRENDA'S REMINDER, JACK HAD FORGOTten to pick up the tickets for Friday night. They were eating dinner in the dining room, halibut steaks with zucchini and mushrooms, when he remembered.

'I'm too beat to go, anyway,' Brenda said. She was expecting her period, and besides, she was going to Philadelphia in the morning; she'd spent all day packing. 'I'd just as soon skip it.'

'Are you sure?' Jack asked her, helping himself to salad. 'Tonight's the last night.'

'I'm sure.'

Thank God, Jack thought. He and Brenda went dutifully to all the Elm Park Little Theatre productions, but he wasn't in the mood for *Hamlet*. Not tonight. The seats were rock-hard – the Little Theatre had taken over the old gym at Roosevelt School – and someone had told Jack that Larry Carpenter was a lousy Hamlet: he overacted, overreached, hogged the stage, just what you'd expect.

'What if Mr. Carpenter wants to know how you liked the show?' his daughter Laurie asked him. She had just turned twelve and had a twelve-year-old's knack for spotting future embarrassments.

'That guy's a turkey, anyway,' Rob announced.

'And what do you mean by that?' Jack looked at his son sharply, took in his slovenly adolescent posture and the arch theatricality with which he tossed back his long dark hair. Jack thought: once I loved this boy.

'The guy's a jerk,' Rob said sullenly, staring at his fork.

And just who the hell do you think *you* are, Jack wanted to yell. He had no love himself for Larry Carpenter, but he hated the shallowness of his son's bombarding judgments. And he could easily imagine that he himself fared no better than Larry Carpenter in this boy's eyes – my old man's nothing but a stupid jerk, a royal prick.

'I like him,' Laurie said anxiously. 'Sort of.'

16

'He thinks he's such a dude. Hot-shot newspaper guy. Zapping around in that Porsche. Like the way he squeals into the driveway.'

Ah, jealousy; Jack might have known; Larry Carpenter next door with a brand new Porsche and he with his three-year-old Aspen. Pure jealousy. Or was Rob, in some clumsy way, being protective? Probably not.

'What'll you say when he asks you about the show?' Laurie asked again.

'We'll think of something,' Brenda said. Her eyes were cool and unclouded – tomorrow she'll have left all this far behind. Lucky Brenda.

'This crummy fish is dry,' Rob said. 'Why do we have to have fish all the time?'

'Mine's not dry,' Laurie said.

'Have some tartar sauce.' Brenda handed him a bowl.

'It's got mould on it.'

'That's parsley,' Brenda said. Such calmness; how did she do it? Couldn't she see that at fourteen Rob's behaviour had become intolerable? It's just a phase, Brenda said. He'll grow out of it. When?

The problem was, his children didn't appreciate how lucky they were. They were strong and healthy; did they ever stop to compare their health and intelligence with that of Bernie's daughter Sarah, a vegetable in the vegetable bin at Charleston Hospital? His children had three square meals a day, parents who were liberal and caring, a real roof over their heads. Whereas he and Brenda had both grown up in city apartments, Brenda and her mother – she'd been Brenda Pulaski then – in three rooms over a dry cleaner's in Cicero, and Jack's family in a six-room triplex in Austin, across the street from Columbus Park. The house in Elm Park, in fact, was the first real house Jack had ever lived in.

On the day they moved in – Rob was only a baby that summer – Jack had wandered through the empty rooms, dodging the moving men, feeling effete but triumphant. 'Domain, domain,' he'd whispered to himself, loving the sound of the word; my window ledge, my front door. Fences, hedges, shutters, gates, railings, vines – all spoke of a privacy of outlook that neither Brenda nor Jack had been schooled in. There was also a beguiling density of shrubbery and a quiet, furred rolling of twilight across the damp lawns and well cared-for flower borders. The heavy General Motors cars backing out of Elm Park driveways on Sunday mornings on their way to eleven o'clock services persuaded him that post-Vietnam America was not spiritually bankrupt. There was an America that persisted despite popular notions; serious, quiet-spoken, contemplative men and women attended to their obligations and guided their children along productive paths. (A family on the next block subscribed to *Encounter*; it had once been delivered to the Bowmans by accident.)

The first thing he did when he moved in was edge the flower border in the backyard. 'If middle class means that people water their tulips,' he had told Bernie Koltz, 'then maybe middle class isn't all that bad.' Bernie had been unimpressed by this remark; deservedly, Jack had felt at the time, since he had partially lifted it, or something like it, from an article in a recent *Atlantic* – his own phoniness occasionally reared up and appalled him. Jesus!

'I'd like to live in this house for the rest of my life,' Brenda had said the summer that they moved in, lifting her bare arms to take in the varnished baseboards and the cast-iron radiators. Eight rooms of their own – his father had told him he was crazy to take on a mortgage at his age – at 576 N. Franklin, a two-storey brick house; the colour of pickled beets, Brenda had described it.

Bernie had warned Jack and Brenda when they moved to Elm Park that they might have Republicans for neighbours, but Jack had loved it from the start. Of all the Chicago suburbs it was the oldest (and the least suburban, Dr. Middleton's wife, nodding wisely, told Brenda when they bought the house). Even the street names glowed with a kind of radiant idealism. North Franklin intersected with Emerson and Horace Mann. Bud and Hap Lewis lived behind them on Oliver Wendell Holmes. Brenda bought groceries at the A & P on James Madison. Jack followed Shakespeare Boulevard to work in the morning and returned by the Eisenhower Expressway, his working day sandwiched between the poetic and the pragmatic, as he had five or six times observed at parties – a remark that he later loathed himself for having made and that he resolved never to repeat.

But did his children, especially Rob, appreciate the good

schools, the tidy green parkways, the supervised playgrounds, the well thought-of Handel Society, the reasonably accomplished amateur theatre group currently presenting *Hamlet* with Larry Carpenter in the lead role? No.

'I like Mrs. Carpenter better than Mr. Carpenter,' Laurie said, her mouth crammed with zucchini.

'She's nothing but a dumb blonde,' Rob said.

'I don't know about that,' Brenda interjected mildly.

'Doesn't anyone have anything interesting to say?' Jack tried.

'At least the Carpenters have nice dogs,' Laurie said. 'Especially Cronkite.'

'Cronkite's got fleas, the dumb mutt. They've both got fleas.'

'All dogs have fleas,' Brenda said placidly, rising, gathering plates. A section of brown hair swung across one eye.

Jack followed her into the kitchen. He put his arms around her from behind, slid his hands inside her sweater, registered warmth.

'It's only a week,' Brenda said, turning, smiling.

'I know, I know.'

Later, in the living room, they watched an old Barbra Streisand movie. Rob sprawled lewdly in a chair but kept silent, and Laurie yawned in her bathrobe. It turned out to be an unexpectedly peaceful evening. Once or twice Jack came almost to the point of telling Brenda about Harriet Post's book, but held back out of a reluctance to disturb this rare tranquillity. They ate apples, and crackers and cheese, and by midnight they were all in their beds.

Chapter Four

EARLY SATURDAY MORNING BRENDA FLEW TO PHILADELPHIA for the National Handicrafts Exhibition. She left them a casserole for Saturday night, Spanish rice with cheese topping. 'After that you're on your own,' she told Jack at the airport. She said this briskly, but with a certain rising sweetness of tone she had. She was wearing a new red raincoat with a zip-in lining, belted and notched and top-stitched, and her short brown hair, tinted a lighter shade than usual, had been freshly washed and blown so that it flew out like the tipped fur of a small animal. Ebullient, giddy, she seemed to Jack to be spangled all over with nerves: she couldn't stop talking.

'I'll phone Tuesday night, Jack, and see how everything's going. Listen, you've got the name of the hotel, haven't you? The Franklin Arms. It's on the bulletin board in the kitchen.'

'Okay.'

'Damn it, damn it, damn it,' she moaned, almost, Jack thought, like a song,' where did I put that boarding pass? I had it right here in my hand two minutes ago and now – here it is, I've got it. Laurie can fix pancakes one night, she'd love that, it would give her something to do. And there's always Colonel Sanders if you get really desperate and there's no reason Rob can't pitch in a little. And, who knows, maybe the Lewises will have you over one night, though I don't know, they're both so busy at the moment. And you've got that party at the Carpenters' tonight. *If* you decide to go, that is. Anyway, you can always get hold of me, Jack, it's not like Philadelphia's at the end of the world. If there's an emergency, I mean, knock wood there won't be, but if –. Anyway,' she drew her breath in sharply and floated him a brief dazzle of a smile, 'anyway you'll get lots of writing done with me out of your hair.'

This last remark, blithe, self-mocking, sounded to Jack like a sop. 'Don't worry about the book,' he told her, chagrined at the tone he struck, astringent and grudging.

'*I'm* not worried about the book,' she said. 'You're the one who worries about the book.'

'I'm the one who's writing the book.'

'I'm just saying, the world won't end if you don't finish that book.'

Was this lack of faith, he wondered? Or sixth sense? He should have told her about the announcement in the *Journal*. 'I meant to tell you yesterday – '

'Was that my flight they called, Jack? Did you hear what the girl said on the loudspeaker? I can never make out what they say on those loudspeakers, it all runs together. This is a real change, isn't it, you seeing me off instead of the other way around. I think that was it, Jack. Didn't she say Flight 452? It sounded like it. Well, then. See you Thursday. Seven o'clock. Okay?'

The kiss she gave him was nervous, close-mouthed, distracted. They were accustomed to short separations since Jack's work at the Institute often took him out of town. 'Good luck,' he called after her, aware that he was falling short of genuine heartiness and that he owed her something more in the way of a fulsome send-off. He should have brought flowers; why not? Or did you only do that at sailings? He glanced around; not a flower in sight, nothing.

Poor Brenda; it came to him suddenly that she had almost never, in her forty years, travelled alone. A few minutes earlier, when asked her seat preference, she had declared with pressing earnestness, 'Non-smoking please,' and the attendant, scanning the seating plan, had informed her that he was sorry that there were only middle seats available in the non-smoking section. Brenda, chin up, bright and amiable, had replied, 'Oh, that's okay, just so it's next to a window.'

'No, Brenda,' Jack had interrupted. 'He means that there aren't any window seats.'

'Well then,' she said with a complacent shrug, 'whatever.'

She had a way of shrugging with her voice, a kind of Slavic arching of vowels which made her appear to her friends to be a woman of great reasonableness. She could also, when she chose, suppress this same open, yawning amiability of voice, replacing it with a startled, rapid, pared-to-the-quick sensitivity – Jack had sometimes seen her switch gait in mid-sentence.

Today he had been pricked by a needle of tenderness, watch-

21

ing Brenda balance her leather handbag on the X-ray belt and then, carefully, tentatively, step into the walk-through metal detector. Standing there, framed by moulding, she had turned slowly around and waved uncertainly as though suddenly touched by thoughts of danger and separation. Jack had waved back, rather wildly, and for no reason that he could think of, sent her a boxer's overhead salute.

In response she lifted her arms in a wide hands-up shrug of helplessness. She was smiling. At what, he wondered – at the ludicrous idea of herself smuggling a bomb aboard – or a gun or a cylinder of heroin? Isn't this absurd, she seemed to be marvelling across the barrier, isn't this crazy to be standing here in a make-believe doorway – almost a stage setting, it's so phony – and getting riddled with rays, me, Brenda Bowman.

Departures and arrivals depressed Jack; the disturbing mixture of the significant and the trivial aroused in him a blunt sense of betrayal; why should moments of archetypal solemnity be undercut by the picayune commercial clutter of duty-free shops and mechanical scanners? Leave-taking was meant to be immensely mythical. Voyages – he thought of LaSalle's last journey on the Mississippi – should overwhelm with vast opening silences, not this noisy, amplified, greedy shuttling of human bodies. No flowers, no brass bands, no flags waving, not even an embrace worthy of the name. And especially he loathed O'Hare with its helpless public struggle to remain clean and contemporary; who were they trying to kid? If you swept the floor fifty times a day you'd never in a hundred years get the whole place free of gum wrappers. The indestructible vinyl surfaces were gouged with cigarette burns; someone had taken a razor to one of the Mies van der Rohe chairs; someone else – cretins, hoodlums – had twisted the branch of an artificial palm so that it hung grotesquely by a thread. Faint gusts of hamburger grease blew through the departure area, and a weary, blue, carnival sleaziness creased the eyelids of the girl who peddled flight insurance; *three bucks on your wife's precious body and you, Jack Bowman, could be a rich man.* Oh, yeah?

He managed, as always, to resist flight insurance; superstition kept him reluctant, and anyway, his belief in Brenda's indestructibility was complete. ('I'm going to live to be a hundred,' she'd said more than once, and she said it not with whimsy, but with powerful, persuasive certainty). Jack thought

22

of her purse, pierced by X-rays and showing up on some out-of-the-way screen as an innocent, open assembly of coins and lipstick cases, a nail file, a notebook with a spiral edge, a pen; they were all there, the lucky familiar charms that kept her safe. In his mind he saw her body spreadeagled under the sweep of the mechanical eye: skull, vertebrae, arms, legs, a luminous framework of bones spiked by a wedding band, a hair clip, a stray safety pin – well, perhaps not a safety pin.

His wife's body, Brenda's body; the thought of it pressed compellingly as he drove home through the light Saturday traffic: her familiarity, her particular resin fragrance and a frail, busy muscularity about her that made her seem both industrious and remote, so that the outlines of her body were difficult to hold in the imagination. (Harriet Post's body, paradoxically, with its slightly roughened skin and slack joints, was incised on his brain.) Did he actually perceive Brenda's body, he wondered, after all these years, or was his perception of her reduced now to touch and sensation, abstraction and memory? He had touched her body in a thousand different ways. Twenty years, in fact, of highly specific touchings. But this morning, Jack thought, suspended inside the arc of the metal detector and bombarded by busy rays, Brenda had seemed, momentarily, to lose possession of her body, as though some vital supporting fluid had leaked away, flattening her, making her seem for a moment like someone else's wife wearing a red coat and waving her hand at her anonymous klutz of a husband who foolishly, pointlessly, clenched his fists in a victory salute; ah yes, a man still young enough at forty-three (though faintly, furtively balding) whose wide, unbusy face marked him as one who belonged, unmistakably, to the vague, unspecified professions; a man with a steady eye, ah yes, a man of slow reflexes. He had let his hands fall to his sides, seeing clearly as he dropped them a vision of himself, a soft-looking Saturday-morning man, husband and father, responsible, honest, a trifle bulky in a tan trenchcoat, a man defined by nothing at all except the invisible band that connected him to the woman he had just brought to the airport and waved off, the woman in the red raincoat. The husband of the woman in the red raincoat.

He gripped the steering wheel, and with a careful and deliberate effort of will – he prided himself on his fantasies, their colour and secrecy – imagined the soft inner ridges of Brenda's thighs. (He always began at the thighs.) Blue-white, tender but with a particular spongy resilience. His thumbs rotated, stroking upward into the conceived hollows of flesh, tipping toward the taut triangles of skin over softness, a giving resisting softness. Hold it, hold it still, now it was coming. Her body was taking shape again, re-establishing itself limb by limb, gleaming skin, a firm coalescence, the distinct anterior presence of – what was it – fresh lettuce, Boston lettuce? Or something.

A red light. He braked with fury. There was a splutter of rain on the windshield and a harsh-ribbed washboard wind thudding against the side of the car. Next year, he raved to himself, when the book's finished – if the book's finished – I'll turn this bitch in. Get something with guts, something that jumps when the light turns green. Zoom.

Chapter Five

IT WAS A LITTLE MORE THAN FOUR YEARS AGO WHEN BRENDA took up quilting; where had the time gone? Jack had forgotten how she got started – another case of blurred beginnings – but it must have been that out of boredom or restlessness or perhaps a frenzied half-conforming, half-angry reaction to the many women's magazines she seemed to read at that time ('How to Put the Essential You into Your Home,' 'How to Chase the Drearies from a Blah Corner') that she decided to make a bedspread for Laurie, who was then eight years old.

The design of joined squares had been cautious, primitive, almost childlike; Jack still had a memory of Brenda, a fugitive smile flickering on her face, taking him by the hand early one evening and leading him upstairs to see what she had been working on. He had been prepared to be generous. (At that time he nourished a particular belief in his own generosity, a guilty hand-me-down, no doubt, from the continuous stream of generosity pouring from Dr. Middleton, a belief that he now saw as somewhat oafish, even quaint, but that had seemed at the time humane and productive.) As it was, Brenda's quilt had surprised him. She had counterpoised the pinks and oranges and purples in such a way that they gave off a dancing, almost electronically edged vividness, and in Laurie's small dark northeast bedroom, furnished chock-a-block with Ethan Allen components – desk, dresser, bookcase – the new quilt leapt out with an insistent claiming presence. 'Very nice,' he told her. 'Terrific, in fact.'

'Brenda,' her friends said when they saw it, 'you've found your thing.'

'Brenda's an artist,' Hap Lewis told Jack at the time, as she slapped down a bridge hand in front of him. 'Not a craftsperson like the rest of us slobs, but a goddamned artist.'

From the start he had been encouraging. The children had both been in school for years and were starting to have lives of their own, at least he hoped they were; his own work at the

25

Institute kept him fairly busy. He'd done a number of papers on the LaSalle expeditions, some work on Indian settlement, and he had told himself that the time had finally come to get going on his book; it was now or never. He hadn't been consciously worried about Brenda at the time, but he had noted a number of small worrisome signs: her mother's death had hit her hard. And since passing her thirty-fifth birthday she had grown more compulsive and even a little demanding, though in bed she had become, each day, less ardent, less sure of herself. She pushed at her cuticles in front of the television, and seemed to spend an inordinate amount of time shopping; sometimes during that period Jack had come across lists of her errands tacked up in the kitchen – measure shoe laces, return coat, toothpaste, post office. One terrible and memorable Saturday morning, four years ago, she had gone downtown to Stevens and bought six guest towels for the downstairs bathroom, then discovered when she got home that they were the wrong shade of blue, too purple, too dark. Her response had been to weep, ferociously, helplessly, and at length. Jack had lain with her on top of the striped comforter in their bedroom, holding her in his arms, murmuring into her hair the litany of comforts that he had once chanted to Rob and Laurie: there, there; it's all right; it doesn't matter.

That Brenda should expend authentic energy on such trivia shocked him into guilt; had he done this to her? Menopause – when did that begin? Not for a few more years, please God; he couldn't bear the thought of its terrible unknown and wambly aberrations blowing his poor Brenda up like a balloon and making a loose-bosomed, boxy-jawed matron of her, pouring poisonous damaging hormones into those slender receptive veins at the backs of her girlish knees, knees which he had kissed, please not yet. (She recovered from the weeping fit; they took a long bath together, locking the door; later they took the children to McDonald's for hamburgers, which they ate in a state of giddy exhaustion.)

Jack had, in fact, been pleased when Brenda took up quilting seriously, especially when he considered the alternatives. For a while she'd talked about going back to secretarial work, and she'd even sat down at his old Remington in the den and banged away for a week or two. But in the end she decided against it; she was too rusty; she would have to learn to use an electric model; on top of that the whole thing was unbelievably tedious. And it made her back ache.

Just as well, Jack thought; he was no snob, he said, appreciating as well as the next person the value of a good secretary, but Brenda's returning to the job she'd left when Rob was born seemed to him to be dismayingly wasteful. Cycles of any kind alarmed him; he'd got that from his father, the belief that you never go back, never read the same book over again, never rent the same summer cottage two years in a row, never retrace a mile of road if you can find an alternate route. Life was too short, his father always said, and now Brenda at thirty-five was saying the same things: life was too short to spend it hunched over a typewriter, especially when making quilts was so much more rewarding.

Jack agreed. There was something he found rather pleasing about the idea of quilts, about the combination of practicality and visual satisfaction – he liked that. He could even half-way understand the satisfaction Brenda found in bringing hundreds of separate parts together to form a predetermined pattern; in this respect, he told Brenda, it was not so different from his own research on Indian trading practices. (She had smiled at this analogy – what an ass he was at times!) Quilting seemed to him more substantial, more robust than the needlepoint his mother had once done, those chair covers, those stitched birds in tiny frames; it was more than a question of fashion or scale – it amounted to a whole attitude. Quiltmaking had a built-in generosity: quilts were made to give to brides, to cover children, to wrap about the legs of the elderly and infirm. And as an art it was less deliberate, less abstract, less *artsy* than the batik and copper enamelling and abstract sculpture that some of Brenda's friends did. Hap Lewis's wall weavings with their loops and swags of wool reminded Jack of obscene bodily processes. Quilting, on the other hand, had a tradition which he as a historian could appreciate, New World in its boldness and in its blend of utility and design, in tune with the past but in harmony with the recycling psychology of the seventies, *et cetera, et cetera,* a craft, he had once told Bernie, that had powerful historical resonance. (Medieval knights wore quilted material under their armour for warmth and to prevent chafing. Mary Queen of Scots quilted in her prison to pass the time.)

For Christmas Jack bought Brenda a fairly expensive illustrated history called *Quiltmaking in America*. And it was he who had pointed out to her the quilting design course offered at the Art Institute, urging her to sign up. She had been hesitant, she hated night driving, especially downtown; it was on her bridge night, anyway. 'What have you got to lose?' Jack said – then wildly added, 'Who knows, you might even want to get into it professionally someday.'

In the end she had gone. Two of her friends registered with her, but only Brenda stuck it out until spring. A year later her design project, *Spruce Forest*, won first prize in the Chicago Craft Show and was sold for six hundred dollars.

Six hundred dollars! Jack had been astounded – though he managed to conceal his amazement from Brenda – that anyone would lay out that kind of money for a quilt; it was incredible, he told Bernie Koltz over lunch, six hundred bucks for a *quilt*. And even more amazing was the fact that the couple who bought the quilt, a fairly well-known nightclub comedian and his singer wife, planned to put it not on a bed, but on the living-room wall of their Oldtown house. 'When I look at that quilt,' the comedian told Jack over drinks at the craft show reception, 'I feel as though I'm entering a green cube of the absolutest purity.'

The nonchalance with which Brenda had parted with *Spruce Forest* ('So long, pal,' she'd said, wrapping it in tissue paper and folding it inside a Del Monte pineapple carton) forced Jack to revise his idea of her as a sentimental collector of trivia: Brenda with her wedding photos, her baby scrapbooks, her boxes of old birthday cards and theatre programmes – where had all that gone, Jack asked himself; where was the Brenda of old? Her success at the craft show, instead of weighing her down with solemnity, had seemed to loosen in her a jingle of newly minted mirth, investing her familiar daily mannerisms, her comings and goings, with a spritely cheekiness; she had tossed her first-prize certificate (with her name, Brenda Bowman, printed inside a circle of stylized oak leaves) into a desk drawer where it lay beneath a clutter of old letters. She began to work on another quilt, spending up to three or four hours a day on it, and at night, instead of being tired, she became suddenly flippant and ready in bed, chucklingly irreverent even at the peak of orgasm. She seemed newly gifted with a random knowing; ten or twelve times in the last three years they had experienced nights of extravagant sexual adventure. Something had happened, something untellable. Once it had been otherwise; once she had demanded soft words, endearments, subtlety, and all the patience Jack could muster. Now she roared and bounced and moaned and then, later, in a post coital embrace, the same sort of embrace she once sought to prolong, she frequently signalled her desire for release by giving Jack's shoulder a light dismissing double pat. There was a consumed gaiety in that simple patting gesture. He had been surprised at first, then amused. Pat, pat, he waited for it now. She stopped worrying about the children, about Rob's social adjustment (all children are basically self-centred) and Laurie's weight problem (all children are either too fat or too thin). When she fried eggs in the morning she hummed *Greensleeves* or *Amazing Grace*.

Eventually, after she'd finished half a dozen quilts, she made up her mind to turn the fourth bedroom into a work space. It was on the south side of the house; the light would be just right. 'Besides,' she told Jack, 'no one has a guestroom anymore.'

'Really?' he asked, doubtful, but, at the same time ready to take her word for it; she had always had a knack for summing up. And for firmly, though off-handedly, keeping him up to date on her social readings. No one, she told him, except maybe Bernie Koltz, wears poplin windbreakers anymore; no one gives those Saturday-night dinners for eight anymore; no one goes to Bermuda nowadays, what with the political mess; no one who lives in a city keeps two cars when the world is running out of oil; no one, with the exception of Janey Carpenter next door, goes out every spring and buys a new golf skirt, a golf skirt!

Jack lacked, it seemed, Brenda's talent, the specialized sensitivity to qualify as a decoder of modern life; his conclusions were slower to ripen, and Brenda's pronouncements, though delivered with chiming friendliness, carried with them a faint whiff of custodianship. And the suggestion that he, Jack Bowman, was something of a social retardant, a woolly academic type for whom she was, nevertheless, willing to take responsibility. She was usually right – he had to admit that – and certainly it was absurd to maintain a guestroom when Brenda needed the space. He, after all, had a den where he kept his papers and research files and where he was supposed to be polishing up his book on Indian trading practices.

Her new workroom – he was grateful she had resisted calling

it a studio or, worse, an *atelier* – was hectically, openly cheerful. (Brenda is such an 'open' person, Hap Lewis was always saying.) Her quilting frame filled all of one wall with brilliant transitory colour, and a waxed pine dresser of considerable beauty (his mother's) held her sewing things, her patterns and sketches, her shears and spools; at the sunny uncurtained south window, overlooking the Carpenters' new cedar deck, hung a rapidly multiplying, immensely fertile spider plant. Yards of printed fabric – she was working her way into the yellow family, she said – swirled out of baskets and drawers. If her friends happened to drop by in the afternoon for coffee she brought them up to this room, which had become, almost overnight it seemed to Jack, the radiant core of a house that now felt timidly underfurnished and strangely formal.

Sometimes when Jack got home from work at six he would find them still there, Andrea Lord or Leah Wallberg or Hap Lewis – Hap Lewis with her wedge of ginger hair and her gift for unanswerable pronouncements – drinking out of Brenda's pottery mugs and talking the particularized politics of the craft world: guild showings, co-operative kilns, the aesthetics of mounting, the intrusion of technology, the ramifications of texture, the evils of adjudication. They would sit on the floor, these women, all of them in their late thirties or early forties, with their knees drawn up, ankles still trim for the most part, drinking their coffee in excited sips and jabbing the air with their filter-tipped cigarettes. Their voices arched soprano, searching over the mysteries of the things they made with their hands.

Things. That was what Jack could never reconcile, the fact that all their finely channelled sensitivity was spent on the creation of *things*; couldn't they see that? In their headlong rush to looms and silk screens (and in Andrea Lord's case to a spinning wheel) hadn't Brenda and her friends lost sight of the fact that all their energy led back, in the end, to things?

Because it did seem to Jack in his more clear-headed days, his wise days he called them, when the Aspen was washed and greased, his overcoat despotted, the morning coffee hot and dark and plentiful and poured by Brenda, looking thoughtful and tender in her belted robe, that this worship of *things* ran counter to the whole struggle of the race. The thought came to him, now and then, of a particular ancient earthenware bowl which had been on permanent display at the Institute since he'd started there years ago. Much mended and badly faded, it was estimated by the ceramics people to have been in continuous daily use for more than three hundred years. This particular bowl, brought from France it was thought, was of rather remarkable delicacy – considering the crude state of provincial pottery in that period – and had doubtless survived because it had been handled with the care normally given a holy object. It may even have *been* a holy object, since sanctity, as Dr. Middleton frequently reminded the staff, tends to attach to those objects which are most clearly matched with human need. That poor brown stupid bowl had done all that was asked of it, and it had done it day after day after day. Its importance was earned, and Jack could freely acknowledge its value to a pre-industrial society; if he'd been one of them he'd gladly have got down on his knees when the bowl was passed his way, gladly have lifted it to reverential lips. But haven't we – and in his brain a quizzical eyebrow went up – haven't we gone beyond all that? What about the spirit behind the bowl? What about the platonic idea of truth behind all objects? Wasn't the refining and shaping of ideas the important thing, and not filling up the world with more and more objects?

He would like to have discussed this seeming contradiction with Brenda, and he had even got as far as imagining when this discussion might take place: on a Sunday morning, the two of them waking late to the swell of music from the clock radio – he loved the comforting sound of full-bodied hymns launched clumsily into the airwaves by untidy, untrained mixed choirs; the sun from the east window would throw tipped parallelograms of light across the bed, and Brenda, languorous in the blue-printed sheets, propped sleepy and froggy-voiced on one elbow, would attend thoughtfully to his argument, nodding slowly, reflectively. Little softenings would appear around her eyes, her mouth. 'I see what you're getting at Jack. Yes. You know something, you've got a point there.'

But the time when he might have begun such a discussion had passed. For some reason – slow reflexes perhaps or simple absent-mindedness – he had failed to seize the moment when the question had possessed relevance or promise. This one small silence on his part had opened to a series of silences; acceptable silences on the whole, topics too delicate to touch

31

upon (such as the news about Harriet Post's book) or too small to be given distinction. The name of Brenda's latest quilt, the one she hoped would win her a prize in Philadelphia, was *The Second Coming*. Was there something symbolic in that title, Jack wondered; something sexual? He hadn't asked. A soft whittling away of truth, or at least of confrontation, had placed the two of them in the safety zone: with the happily married, with the reasonably content, the spiritually intact.

Another thing: he was not altogether certain about the philosophical underpinnings of an argument about materialism; he would have to think about it, work out some of the details, discuss it with Bernie, get a few quotes from, say, Tolstoy or maybe Thoreau. Nor was he sure he could defend a life based on the abstract without sounding like a puerile hypocrite, he who last month had bought himself a sixty-dollar suede vest, he who yearned after Italian sports cars. Yeah, yeah, we know your type, some big man of ideas. Hah!

It had even occurred to him from time to time that Brenda, and not he, might be the one who was on the right track; by accident she may have stumbled ahead and laid her hands on what really mattered in the world – things, things. Historical potency and all the razzle-dazzle that went with it might reside not in amorphous systems of thought at all, but in the concrete, the measurable, the patently visible. Pots and quilts just might, in the end, lead to the final knowledge, whatever the hell that meant.

He doubted it, though.

Still, Brenda's contentment flowed from the kind of innocent vision for which one did not set traps, and her faith was too matter-of-factly assured anyway to be threatened by casual intellectual scepticism of the Sunday morning variety. Especially, he admitted to himself, especially coming from him.

Chapter Six

FOR LUNCH HE ATE A BANANA, STANDING IN THE KITCHEN, looking out the window. A grey comfortless sky pressed through the trees with the density of packed satin. It was headache weather, manic-depression weather, but at least the rain had stopped. The two backyard maples and the ornamental cherry, leafless and frenzied and wretched, snapped back and forth in a continuous tearing whorl of wind. The storm windows rattled and whined in their old wood frames, letting in, around the edges, blades of cold air.

Jack found a new package of Swiss cheese in the refrigerator, unwrapped it slowly and broke off a chunk. The garage roof was in bad shape; even from the kitchen window he could see where the shingles had blown off. Heights worried him; he secretly dreaded the twice-yearly manoeuvring of storms and screens, but the garage roof was fairly low and not too steeply pitched; he might have a crack at it himself in the spring if he got the time. Bud Lewis, after all, had put a new roof on his garage. Come to think of it, he had reroofed the whole house – had done the whole thing in a week; Jack could see the neat grey edges of the Lewis roof from here.

Quite a number of the old dark Elm Park houses with their clumsy porches and yawning hallways had been patiently restored as Hap Lewis and her husband Bud had done, the good brass hardware around the windows revealed, layers of paint scraped from the mouldings and banister, an old stone fireplace rescued from behind a sheet of wallboard. A few had gone the other direction, as Larry and Janey Carpenter had done, and gutted the house, discriminatingly exposing a brick wall here and there, painting the dining room a soft oyster, putting a skylight in the bathroom and pointing up the old bathtub with aubergine enamel; the dim awkward corners could be filled with creamy suede sofas and smoked glass tables and rough-weave cushions and primitive Inuit sculptures and healthy potted ferns until they gleamed and glittered with restraint and energy and a sense of caring

Jack was no handyman like Bud Lewis – there was no sense in fooling himself – but it might be nice, hammering away up there on the garage. Early spring maybe. A Saturday. He longed suddenly for spring: he in a light jacket, kneeling on the roof while pale fronds of sunlight fell through the branches, warming his back and shoulders; there would be birds warbling in the unfolding air; the grass would be freshly raked after the winter; there would be Brenda, a cotton scarf on her head, sweeping out the corners of the patio, and the children jumping over the flowerbed – no, that was ridiculous; they were almost grown up. Rob was fourteen and Laurie was twelve; neither of them had jumped over the flowerbed for years.

He chewed his cheese and thought how possibly destructive it might be to stand around staring out of windows; it was something to discipline yourself against. It interfered with that fine-toothed mechanism that measured and accounted for time. You lost track of reality; you could become hypnotized by electric lines and the almost imperceptible way they crossed and recrossed each other; you could go crazy counting roof shingles. After a while, if you didn't watch out, you started swaying back and forth, back and forth, in rhythm with the trees, and then you'd really had it. No doubt lots of people, thousands of them, had gone down the drain just standing around looking out of kitchen windows. Like this. Boredom had its seductive side, an allure that had to be resisted.

The house was quiet, stupefyingly quiet. Laurie had gone off to perform her Saturday-afternoon job, which was to exercise the dogs from next door. The image of his daughter Laurie filtered sadly through Jack's head; she had inherited something of his weakness, his dependence on the good will of others; it was too bad, really it was too bad. For a buck the poor kid willingly, cheerfully, stupidly kept those two mutts out all afternoon while Larry and Janey Carpenter (The Prince and the Princess, he thought of them) pleasure-mongered indoors, rolling around, no doubt, on one of their white sheepskin rugs, trying it now this way, now that, now standing on their heads. The poor kid, round and round the cold streets with Cronkite the spaniel and Brinkley the airedale; she'd cover several miles before she returned. Sheer exploitation, Brenda called it, a crime, but it kept Laurie occupied and seemed to make her happy. She looked forward to Saturdays; she'd do it even without the dollar, she once told Jack; she loved it, she really did.

Rob had gone off to the track meet at the high school. 'Who you going with?' Jack had asked him as off-handedly as he could, but Rob, bending to do up the zipper of his jacket, had mumbled something incoherent. 'See ya,' he said, making for the back door.

'Hope they get slaughtered,' Jack had called out loudly, straining for a tone of comradeship.

'Huh?'

'The other team. Hope they get slaughtered.' Did he really hope anything of the kind?

'Yeah, well . . . ' The door slammed shut.

Peace, quiet. If Brenda were here there would be coffee on the stove. Instead, in the back of the refrigerator, behind the cottage cheese, he found a can of beer lying on its side. It was only one by the kitchen clock. He would be able to work on the book until six. What he really should do, he thought, is take the phone off the hook; that would give him five full hours, a good solid afternoon's work for once, with no interruptions and no obligations. Whatsoever. On the other hand, Brenda or the children might phone, something might happen, some emergency – better leave the phone on.

He looked again at the clock, whistling sharply, almost savagely through his teeth. Five full hours; a rare event; he was in luck. Outside the window a small colourless bird of indistinguishable species perched on top of the telephone pole. When it flies away, Jack promised himself, I'll get down to work.

For a full minute the bird sat completely still; then it twisted its bobbing, round golfball of a head sharply to the right, abruptly raising and then resettling its wings. It shuddered crazily and peered straight down so that it seemed to Jack to be looking directly into the kitchen window. Maybe it's hungry, Jack thought, thinking of his mother, who put a slice of bread out for the birds every day of her life. He made a move toward the breadbox, but at the same instant the bird darted from its perch and fluttered, against a current of air, in a graceful arch down onto the Carpenters' garage.

'Tough luck, birdie-boy,' he muttered out loud, obscurely betrayed. 'No lunch for you, kiddo.'

Five minutes had passed – only five? A short sigh escaped his lips, and since he was not normally given to sighing he felt a twinge of alarm; sighing, like yawning and scratching and whining, could become habit-forming, he'd have to watch that. Four hours, fifty-five minutes to go. The span of time opened before him like a body of water; he had only to glimpse its surface and he was stricken, instantly, by a familiar rising of pain, a sharp, acid-coloured clove of pain that entered at his chest and rose with swift suddenness to his head, his arms, even the tips of his fingers. Beneath the pain, he recognized, and surrendered to, a subtext of panic, a shallow void that sucked and taunted and seemed unbearable. For the moment at least there was no escape; he could have wept. There was nothing he could do to contravene the certainty that awaited him: a whole solid clock-ticking afternoon buried alive in the dark, lonely den with that goddamned book.

Chapter Seven

O N HIS DESK JACK KEPT AN OLD WIND-UP ALARM CLOCK, more for company than for anything else; its ticking was a reproof, but at least it picked away at the silence. Today, as always before settling down to work, he wound it tightly and set it down, making it serve as an island or a kind of territorial flag in the midst of heaped notes, sliding stacks of paper, chewed pencils, chains of paper clips, odd envelopes and index cards, apple cores so dehydrated they blended indistinguishably into the dry papery swirl.

From his briefcase he took the stapled manuscript copy of Chapter Six. 'Symbols and Solecism – the Concept of Ownership.' Dr. Middleton was anxious to see how this particular chapter was coming along, and Jack had promised, or nearly promised, to bring it in on Monday morning. Glancing at the title, which now seemed to border on the precious, he caught himself, for the second time in one day, sighing.

The opening paragraph – he read it over silently, nodding rhythmically at every comma – wasn't bad; not what you could call scintillating, no, certainly not scintillating, but it did seem to catch the point about the connection between ownership and status, and wasn't that what mattered in the long run? This was scholarship, after all, not Walt Disney. Keep your readership in mind, Dr. Middleton was always telling him.

But the second paragraph. No! God, no! He fished in a drawer for a pencil; paragraph two would need a little work; a lot of work. Somehow he'd wandered away from the subject and had got into the part about relative values and ritual which wasn't supposed to come in until Chapter Nine at least.

He'd have to go back again to the bloody outline, which was floating around somewhere under all these other papers. Christ, what had he been thinking of? A real digression, unforgivable, but then the mind worked like that sometimes, which was one of the problems with scholarship, the way it flattened and confined the speculative impulse. Should he leave it or cross it out? If he did leave it in he would need an elaborately detailed justification, and the thought of organizing a footnote on that scale was too oppressive to think about; it would have to be removed.

In a drawer he found a fresh sheet of paper and rolled it carefully, evenly, into the typewriter. Margins set. Page number. Indent. Now –

The little clock ticked. Ten minutes went by. Jack wrote a sentence, which was: 'The Indian concept of trade was vastly more sophisticated than previously thought for at least three reasons.'

The room was quiet. Through the walls he could hear the grim blue gnawing of wind. Brenda would be in Philadelphia now. Odd, how he'd never been to Philadelphia; all the places he'd been, but never once there. She would have checked into the hotel and registered at the exhibition centre. Probably she'd been given one of those little plastic name cards to pin to her shoulder – Brenda Bowman: Chicago Craft Guild. She'd be standing somewhere, a little to one side, but still well within the swelling flow of delegates who would be greeting one another, sizing each other up, smiling, making facile but cheerful connections – 'Well, I don't know him personally, but I certainly know his work.' Or 'You say you're from the Windy City, I have a brother out there in electronics.'

Painfully he rewrote paragraph two: the syntax wobbled, but the essence was there as long as he remembered, when he came to the final draft, to refer to the Iroquois in a note. He'd have to look up the exact reference, but he was sure he had it somewhere on an index card. It didn't seem to be on the desk, though; he'd have to leave it for the moment, get back to it later.

He wondered at times if his writing might go better if he had the advantage of more agreeable surroundings. These porous walls seemed to exhale the deadly gas of inertia. There was a chilly cramped look of underachievement about the den; instead of built-in bookshelves that would have warmed and settled the room, he and Brenda had made do with a pair of tentative unpainted bookcases from their student apartment. The file cabinet of painted metal was utilitarian and non-threatening.

Jack's desk was the same blocky, reproachful oak office desk of his childhood; his father had bought it for five dollars in a second-hand store in Austin when he was twelve, and it was somehow too solid to throw away. ('The wood alone is worth twice what the old man paid,' he told Brenda.) Jack had wanted to paint the walls the same apple green as the living room, and Brenda had wanted a sunny yellow, since the north side of the house was dark. They'd settled on a bargain gallon of eggshell latex which rapidly darkened to a streaky cream. It was a gloomy room, anyway; the windows were narrow and leaded, insistently serious, and the radiator, which was small and corroded, never felt more than faintly warm to the hand. At this time of year, January, the room was both cold and damp.

Their house, though he loved it, especially in summer, lacked style; it was one of Jack's mild regrets that he and Brenda hadn't quite managed to pull it off. The house – except for Brenda's workroom, which was a mutation from a much later era, had never really fulfilled its promise. What was missing was a vividness and direction that was the essence of style. Could it be, Jack sometimes wondered, that he and Brenda were people who had no real style of their own? It seemed to come more easily to others. The Carpenters with their cedar planking and pottery planters. Even the Lewis house across the way had a kind of style. It annoyed Jack a little to think that Bud Lewis had, by dint of his joyless versatility, his expert home carpentry, and his knack for landscaping, brought a glow to the narrow old house he and Hap had bought on Holmes Avenue. There must be *something* in Bud Lewis, a smouldering of imagination, barely visible, which he himself lacked. Once, at the Institute, he had chanced upon a copy of a letter of reference addressed to Dr. Middleton in which he, Jack Bowman, was described as a 'hard-working young man but rather colourless.' Colourless; the wound had lingered for months; the injustice of it stung him to the heart. Did Brenda, he wondered, perceive this terrible colourlessness? (Later the pain subsided, became a memory, a portion of suffering concluded and filed away.)

'What we really should do is start from scratch and do the whole house over,' Brenda said from time to time, eyeing the beige grasscloth in the hall and the apple-green living room with its darker green open-weave curtains and chocolate-brown corduroy sofa (if in doubt, choose chocolate brown, someone had advised them). But so far they hadn't managed to get around to it. They were busy with other things. Or else it cost too much. It might be best, they said, to wait until Rob and Laurie were older.

There might, Jack sensed, be another reason: an unspoken wish not to interfere overly much with the substance of the house, with its still obstinate purity. He and Brenda wanted, half consciously, it seemed, with their neutral colours and sheer curtains, to do the house the minimal amount of harm. 'Your trouble,' Brenda said once, nudged by a flash of insight, 'is that the historian in you resists corruption.' In the early days of their marriage she had frequently mentioned his historian's calling, deliberately, proudly, interjecting it into conversation as one does the name of a loved one.

There was some truth in it; he was, in fact, hesitant about imposing the vernacularism of decoration on what had once, in another time, existed as an idea. This house – he could see it clearly in his imagination – had once, briefly, stood as a skeleton of fresh lumber, and before that it had stretched, two-dimensionally, on a sheet of blueprints. But first it had been someone's idea, someone anonymous and long-dead, but nevertheless someone by whose leave he and Brenda held their occupancy. They should have bought a new house, he sometimes thought, and written their own history. As it was he could never shake off completely an uneasy sense of tenancy, especially sitting here in this chilly, depressing den.

Brenda thrived in her sunny workroom upstairs; *she* never complained of feeling lonely and shut off; she liked nothing better, it seemed, than to shut herself up with her quilts for hours at a time – in these last weeks before the exhibition she had sometimes spent up to five or six hours at a stretch. There were thousands of stitches in *The Second Coming*. Of course, hers was a different kind of work, less demanding in some ways, less intense, but still it wouldn't hurt to think about redoing the den, putting in a larger window as the Carpenters had done, opening the place up a bit, painting this gloomy woodwork, at the very least have something done about the heating system.

Harriet Post. He wondered what kind of room she sat down in when she began to write her book. Had all those maps and rare woodcuts been assembled in a trim modern university office? At her kitchen table? – it was difficult to picture Harriet at a kitchen table. In a basement study panelled in knotty pine with an electric heater sparking away in a corner? He knew nothing of her life after she left Chicago except that she was living in Rochester; he had seen her address year after year on the alumni list, Rochester, New York, the same street, the same number. And he knew little about Rochester except that it was said to be ugly and have bad winters, but perhaps Harriet lived in a good part of the city; every city had at least one decent section. Probably she was married. (He thought of the springiness of her oddly shaped breasts, the narrow blue-tipped nipples, the colour of washable ink.) It would have been typical of Harriet to keep her maiden name. Perhaps, like Brenda, she had taken over the family guestroom for her work, hung plants in the window, hummed *Greensleeves* while she pored over her notes. God, the afternoon was slipping away; he'd better get going.

Paragraph three. He read it slowly, unwilling to believe he'd really set down these words. Could he actually have written this parsley-strewn clutch of sentiments about the purity of the Indian mind ('Trade approached the gracefulness of giving'), committing to paper what Dr. Middleton – chin stroking, lip licking – would call a romantic indulgence? It would have to go. Zap. Wham. Out.

But he paused, reading it over; could he afford to take it out? He needed every word; as it was, Chapter Six was fairly thin, thinner even than Chapter Five had been.

Concentrating, shoulders back, eyes level, he read it once more. Christ! Then, because he felt a desire to pierce the unmoving air in the room, he tried reading it out loud. His voice caught, a strangled squawking; he could hear a distinct Boy Scout earnestness. Jesus.

He cleared his throat, tipped back his chair, and read it again – much louder this time – in stage British, clutching himself at the throat, squeezing in the vowels, plunging from phrase to phrase, from curdled outrage to wet sobbing sweetness. He should have been an actor, he thought, brightening; he should try out for the Elm Park Little Theatre, must make a point to speak to Larry Carpenter about that one of these days. If a solemn prick like Larry Carpenter could be an actor – of course, he'd bombed out on the Hamlet thing – then why couldn't he, Jack Bowman, take to the stage?

No. Absolutely no. There was no question about it, the paragraph would have to be completely redone. He grasped the pencil, feeling stiff waves of refrigeration settle around him. The whole thing would have to go; tears stood in his eyes. 'I have no faith in this,' he thought, sighing.

And this time his sigh took in the deskful of papers, the cold room, the emptied house.

'I'm a man who has lost his faith.'

He said this aloud, knowing he was giving way to the cheapest kind of self-dramatizing, but recognizing at the same time that what he uttered was perfectly true. His previous and frequent – especially lately – midnight encounters with the spare unlovely belly of truth were nothing compared to the heft of this announcement. He was, had chosen to be, powerless. Avoidance had led him to a dead end; a gigantic spiritual pratfall awaited him. He repeated: 'I am a man who has lost his faith.'

As he spoke he listened to the curious lifting tendrils of his voice; the tone was bleak but unmistakably decent, and the words, let loose in the air, carried with them a certain richness of decision. Well, it was established then, his loss of faith. Officially.

Then, far away, he heard the doorbell ringing. It rang only twice, long enough, though, to send him stumbling, joyfully reprieved, out of the room to answer.

Chapter Eight

'BERNIE!'

'Hi.'

'What're you doing out this way? On a Saturday?'

'Just thought I'd drop by. You busy?'

'No. Not at all. Well, I was working on the book, but I was just thinking of taking a break anyway. C'mon in, come in.'

'You're sure you're not – '

'No, absolutely, I mean it. Come on in out of the cold.' Jack held the door open, dizzy with hospitality.

'Christ, it's cold.' Bernie, in a light navy windbreaker, was shivering. Bareheaded, his ears a bright pink – Jack had heard him boast that he didn't own a hat – he moved into the hall and set a suitcase down on the floor.

'Winter's really here,' Jack said with inane, florid, furious good cheer. Thank God, thank God for Bernie, the afternoon was saved, *he* was saved.

Bernie's round nose glowed red from the cold. 'When winter comes,' he said, rubbing his hands together, 'it comes with a vengeance.'

'And you're the one,' Jack challenged, happy now, though puzzled – weather was something they never discussed, 'who's always giving me the bull about the Windy City myth being an exaggeration.'

'Why is it we stay here in this city and live with all this grit?' Bernie produced a Kleenex and blew his nose loudly. 'Tell me, is there any material in the universe that is as hard and compacted and flinty as a piece of Chicago grit? God, you know something, I've got grit in my bloodstream, grit in the joints, grit in the groin, give me a few years and I'll have grit lodged in that little spot in the back of the brain, what do you call it – the seat of the involuntary nervous system?'

'The medulla.'

'The medulla! How'd you remember that Jack?'

'God knows.'

43

'That little black thing shaped like a cigar. It all comes back. First-year Psych. Actually, that's why I'm here. My medulla is acting up again.'

'You need a beer. How about a beer? If you don't mind a warm one, that is. I was just going to get one myself.'

Bernie stood silent and unmoving in the hall.

'Well, what about it?' Jack pressed. 'It's Saturday afternoon. Surely you've got a little time.'

'I've got time,' Bernie said, coming to life and slowly unzipping his jacket. 'Time, if you want to know the truth, is what I've got. I've even got time, in case you're interested, to deliver a lecture on the nature of time, *kairos* and *chronos*, extemporaneous, without notes even. I could go on and on. There's the human concept of time, the dimension of time, the incumbency of time, the sovereignty of time, the incursions of Chicago grit into the manifold layers of time – '

'Time to sit down?'

'But have *you* got time? You've got that woozie out-of-joint look. You're in the middle of writing. I see you haven't thrown in the towel after all. And I'd hate to interrupt when you – '

'Since when did you start being deferential about – ?'

'Since this morning. When Sue – you remember my wife Sue – when Sue informed me I was insensitive to the feelings of others. I tried, God knows, to tell her it was the grit in my medulla but – '

'Where are you off to anyway?'

'Me?'

'With the suitcase?'

'That, as they say, is a long story. A longish story. With many and manifold layers of meaning.'

'You're drunk,' Jack said appraisingly, stepping back.

'You're absolutely wrong.'

'Weren't you and Sue going to Fox Lake today?'

'She had to work. She got a call from the hospital this morning, could she come in and relieve somebody or other.'

'Again? Didn't that happen last time?'

'And the time before that. And here we are back on the subject of time. Remember the year we did time? When was that? 1969?'

'You may not be drunk but there's something wrong.'

'It's probably the tranquillizers. They take off the old sardonic edges. Give me this nice, easy-going, adagio style.'

'Tranquillizers? You? What do you mean, tranquillizers?'

'Sue gets them at the hospital. Freebies. Every profession has its perks, and hers are those little blue-and-yellow pills. They keep the libido trimmed down a bit too. Sublimation, you know. It's the thing now. Sublimation is sublime – it's the same word, you know.'

'I'm going to make you some coffee.'

'You're going to sober me up. Ah, the good host. You're wrong though. I'm not even slightly high.'

'Stay here. I'll be right back. You don't mind instant, do you. I'll make us both some coffee.'

'Did Brenda get away?' Bernie asked bleakly, lowering himself onto the brown sofa and pulling at his eyebrows mutinously.

'I put her on the plane this morning.'

'*You* put *her* on the plane? Now there are those who would see a hint of chauvinism in the way you put that.'

'Oh?'

'So here we are,' Bernie paused. 'You and me.'

'Just make yourself at home.' Jack called from the kitchen, running water into a pan.

'And the kids?' Bernie called, more feebly now.

'Out for the afternoon. Rob's at the track meet and Laurie's out walking the dogs next door. This place is a morgue. I'm really glad you came by, in fact.'

'Good,' Bernie said with a flatness of tone that Jack found curious and alarming. 'That's good.'

The water came slowly to a boil. From the living room there was silence. Jack found mugs – Brenda must have twenty odd coffee mugs, most of them in earth tones with rough unglazed edges that made his tongue curl back. He measured Nescafé and stirred in water. Cream? He'd known Bernie all his life but couldn't remember how he took his coffee. Anyway, there wasn't any cream. And black coffee was what he really needed at the moment.

Taking a cup in each hand, spilling a little on the hall rug, he came back into the living room.

Bernie had stretched himself out on the sofa. His Adidas, mud-spattered, had been removed. His eyes were closed.

'You asleep?' Jack asked, hesitant.

'No.' The voice sounded plugged and dangerous.

'Look, do you want your coffee? I made you a cup.'

'No.' Bernie turned his face away. 'Thanks anyway.'

'What then? How about a salami sandwich? Have you had lunch?'

'Sue's left me. For good. This morning.'

'Sue? I can't believe – '

'For good.'

'Let me get you a drink, Bernie.'

'No. Christ, no.'

Softly, solicitously, Jack asked, 'What do you want then?'

'Actually,' Bernie said, his face pressed into the soft brown cushions, 'actually, I want to cry.'

Which he did, to Jack's horror and disbelief.

Chapter Nine

WITH JACK'S ARM ACROSS HIS SHOULDERS, BERNIE FELL asleep at last, and Jack went upstairs to find him a blanket; the living room with its new storm window was several degrees warmer than the den, but still decency seemed to demand that Bernie's sleeping body be covered. He was adequately enough dressed in his jeans and sweater (a maroon acrylic, stretched at the wrists, pulled thin at the elbows) but the position in which he lay – his legs pressed together and drawn up slightly at the knees, an arm thrown awkwardly (grievingly, it seemed to Jack) over his shoulder – gave the impression of helpless nude exposure. In fact, at the back, where Bernie's sweater had pulled away from his belt, there was a curved, tallow-coloured moon of hairless flesh. Jack, arranging the blanket over the sleeping form, felt a shock of love. This man, this person, Bernie Koltz, was his oldest friend. Almost, in fact, his only friend.

Only one friend? There must be a measure of failure, Jack supposed, in the admission that he had gone this far in his life, forty-three years, and achieved only one friendship.

For Brenda it was different; it had always been different for Brenda. To begin with she seemed to have no instinct for discarding; Jack had always felt amazement at the way she managed to carry her friends like floating troops in and out of the openings of her life. It puzzled him that she was still in touch, after all these years, with her girlhood friends from the old Cicero neighbourhood, with Betty Schumacher and Willa Reilly and Patsy Kleinhart and even Rita Simard. And at least twice a year she got together for lunch in the Fountain Room at Field's with friends from Katherine Gibbs, where she'd taken the two-year course in Secretarial Science, as it was called then. Furthermore she frequently saw the three girls – these girls in their forties now, married and with children – from the typing-pool days at the Great Lakes Institute; Jack had once known these women too, but for him they had faded to the faintest of

47

images – he heard their names, Rosemary, Glenda, Gussie, and their faces rose up briefly from a white mist, then immediately receded. Brenda got phone calls, fairly frequently, from couples they'd both known when they lived in the Married Student Complex; it was usually Brenda, and not Jack, whom these nostalgic couples, passing through town, asked for. Not that he minded; Brenda was the one with the patience for friendship; he admitted it; she remembered names; she kept in touch; she had the impulse – or was it imagination? – to invest in people a clear corporeal sense of intimacy. So-and-So, she was forever saying, was one of her closest friends.

Close. A troubling word; it mystified Jack, and occasionally caused him a degree of disquiet – could it be that he was missing a piece of sensory equipment? Or was it a question of definitions? It might be, he reasoned, that Brenda's concept of the word close was altogether different from his, more innocent, or a little uncomprehending. Did closeness mean, as Brenda seemed to think, remembering birthdays and keeping the names of people's children straight and murmuring over and over those difficult healing phrases, *I know how you feel, it's not half as bad as you think, it'll look better in the morning*. It occurred to him at times that Brenda's friends with their confidences and instructions might be simply slicing the fat off each other's backsides. There was something inherently selfish about the idea of closeness when he thought about it; the long drawn-out confidentialities, damp and demanding, the giddy, wilful letting down of hair. Let my grief be yours. Let my anxiety rest on your head tonight, old pal, take my weakness, give me your strength in return.

And secrecy, always secrecy, the abrupt, theatrical, almost literal running down of a curtain. When Brenda talked to one of her 'close' friends on the phone – to the braying, wild-haired Hap Lewis in particular – she invariably cupped her hand over the receiver and spoke in a shallow, anxious, breath-wedged voice. Whispers, subterfuge, weighty suggestions, meaningful pauses. Once or twice Jack had chanced upon a roomful of Brenda's friends, and the conversation, warmly flowing before he entered, had lapsed awkwardly into a secretive, bitten off, embarrassed silence.

'What do you talk about all the time?' he'd asked her.

'Everything,' she'd answered. And then, seeing his expression, smiled cannily and added, 'well, almost everything.'

'Such as?'

'It's hard to say.'

'Why?'

She looked at him. 'Well, for one thing, we don't assign topics the way you and Bernie do.'

Her tone was reasonable but pointed. Her eyes watched his. He knew, of course, and had always known, that she lacked faith in his friendship with Bernie. 'Is Bernie really a *close* friend?' she'd asked him not long ago.

'Of course he's a close friend. Jesus.'

'How can he be if you never really talk?'

'We talk. You know we talk.'

'But you never . . . you never reminisce.'

'Maybe not, but we talk.'

'Do you talk about Sue, for example? About her, what do you call them – her adventures?'

'Affairs, you mean?'

'Yes.'

'Once or twice. Obliquely.'

'Obliquely! And I suppose he never mentions Sarah.'

'Good God, Brenda, it's a somewhat painful subject, for both of them. Can you really blame Bernie if he doesn't – '

'Pain is supposed to be shared.'

Jack stared at her. 'Isn't that a little pious?'

'Is it?'

'Well, here you sit with two normal, healthy, intelligent kids – '

Brenda was unmoved. 'Sarah's his child. Regardless. And here you are, Jack, his so-called friend, and he never mentions her to you.'

'What I said was he doesn't talk about her directly, but he mentions sometimes when they've been out to Charleston to see her – '

'It's really incredible.' Brenda shook her head. 'Incredible! And this is your closest friend.'

Jack had tried to explain, but it wasn't easy. He'd grown up on the same block with Bernie Koltz. Once, an impossibly long time ago, their parents had played euchre together. Jack and Bernie had gone through Austin High School, both non-ath

49

letes, both non-joiners, and after graduation they'd taken the 'El' downtown every day to Illinois Extension at Navy Pier and later to De Paul where Bernie eventually did a Ph.D. and where he now taught in the Math department. (He had never lost his busy, meticulous sense of prodigy.) Bernie had been best man at Jack's wedding – treating the occasion with enormous seriousness – and Jack, several years later, when Bernie met Sue, had done the same for him.

For a while the four of them got together fairly often in each other's apartments for dinner, but Brenda and Sue had not, even in the beginning, taken to each other. 'I can tell she thinks I'm a complete moron,' Brenda complained. 'She's always asking me what I think about disarmament or something.'

'You're projecting,' Jack said.

'I'm too dumb for her,' Brenda said.

'You're not dumb,' Jack said, 'you're oversensitive.'

'I'm sorry, Jack,' Brenda said. 'I really am sorry.'

They persisted for three or four years, and then the dinners gradually became less frequent. Sue was qualifying for medical school and, at the same time, was getting heavily into gourmet cooking. Several times in one year she served them strange, small, bony birds: pheasant, Cornish hen, quail, flamed in different kinds of brandy. Once, at one of these dinners, Brenda extracted a wishbone the size of her thumbnail; she slipped it into her pocket and showed it to Jack when she got home. 'This is crazy,' she whispered, 'this has to stop.'

Jack saw the hopelessness of it, but was nevertheless disappointed. He had no brothers or sisters of his own, and it had given him an odd thump of pleasure to hear Rob and Laurie, babies then, talk about going to see Uncle Bernie and Aunt Sue. In fact, though the children saw Bernie only occasionally now, they still spoke of him as Uncle Bernie; *Aunt* Sue had been dropped – Sue was nervous with children, once, years ago, asking the two-year-old Laurie, 'What did you do today?' After Sarah was born, Sue and Bernie decided to forget about having a family. (Sarah, five now, had never achieved consciousness. She was better off, Sue said, at Charleston, where they knew how to look after her; life was such a waste; Sarah probably wouldn't live long, Sue said; there was a pattern in these cases.) Sue and Bernie stayed on in the apartment near Lincoln Park, an apartment that had triple locks on the doors and smelled of cats and frizzled garlic, and Sue started back to medical school. Abruptly, to Brenda's relief, the invitations stopped completely. Bernie and Sue had a different group of friends – Jack scarcely knew them, but they seemed to be lean, energetic couples immersed in unpronounceable specialities, branches of Psychiatry or Demographic Studies or East European languages. Except for the Friday lunches and one or two evenings a year, he and Bernie had gone their separate ways. But despite this, Jack had never for a minute stopped thinking of Bernie as his closest friend.

A close friendship. Every year at Christmas he gave Bernie a bottle of rye, and Bernie gave him a bottle of scotch; it was a tradition, aside from Friday lunches at Roberto's, their only tradition, the outgrowth of a private and dimly remembered joke. The annual whisky exchange never failed to send Brenda into one of her rare hand-waving fits of atavism, full of Slavic inversions and lamentations. 'And this you call a gift. Between friends! A brown bottle for him and a brown bottle for you, this is a gift? This is caring? Jack, you amaze me, you really amaze me.'

Perhaps it was really true that men seldom make close male friends after the age of twenty; Jack had read something along that line recently. Was it in one of Brenda's magazines? Or a *Time* essay? Maybe in a *Reader's Digest* – he sometimes glanced through them when he stopped in to see his parents. Men were failures at friendship, the article said. The drive to compete and conquer or something like that was what did it. It froze the spontaneous bonds of affection that eased the friendships between women. (He had observed Brenda closeted with her friends; even on the telephone she leaned, sympathetic and nodding, into what seemed a sealed, privileged bathysphere.) Men, it appeared, were forced to make do with uncertain professional associations or with old, imperfect friendships formed in youth, unwieldy friendships that required constant efforts at resuscitations – the visiting of old haunts, or conjuring through the circuitry of alcohol, ancient, riotous adventures, staying up until two or three or four in the morning trying to remember what happened to old What's-his-name who grabbed them in a back alley one Halloween night back in 1944 and shook the living shit out of them; Jack's friendship with Bernie was the only friendship he had that transcended this.

Brenda seemed to have the idea that close friendships had something to do with the baring of souls; somehow she'd never grasped the fact that something else was involved in his friendship with Bernie. And, having this single and unique friendship, he realized that he was more fortunate than many of the people he knew. His father, for instance; most of his father's friends had died – not that he'd ever had that many – and as far as Jack knew he hadn't made any new friends in years. His father read paperbacks now and watched television and waited for Jack's visits. When Jack's mother went shopping, he tagged along with her and carried the bags; he never used to do that; it was something to do, he said. It was the same with other men Jack knew. Calvin White at the Institute was a man of single-ply emotions who had the soft look of a loner; he spent his weekends working on his model railway. Even Dr. Middleton seemed to have no real friends. Jack had heard him refer often to certain associates or colleagues or co-workers, and though he spoke of them with warmth, Jack couldn't recall that he had ever mentioned anyone as being a friend.

He, at least, had Bernie – and how many friends did one person need? There were the Lewises, of course, Hap and Bud. He and Brenda had known them for more than ten years now, and for the last six they'd played bridge with them twice a month, relaxed Sunday evenings in the Lewis living room, 1950-ish evenings, Jack thought: a cardtable and chairs, a bottle of Spanish wine, a dish of cashews. But he had difficulty thinking of them as friends. Hap Lewis had hairy legs and a coarse slamming way with a deck of cards and a rollicking aptitude for opinion-letting – she made a hobby of vivacity – and Jack came away from these evenings sick with pity for Bud, who was obliged, he imagined, after the cards were put away and the cardtable folded, to mount the stairs and take the braying, gesticulating, cursing Hap into his arms. (Though Brenda confided to Jack that Bud and Hap actually had a good sexual relationship and that Hap was basically very vulnerable. 'Really?' Jack had said, unwilling to think how this information had been transmitted and at what cost.)

As for Bud Lewis, he was a lean man with a dark wolfish face, a year or two older than Jack. He worked in the sales department at a chemical firm. His hair was heavy and cut in bangs like a stage Roman and his face was blank as an athlete's. He moved slowly, abstractedly, with a density of patience. An expert bridge player, he arrived at his trumps with a menacing, laconic bending of the final card. He also grew tomatoes from seed under glass and, on Saturday mornings, soberly tuned and adjusted the motor of his 1976 Pontiac. He coached his son's soccer team – Jack had never got over thinking of soccer as an exotic sport – and played a fair game himself. When he spoke it was in flat grammatical English, ploughed with mid-western half-tones; but also with nimble transpositions of phrase that Jack supposed came from his early immersion in the Chicago Lab School. Hap and Bud. Their closest friends. Or so Brenda described them.

Jack had doubts. How could it be true when, after all these years, the bridge nights still commenced with a good quarter-hour of heavy ice breaking? There sat Brenda, stiffly centred on the Lewises' American Provincial sofa with her hands in a worried knot, Hap flying back and forth across the room looking for her cigarettes, and Jack and Bud Lewis facing each other over the coffee table and saying: Have a good week? Not bad. What's new at work? Same old thing more or less, what's up at your place? Same old headaches with the additives, lobby group after us all the time, political thing, we think. Speaking of politics, what do you think of Carter hoisting the dollar? He'd better or we'll go smash, never mind the so-called line of defence. Nothing's going to save us but our own efforts in the end, I don't know.

At last, at last, Bud, with a look of chilly eagerness in his eyes, carried in the bridge table and snapped open its legs. Ready? He positioned the cards on the table. Then Brenda relaxed, Jack pulled his chair forward, Hap lit up, and Bud said, fanning the cards into a semi-circle, 'Here we go.'

The evenings always ended better than they began, and Jack, at times, almost believed Brenda when she referred to the Lewises as their best friends. Bud wasn't half bad, he'd think to himself at the end of a rubber, at least he didn't gloat over his slams, at least he didn't bore hell out of them with office politics. He seldom, in fact, referred to the office, though he did drop occasional clues about what went on in the strange world of sales, confiding to Jack a week ago that since business was slow at the moment, he had been concentrating on cold calling. Cold calling? Bud explained: cold calling was when you initiated a new contact, when you call unannounced on a potential client. Jack had nodded, *Of course, of course,* but imagined curt refusals, doors slamming. Christ, how had *he* been so lucky? His small comfortable office at the Institute. Dr. Middleton, ease, courtesy, open schedules, plenty of time, tea served in china cups at staff meetings. Tea! While Bud Lewis was out making his cold calls, the poor sap.

And who else could he call a friend? There weren't many. Brian Petrie at the Institute, Brian with his egg-rich aura of expertise? Brian had once confided to Jack that he spent ten minutes a day under a sun lamp; that had been years ago, but Jack had remembered, and the small confession of vanity on Brian's part had put a curse on any possible friendship. Who else? Larry Carpenter? He hardly knew him after two years, and had the suspicion anyway that Larry felt for him the same kind of condescension that he felt for Bud Lewis. To Larry *he* was the dull plodder, the man who performed inconsequential and unimaginable daily acts. The thought struck him that everyone might be a Bud Lewis to someone else, tolerated, examined for 'good points.' No, he could never be a friend of Larry's. Certainly he could never talk to Larry Carpenter in the same way he did to Bernie at Roberto's on Friday afternoons.

The Friday lunches: they were in a low period now, of course. And occasionally Jack saw himself and Bernie as they really were, absurd and a little pitiful in their scrambling for the big T Truth, a couple of self-conscious, third-rate, midwestern pseudo-intellectuals, tongues loosened on cheap wine and cliché nihilism, playing a game in which there was more than a suggestion of posing. Much more.

But, on the other hand, the Fridays, at their best, had given him some of the most profoundly happy moments of his life. There had been Fridays when he'd struggled around the corner to Roberto's through sleet storms. He'd turned down invitations from Dr. Middleton to lunch at the Gentleman's Cycle Room. At Roberto's he'd suffered bad service and cold food, and twice his coat had been stolen. But the pleasure, the sweet, reassuring pleasure of it!

Even the regularity of the meetings was preserving. Once a week. It made a time frame of easy proportions, effortlessly adhered to, having the grace of continuity without the weight of appointed occasion. On good days, on lucky days, the antiphonic reverberations heightened like sex his sense of being alive in the world, of being, perhaps, a serious man, even a good man. He felt strange pricklings at the backs of his hands, and a pressure in his chest of something being satisfied and answered. Not that the satisfaction was actually sexual; it was something else, something different but akin to the kind of ecstasy he felt lying in bed with Brenda, holding her in his arms or pressing his face in her shadowy thighs; then his body was invaded by the kind of joy that leaks around the edges of music or from certain kinds of scenery, the singular and untellable sense of arrival.

On Fridays, talking to Bernie, there had been moments when he'd felt a similar kind of arriving, times when he and Bernie had reached out and touched, at exactly the same moment, the identical fragile, inchoate extension of an idea. Of course these moments were rare. They always came as a surprise. You had to get through hours of cold groping; a certain amount of luck was required. But when it happened, Jack felt himself transported to a clean, cool chamber of pure happiness, his heart stopped, his body stilled. The experience – he wondered if Bernie felt it too; they had never discussed it – was something he hadn't attempted to describe to anyone. Why should it be described? It seemed enough that during those rare moments the rest of his life appeared worthy. And possible.

And always, though Jack had never given the thought expression, he had known that the other kind of friendship was there too. Brenda's kind of friendship, caring, dependence, support, consolation. It had always been there, the knowledge that, should he need help, Bernie would supply it. Bernie would stand by him. He had never doubted it. This afternoon, shut up in the den with his lost faith, hadn't the image of Bernie's solace – the possibility of it anyway, brushed past him, lightly promising a form of release? It was there, waiting in reserve. And yesterday at Roberto's he had come close to drawing on it. Harriet Post; rising out of the past with her damned book, the unreasoned treachery of it; he had wanted to weep and beat the table and cry out for deliverance. But he'd held back. He was not one to confide easily in others, having, he supposed, a selfish desire to possess for himself his imperfections. He had grave doubts about the wisdom of casual sharing. Still, there were times when it was hard to hang on alone.

But he had held back, and he was glad now. He'd managed to contain it all, to smooth it over, incorporate the news about Harriet into the formal argument. It would be a mistake to demand too much and too often of his friendship with Bernie; something inevitably was risked, something sacrificed. It was enough anyway to know that the possibility of help existed.

What he had never imagined in his wildest dreams – why was it he was a man with so little imagination? – what he had never imagined was that it would be Bernie who would turn to him. Christ!

It was getting dark. A pool of light from the street lamp outside fell into the room, a faint stippling, bluish-white through the curtains. Jack's hands trembled as he felt for the light switch; the sight of Bernie's flowing tears had shaken and exhilarated him.

It was almost six o'clock. Evening. Time to put Brenda's casserole in the oven.

Chapter Ten

'D^{AD}?'
     'Laurie! My God, you scared me. I didn't hear you come in.'

'I came in the front door.'

'I didn't hear you.'

'What are you doing, Dad?' she said, peering at him across the kitchen. Her face glowed a roughened vegetable-like red from the cold, and her dark curly hair stood straight up.

He held up his hands. 'What does it look like? I'm making a salad.'

'Oh.' She stepped back.

He was always offending her, always speaking with unnecessary sharpness. 'Look, Laurie,' he said. He took a breath. 'Why don't you take off your coat and come give me a hand.'

'Okay,' she said in a larger voice, brightening at once. She was, Jack saw, too easily placated, too easily won back. Watching her unwind her long scarf, he felt his heart clutched with love. There was something soft, something surrendered in this strenuous amiability of hers.

'I wonder,' he said, 'if you happen to know where your mother keeps the salad oil and stuff?'

Laurie's round face with its large, very dark brown eyes beamed confidently at him. There was a suggestion of Brenda in that face, a sleekness about the cheeks that hinted at good nature, and the same wide cleanliness between the eyes. 'Sure,' she said, almost jaunty now, sliding out of her ski jacket and letting it fall on the back of a chair.

'Hang it up,' Jack said automatically, but he made an effort to keep his voice level, 'and by the way, do you know it's after six? I thought you were supposed to get home before it got dark.'

'I was only next door. I couldn't very well get attacked just cutting through the bushes, could I?'

'Hmmm.' He drove a knife through a crisp new head of lettuce.

'Dad?'

'What?'

'Dad. Uncle Bernie's sleeping on the couch. In the living room.'

'I know.'

'Why is he?' She was standing on a stool, rummaging in the cupboard. With sorrow Jack observed the awkward roundness of her body; the soft heft of pre-adolescent thighs and trunk; baby fat, Brenda called it.

'Why is he what?' Jack asked.

'Why's he here? On the couch?'

Her tone, easy, musical, pleased him for some reason. He liked the busy, surprising way her hands were moving across the shelves, and there was something agreeable about her matter-of-factness, as though Bernie's unusual presence on the living-room sofa was no more than an interesting puzzle whose solution she would gladly see solved. She waited, her face ready.

Outside the sky was black and filled with wind; Jack could hear bare branches cracking against the drainpipe at the back of the house. The kitchen felt warm, dry, a cube of light on the dark street, and across the illuminated safety of the table he watched Laurie turn and break an egg into a small glass bowl. 'What are you doing now?' he asked her.

'It's for the salad dressing.'

'An egg?'

'Caesar salad,' she said. Then, entreatingly, 'Is that okay?'

'Good,' he said. 'Great. You know I love Caesar salad.'

'Uncle Bernie –'

'Uncle Bernie's staying overnight tonight,' Jack told her, placing a feather-edge of enthusiasm on his voice.

'Oh.' She turned to him happily and her shoulders contracted with pleasure. 'He's sleeping here? Tonight? On the couch, you mean?'

'I don't know about the couch,' Jack said. 'I haven't thought that far ahead.'

'Because he could have my room,' Laurie said. 'If he wanted to.'

'Well, okay. Maybe. Why don't we ask him when he wakes up, where he wants to sleep.'

'I mean, I could sleep in the quilt room. On that folding bed.'

'Okay. We'll see.'

'Or you know what, Dad?' she said, excited. 'Mother's away, so he could sleep on her half of the bed.'

She spoke urgently, delighted with herself. She had stopped stirring the oil and vinegar around and was waving the fork back and forth in the air, dazed by her own good sense.

'I don't think so, Laurie.'

'Oh.' She began to stir the dressing again, slowly now, absorbing this unexpected 'no.' 'Okay,' she said at last.

Then the back door slammed, letting in a burst of icy air. Rob was home. His blue and white satin jacket radiated with its own cloud of cold. He had grown two inches in the last year, and the kitchen seemed cluttered with his arms and legs. 'I'm starved,' he said, glancing suspiciously around the room.

'How was the track meet?' Jack asked with hollow heartiness, and as he spoke he could feel the question drifting off into the air, apparently unanswerable.

'Not bad. What's to eat?'

'Spanish rice,' Laurie said. 'Who won? Did Elm Park win?'

'When're we eating anyway?'

'Soon,' Jack said shortly.

Rob was opening the oven door and lifting the lid from the pyrex casserole. He grunted, made a face, and gave a ripe snort of disgust. 'Do we have to eat this crap?' he said.

Jack felt the room rock. For a fraction of a second – it couldn't have been more – he was sure he was going to kill Rob. His right hand jerked upward and with horror he saw that he was still holding on to the paring knife. So this was how it happened, kitchen murders, blood on the floor, bodies falling, blind unreasoned passionate rage.

The word crap? It wasn't that; the kids used that word all the time; he used it himself, TV was crap, Nixon was crap, the newspapers were full of crap. It wasn't just today; today's explosion was months overdue. But today, finally moved, he had wanted to smash Rob's face in, to bring his fist up against Rob's nose; he wanted to knock those teeth right out of his head. He made himself take a deep breath and then, trembling, he brought his arm down, carefully placing the knife on the

59

counter, parallel to the edge of the cutting board. The room seemed overbright, blazing. He stared at his son.

Rob stared back, a little frightened now. He was almost as tall as Jack, but a good twenty pounds lighter. 'I hate Spanish rice,' he said weakly.

'You can damn well go hungry then,' Jack said, breathing out sharply. Lout. Insolent lout. Barbarian. Stomping in, as though he owned the place. He could feel his heart pumping blood; there were kids in the world who were starving to death.

For half a minute or more no one spoke. Rob stood, fixed to the floor, his face, with its roughened acne mask, gone suddenly formless, uncertain, and Jack could feel like a physical force his son's instant contrition. He could also sense, and was frightened by, his own inability to let the matter drop.

'Just who in hell do you think you are, stalking in here like this, demanding – '

'Okay, okay,' Rob said, backing off.

'There's salad,' Laurie croaked tearfully from the corner, 'Caesar salad.'

'He goes without dinner tonight,' Jack said stiffly, taking up the knife again and hacking off another wedge of lettuce.

'I said okay, didn't I,' Rob shot back as he dashed from the room and up the stairs.

Silence. The kitchen was stilled. Jack stared unbelievingly at his daughter, who had stopped stirring; her poor mouth sagged open; her hands hung dead in her lap. What in God's name had happened, he asked himself. The bubble of gaiety that had contained the two of them a minute ago, only a minute ago – where had it gone? What in hell – he surveyed the silent kitchen – what in hell had happened, anyway?

The oven was set at four hundred degrees, and the smell of Spanish rice rose in the room. He remembered, with something like anger, that he didn't like Spanish rice. It was one of those budget dishes Brenda used to make when they were first married, hamburger stroganoff, tuna-noodle pot, corned beef pie. Brenda was a good cook, more than a good cook; why, when she was away for a meal, did she leave them bowls of pallid, insipid, impossible food? Was it a punishment of some kind, a way of reminding them of the enormity of her absence?

Upstairs he could hear Rob stomping about, slamming doors. Laurie sniffed in her corner.

'Never mind, kiddo,' Jack said, patting her soft round shoulder. 'All the more for the rest of us, as your Grandpa would say.'

Then, briskly, he made himself a gin and tonic, finding in the dining-room cabinet, the tall frosted glass he liked, shaking ice cubes out of a tray, measuring out a good double ounce of gin. Outside the wind whistled and blew. Usually about this time of day he could see the moon rising over the garage roof. There it was, behind a bank of dark marbled cloud, a scattered, impressionistic luminosity. Maybe it'll snow, he thought idly.

He was about to carry his glass into the living-room; he was halfway there when he heard the soft breezing sound of someone snoring.

He'd forgotten. Bernie was here.

Chapter Eleven

As it happened Bernie loved Spanish rice. He hadn't had it in years, he said, not since he and Sue were first married. 'Glad you woke me up,' he told Jack. His eyes were dull and rimmed with a watery line of red, but his voice was, steady enough. To Laurie he said, with sturdy, dutiful blandishment, 'You know something – I think this is the best salad I've had since I don't know when.'

Laurie had set the table in the kitchen. 'It's cozier in here,' she explained. She closed the red denim curtains at the window over the sink so that the room seemed warmly sealed and softened. She put three woven placemats on the kitchen table, and then she folded paper napkins into fans, weaving them in and out of the tines of the forks. She carried an African violet in a clay pot from the window sill and positioned it in the middle of the table.

'Hey,' Bernie said to her, 'you didn't tell me this was going to be a party.'

Gravely ceremonial, she placed Bernie at one end of the table, Jack at the other, and herself in the middle, collapsing into her chair with a noisy hostessy flounce. 'There,' she puffed, surveying the table, her face open and expectant, her dark curls shining.

Rob stayed upstairs in his room; they could hear his radio playing loudly. The Rolling Stones. A driving beat. Jack cleared his throat – he felt compelled to explain. 'Rob's not eating tonight,' but Bernie only nodded and reached across the table for the salt.

It was then that a numbing gel of self-consciousness came over Jack; he could actually feel the cold, slow tensing of his skin and outer muscles. It reminded him of being at the dentist and having an injection of novacaine and then losing, by degrees, control over his face. His hands, clumsy as boxing gloves, gripped the fork, and his knees, suddenly bulbous, knocked against the table leg. A calm disbelief seized him – this embarrassment of intimacy had come too quickly; how had he arrived at this motionless disarray, this unjointed unreality?

His relationship with Bernie, with its limits and rules of procedure and orderly, trudging self-restraint – had all that been so quickly overturned? It was Saturday night; he had suffered the spectacle of Bernie's tears; he had put an arm across his heaving shoulders; now he was sentenced, it seemed, to total disorientation. Here sat his oldest friend, yet it was impossible to meet his eyes. Should he, he wondered wildly, attempt to restore the old sense of balance by picking up the threads of yesterday's discussion, go on with his idea about history being a matter of endings? No, the idea seemed suddenly childish. It would be too obvious a diversion. It would be insensitive. Why would a man, abandoned by his wife, want to dwell on a chilly abstraction like history? Better just keep quiet and eat.

He chewed on, engulfed by his own lumbering silence. He had always had, he knew, a disabling lack of nerve for new situations, and now, almost unconsciously, he cursed Brenda for abandoning him on this day of all days. For leaving him with Bernie's tears and with their two puzzling and difficult children and this sticky bowl of pink rice. What had irked him, he realized now, was the assertiveness, the greed, with which Rob had plunged into the house, demanding as his right, food, warmth, clothes on his back.

Bernie's presence – his firm occupancy of the kitchen chair and the rigorous plying of his fork – nudged at Jack. And so did the suitcase still standing in a corner of the hall. What was the matter with him? Was he so uncharitable? And did Bernie perhaps detect a subtle failure of welcome – was that why he was ploughing through a second helping of rice, knocking back a glass of beer, attempting jollity?

This was the kind of silence that could be ruinous, and he was grateful to Laurie who, as she ate, recited for them her recipe for Caesar salad. Oil, lemon, parsley, garlic. She seemed intent on her newly created role, eating with elaborate delicacy and taking masterful, cheerful charge of the conversation. Bernie, blinking, eating, smiling, listened in a daze.

'Have some more rice, Dad,' Laurie urged. Although she had perfect teeth, she had in the last year devised a new way of smiling, a curious closed smile with a demented sweetness about it.

'Doesn't anyone want any more?' she demanded, and Jack could hear disappointment in her voice.

'What about you?' Bernie asked. 'Cooks should get their fair share.'

'I'm stuffed. All that junk I ate over at the Carpenters.'

'I thought you were out walking the dogs,' Jack said.

'I was. Brinkley doesn't heel anymore. Mrs Carpenter says they're sending him to obedience school, and do you know what Mr. Carpenter said?'

'What?'

'He said "in a pig's eye." I thought people only said that in the movies.'

'Uhuh.'

'He's in a bad mood. Mrs. Carpenter said I could open the dog food when I got back, but he said he thought I'd better get a move on. And then Mrs. Carpenter said I could stay and help her with the party food. And do you know what else? She said I could call her Janey. She said because there weren't all that many years between us.'

'She did, did she.' Jack sipped at his beer.

To Bernie she explained, 'They're having an enormous party tonight. Huge. Shrimp and stuff. Lobster salad with guess what in it? Pecans. And these little pastry things with curled up ends and chicken inside. I've been helping her poke the chicken in.'

'And she let you have a taste?'

'A taste!' Laurie rubbed her stomach with enthusiasm and rolled her eyes. 'I've eaten tons. *Tons*. She – Mrs. Carpenter – Janey – kept asking me to taste everything for her. Like she wanted to know if there was enough salt in the dip or too much curry in those chicken things I told you about and stuff like that. She made this neat dip out of sour cream and grated turnip. She said last time they had the caterers do everything, but they always brought the same old stuff and it was kind of soggy. Do you remember, Dad? If the food was soggy at their last party? You were there.'

'Actually,' Jack paused, wishing he could say something that would make her laugh, something that would compensate for the ugly scene with Rob before dinner, 'actually, as I remember that last party, it was the people who were soggy.'

Laurie didn't laugh; she looked puzzled. 'The people?'

'It's only a joke.'

'What do you mean they were soggy?'

'Nothing. I didn't mean anything. To tell you the truth, hon, I can't remember what the food was like. Or the people.'

The Carpenters' last party, and Jack reflected with a mild wave of belligerence that it had been only six weeks ago, seemed little more than a blur. He had been on edge for some reason that night; he had wanted to go to a movie, something trashy and softly coloured with tap dancers, where he could drift off holding on to Brenda's hand, but instead they had got dressed and gone to the party, where he had drunk too many scotches in too short a time, and to complicate matters he and Brenda hadn't known anyone there. Larry and Janey Carpenter had moved out to Elm Park less than two years ago. They had made a few friends, the Lewises and the Wallbergs and the Bowmans. They'd joined the Little Theatre and the tennis club, but most of their friends seemed to live downtown. There were, as Jack remembered, quite a few journalists and theatre people at the party (Larry wrote on theatre and, sometimes, wine, for Chicago *Today*); there were at least two psychiatrists and a handsomely dressed, articulate group of people who seemed to have something to do with raising money for a ballet committee. No one had sat down. Jack, who had spent the afternoon cleaning out the basement, was weary, but it hadn't been the kind of party where he felt he could ease himself into an armchair and fade away. After a while he found a doorway in the dining room to lean against, and he dimly remembered having a long conversation with a young, sharply made-up girl in a dark green corduroy suit who told him she was a troubleshooter for a uranium company. Troubleshooter? It sounded bizarre; he wanted to ask exactly what that meant in terms of the uranium industry, but he hadn't. At the time he suspected she might be pulling his leg; now, six weeks later, he was sure of it. He had felt middle-aged and dull. The backs of his knees hurt. He remembered remarking to her that he was engaged at the moment in writing a book, and she said, shifting into a mock southern tone, 'Ain't everyone?' What was that? He'd opened his mouth, about to ask what she meant, but she had wandered away toward the bar. There was a great deal of food, but it seemed to be hours before it appeared. Then, finally, later still, there was some coffee and a tray of French pastries; he especially remembered the chocolate eclairs because he had been talking in a corner to a political columnist from Chicago *Today* – an older man with a crude knobbled profile and a reputation for having once held hawkish views on Vietnam – who stuffed his eclair into his mouth, and then, carefully, meticulously, licked each of his fingers in turn, first the little finger, then the second finger, and arriving, finally, at his thumb, which he twisted and smacked between thick pink lips. Jack watched him, fascinated. He should start reading this man's column again, he thought to himself, to see if he's softened up on communism. There would be something affirming about such a softening up. He was about to confide the fact that he too was a writer of sorts, in the midst of writing a book on Indian trading practices; but he stopped himself; enough of that for one night. About the rest of the evening he recalled nothing.

Except for one thing. He remembered, in perfect, reprintable, film-like memory, the moment when he and Brenda arrived, a little late, at the Carpenters' front door. (He had put on his new vest; then, at the last minute decided against it.) Janey Carpenter in a calf-length calico dress had flung open the door and astonished them both by dipping all the way to the floor in a strange, slightly tipsy curtsy. She had very pale blonde hair, longer than most women were wearing this year, especially women in their late thirties.

'Enter, neighbours,' she cried over the hubbub. 'Greetings.'

Jack had always thought her a little cool, and the warmth of the greeting had surprised him. From nowhere Larry appeared, steadying Janey with one hand and taking charge. He was wearing a deep brown Norwegian sweater with dropped shoulders and suede patches at the elbow. His softly shining sandy-beige hair lay neat as a wig. 'Jack! Brenda!!' He pronounced their names with the heat of exclamation but not the force. 'Let me introduce you around.' Larry's voice was smoothly elegant, but with a tremulous lack of substance about it, like yogurt packed into a carton. 'This,' Larry said, his hand on Jack's shoulder, 'is our next door neighbour Jack Bowman, an expert on Great Lakes Indians. And *this* is Brenda,'he smiled, paused, slid an arm around her waist, 'who is a quiltmaker in her own right.'

Brenda never blinked, and at the time Jack thought she might have missed it; she had drifted off after that, found someone interesting to talk to, a man who travelled around the world photographing beaches for a tourist agency. Jack had caught a glimpse of her later over the buffet table, had heard the word Madagascar float in the air, but it wasn't until they got home that he had a chance to talk to her.

It was two-thirty in the morning. She had fallen backwards onto their bed, still in her dress, shrieking with laughter. 'A quiltmaker in her own right! Oh, Jack, I thought I was going to burst. Didn't you want to howl? All night long I kept thinking about it, didn't you? Every time I saw Larry going by in that woolly sweater of his I just wanted to die laughing.'

They had held on to each other; their rhythmic laughing made the bed shake. They rolled over and over, and Jack, unzipping her dress, had felt almost mad with gratitude: she had seen how funny it all had been. (She didn't always laugh at the same things; only a week before, early one morning, he had been sitting on the edge of the bed putting on a new pair of socks when he simultaneously found himself in a state of erection. Impulsively he had peeled the sticker off the socks, a little round gold and black sticker which said 'New Executive Length.' He glanced down; it was really quite a presentable erection, and he had stuck the label on its swollen tip. Then, wrapped in a towel, he had caught Brenda off guard in the bathroom and, flicking the towel aside, he'd shaken his hips and cried, 'Ta da.' He had been so sure she would laugh, but instead she'd gazed mildly at him from behind her face cloth and said, 'Oh, Jack, honestly.')

But she had laughed at Larry Carpenter's introduction – *a quiltmaker in her own right* – and for that he loved her. He adored her for that. As late as it was, in spite of all the scotch he had drunk, they made slow, languorous love, more attentive than usual. Thank you, thank you, thank you, he had thought, clamping his mouth onto her breast, while the memory of the preposterous Larry Carpenter kept breaking through their embraces like a prized bubble of craziness.

The joke had lasted for days. 'Here's an egg in its own right,' Brenda said, handing him his breakfast the next morning. 'Here I am,' Jack called, arriving home early from work, 'your husband in his own right.'

Larry Carpenter, with his English raincoat and his wondrously shaped head of hair, dissolved before them, an absurd scurrying grasshopper of a man, deserving every nuance of ridicule they could devise. They watched from the window in the mornings as he climbed in his yellow Porsche and backed out of the driveway. 'A sportscar in its own right,' Brenda announced, making a face.

Within a week the joke had worn thin, all its comic possibilities exhausted. It had seemed, somehow, mean-spirited to go on with it any longer. When Larry phoned on the next Sunday afternoon asking them to come in for a drink, Jack had insisted that it was their turn. Larry accepted quickly, almost with gratitude. 'We'll be right over,' he'd said.

They had sat in the living room in the last of the afternoon light. Jack made screwdrivers, and Brenda passed cheese and crackers. Larry, relaxed, talked mockingly but with good humour about the state of the theatre in Chicago, about the renaissance of amateur local theatre. He had been touched, he told them, to be given the role of Hamlet, he who had joined the group only a year and a half ago. His modesty, so unexpected, was becoming. 'There's something,' he said, 'almost heroic about an amateur group taking on a production of *Hamlet*. They almost know in advance that they're going to fail, but they plod on nevertheless. Amateurism may save us in the end, keep us from washing down the drain on our silver-plated fannies.' Janey had nodded, agreeing; she had been particularly sweet that day, Jack remembered.

And now, already, they were having another party. 'Very informal,' Janey had told them when she phoned. 'More of an open house sort of thing. The whole cast from *Hamlet* and some other people I know you'll enjoy.'

'Here we go again,' Brenda sighed, banging the side of her head with her fist, but then she remembered, gleefully, that she would be in Philadelphia that night.

Jack – thinking of the girl in corduroy and the midnight blur of alcohol – had decided not to go. He would spend a quiet evening at home; they would never miss him in all that crowd.

But here it was, Saturday night. His son was sulking upstairs. His daughter was chattering and humming and washing dishes and driving him crazy with her bottomless fund of good will. Bernie Koltz sat morosely, like a depleted monk, at his kitchen table, puffing air into his cheeks and staring at the curtains.

'Bernie,' Jack said at last, 'do you know what you need?'

'What?'

'You need to meet some new people. Have a drink or two. Three even.'

'Like a hole in the head.'

'Why not? We wouldn't have to stay more than half an hour. It's just a drop-in party, no big deal.'

'I don't know,' Bernie said.

Suddenly Jack knew he couldn't bear the thought of sitting home all evening. 'Bernie,' he said, 'you really should go. I mean it. Sitting around at a time like this is crazy. It's the worst thing you can do at a time like this. People can get seriously depressed. Remember what's-his-name, that guy who used to work in your department? What you need is to get your mind on something else.'

'I've brought a book.'

'Listen,' Jack told him, 'I'll lend you a clean shirt. I'll phone over to the Carpenters' and tell them I'm bringing a friend along. They're not all that bad, and the food'll be good. You might enjoy it. It's Saturday night, you need to get out of yourself, you need to forget for a few hours, you need to get some kicks out of life, or what's it for? Hell, Bernie, we can't sit around like this. Come on.'

And to himself he was saying: a better man would resist, a better man would remain at home tonight. He would carry a ham sandwich and a glass of milk upstairs and enact a reconciliation with his son, who is sensitive, who could never bear to be scolded when he was little, who is suffering, who is hungry. A better man would stay home, play Scrabble with his daughter, make her laugh, thank her for doing the dishes, tell her stories, tell her he remembered being her age and what it was like. A better man – where was he? – would give his full attention and sympathy to his oldest friend, his friend who has today suffered a major catastrophe in his life, who is feeling lost and alone and frightened and even tearful. A better man would carry armfuls of seasoned logs up from the basement, lay a fire in the living room, call the children to watch a ceremonial match being lit – they used to love that once. A better man refused invitations from those for whom he felt a casual aversion, he had better things to do than squander his life on social trivia. A man's time on Earth is limited, it has to be carefully, seriously, spent. There was his manuscript awaiting his patient attention; this day might still be turned to profit, he could still, if he wanted, salvage something.

'Well,' Bernie said, 'maybe – '

'Great.' Jack moved toward the telephone. 'I'll give them a call right away.'

Chapter Twelve

BERNIE ASKED: 'WHAT'S LARRY CARPENTER LIKE, ANYWAY?'
What was he like? Jack hesitated, thinking of Larry's successful, intelligent face and narrow late-thirties body. He liked Larry well enough when they were talking together at an Elm Park party or over the back hedge. At these times, talking one-to-one, he found Larry engaging and even generous in his judgments. But at other times, if he happened to think of Larry at all, his mind conjured up images of distrust; there was an empty field of ennui about Larry, an insouciant fending off of inquiry; the truth was that Jack thought of Larry Carpenter as a bit of an ass, something of a prick, in fact. Even Brenda thought so. How could this be, this seeming paradox?

Perhaps because the Carpenters managed to convert their state of childlessness into an intellectual refinement. Janey, it seemed to Jack, was sulky and coy, with her pale hair and vivid *Vogue* magazine mouth; but at times she showed a fleeting prettiness. Larry treated her tenderly, as though she were a child. He was not an easy man to figure out, and Jack's feelings about him consisted mostly of a vague wariness.

He offered Bernie a version of his first meeting with Larry, which occurred on the weekend the Carpenters moved in. It was late fall, the end of November, in the middle of a Saturday afternoon. Jack had been standing in his backyard with his hands jammed into the back pockets of his pants, breathing in the blackish smell of decayed leaves and woodsmoke.

A young man's voice, buoyant and carrying the unmistakable stamp of the eastern seaboard, floated across the hedge – Larry Carpenter in person, *the* Larry Carpenter. Jack had read his column in Chicago *Today* on and off for the last two years – often, he admitted, with amusement; this was a man who would say anything for a laugh.

Hey, Larry had called to Jack across the lawn that first day, hey, neighbour, anytime you want to uproot this jungle, I'll go halves with you on the demolition cost.

Jack had been immediately thrown on the defensive; he loved the wild bank of nameless, shapeless bushes that bordered and protected his yard, and it was his intention to keep them forever; on the other hand, it had seemed only decent to go over and introduce himself.

So you're a historian, Larry Carpenter had exclaimed in a light, waltz-time voice, well, well, maybe you can tell me, then, something about the history of this crumbling wreck of a house my wife and I've just bought. Lord, lord, Larry had said, we must have been crazy to take this on, it's going to take us forever just to get the place cleaned up.

Carefully, knowing he was meeting Larry's suave resonance with unfelt heartiness, Jack explained to this boyish stranger in the grey mohair sweater – Larry was partly hidden by leafless branches – about old Miss Anderson the former owner, about how many years she'd lived in the old house, it was something of a legend, to tell the truth; about her two cats, Aristotle and Plato, about how her sight had been failing for years, how she tried year after year to find high school boys to look after the yard and wash her windows but they always let her down, how she was forced to live on a teacher's pension granted back in the days when pensions had been peanuts. Christ, she bought meat only once a week, she had told Brenda; she was really quite a terrific old gal, actually, Jack said to Larry Carpenter. He said *this*, he who had loathed Miss Anderson and had found the ridges and sexless elongations of her face appalling and terrifying, he who cringed at the asthmatic whine with which she assailed those – like himself – who called on behalf of the Heritage Committee. Old Cactus Cunt, they called her in the neighbourhood, and now, Christ, here he was, standing in his own backyard, his own turf, his own territory, leaning on a bent branch of maple and creating, involuntarily, a tawdry fiction, a melodrama about this marvellous old crone, this real life stoic and neighbourhood character, this heroine, in fact – the old darling herself, bless her.

Larry Carpenter, listening, nodding, had rummaged in the roots of his neat beige hair; he had fixed Jack with a sharp look of incredulity; a smile started to break on his lips, although all he said was, yes, well, about this jungle, if you ever do decide –

Later, upstairs, Jack found Bernie a shirt. 'I think this'll fit,' he said.

They were dressing together. Bernie, Jack saw, wore orange jockey shorts. They hadn't dressed together for at least twenty-five years, not since the old summer days in the locker room at the Forest Park Swimming Pool.

'Unless you'd rather have that blue shirt. Doesn't matter to me.'

'Anything,' Bernie said shortly.

'Well, at least that one fits.'

'Thanks.'

'You don't want a tie, do you?'

'Just the shirt's fine,' Bernie's voice pulled down firmly.

'Okay.' Jack buttoned a cuff and regarded himself in the mirror.

'What's that?' Bernie asked. 'On the hanger? By the blue shirt.'

'That? A vest.'

'I never saw you wear that.'

'Well, I haven't exactly worn it. Not yet anyway, it's still new. But – '

'It looks like suede.'

'I don't know why I bought it,' Jack heard himself say. 'Impulse or something.'

'Well, look, if you're not going to be wearing it tonight, maybe I could wear it. To go over the shirt.'

'Well – '

'Unless you were going to. It doesn't really matter to me.'

'Well – '

'I don't really – '

'Sure. Go ahead. Someone might as well wear it.'

'We're delighted you came.'

The Carpenters seemed to be genuinely pleased that Jack had brought Bernie along, and why shouldn't they be? Jack thought. Bernie Koltz was more than presentable, possessing as he did the bodily compactness of the true, tensely tuned intellectual. His face, at middle-age, had come into fashion: a quizzing ironic muzzle, handsomely grotesque, with pinkish thoughtful eyes that projected liveliness and rascality. Tonight he looked especially modish and jaunty.

'Come, come,' Larry said, 'let me introduce you around.'

He ferried them around the living room, through the study, into the dining room. To all the people standing in casually formed groups with drinks in hand, he said, 'I want you guys to meet Jack Bowman, our local expert on Great Lakes Indians. Trade customs, beads, and blankets. And this – this is Bernie Koltz, have I got that right? Good. Who teaches at De Paul. Math, you said, Bernie? Would you believe I did my Math with matchsticks, right through fourth-year Economics? I still get out the old matchsticks at tax time, ask Janey. Look, I haven't even offered you two a drink. This is old-wine night, I don't know if Janey explained on the phone. We've got some hard stuff if you'd rather, scotch, vodka, some terrific rum, whatever. But we thought you might like to try some of this stuff Janey and I got in Beaune last summer. You've got to have a taste, anyway, after all the trials and tribulations of getting it into the country. Not to mention a measure of criminality. It's not great wine – we got stuck with a few roughs, but this bottle here happens to be a smoothie, at least my palate says it is, try a little. By the way, have you met Hy Saltzer? He does bricks, come on over and let me do the honours.'

'He's darling, Jack,' Janey Carpenter whispered in the kitchen.

Jack had wandered in looking for ice for his scotch and found Janey taking a tray of cheese puffs out of the oven. She was looking flushed and pretty; he'd never seen her look this pretty. A queer cinnamon perfume rose from the region of her throat.

'I like his eyes,' she told Jack. 'I noticed them right away.'

'His eyes?'

'And that terrific suede vest. That toast colour. Sort of muted. I love it.'

'Uhuh.'

'Is he, well, married? Or what?'

Jack helped himself to ice and nodded vaguely. 'Separated.'

'Aha.' She threw Jack a small shrug that said: sad, but that's how it is these days.

'His wife, Sue, is a doctor,' Jack explained, sipping scotch, 'psychiatric medicine.'

'Have they been separated long?'

The question, or perhaps the way she posed it, seemed indecently curious; Jack hedged. 'It's fairly recent,' he told her.

'I thought so,' she nodded knowingly. 'Something about his eyes. You can usually tell. Have a cheese puff.'

'I will. Thanks.'

'Anyway,' she paused an instant on her way into the dining room, 'I think he's sweet. Sweet.'

This party *was* different from the last one. Jack saw here and there neighbours, faces he recognized. Some of them he knew well. Irving and Leah Wallberg, Robin Fairweather and his new wife – Christ, she couldn't be more than twenty-five. The Sandersons, Bill Block. And Hap Lewis, who asked him about Brenda. 'Did she decide to take all three quilts, Jack? Or just the two?'

'Three. I think that's what she said. The box was heavy enough, anyway. We sent it air-freight.'

'Brenda showed them to me yesterday. All three. But my favourite, my absolute favourite was *Second Coming*. Those colours! And what she did around the edges! Have you ever seen anything like that kind of feathering effect on the edges of a quilt before? It's things like that that Brenda excels at. Jesus, I mean she's got that folk thing down solid, and then there's that Van Goghish vitality spilling out, and all the time it is so goddamned restrained. Like a kind of quietness that's all her own, like a trademark. Unique, kind of. I suppose you could call it energy contained. This feeling of, you know, wildness, but it's a tongue-in-cheek wildness. There's sex in those forms, but order. Like you can sense a pattern in the universe if you know what I mean, an underlying order. That's what I was telling Brenda. Discipline within chaos. But strength, a really tremendous flow of calculated strength, do you know what I mean, Jack? I can never put these things in words, it's all so fucking abstract, but that's what I felt, I really did.'

Jack listened. He nodded and sipped. 'Yes,' he said. 'I think so, too.'

'I work for a Chicago-based mining company,' a woman in a velvet skirt the colour of blue plums told Jack. She was standing by the fireplace smoking a small cigar. My God, he thought. Her again.

'Oh?' Jack said. 'Sounds interesting.'

'Uranium. It's shitty work if you want the truth. I have to take nothing but shit.'

75

'Doesn't everyone?' What did he mean?

'It's a PR kind of thing. A troubleshooter, they call me. Ha.'

'Why do you do it?'

'I have to do something. Jesus, I've got a kid to support. A boy. Eleven years old. I'm the sole support.'

'I have a daughter who's eleven,' Jack said, remembering as he spoke that Laurie had turned twelve.

'You do? Really? What did you say you do?'

'I'm writing a book. About Indian trade practices.'

'My God, that sounds fabulous, I mean it. Tell me about it.'

Did you and Brenda see the play?' Leah Wallberg asked him.

Of all Brenda's friends he liked Leah best. She had a wide pink apple-shiny face and a plump body filled with soft slopes. When she talked she had a trick of lifting her hands into small shapely gestures, the gestures of a much younger and more slender woman, exquisite, precise, as though she were inscribing words on sheets of air. By profession she was a designer, and it was she who had designed the stage setting for the Little Theatre production of *Hamlet*.

'No,' Jack told her, 'we missed it, I'm afraid. Brenda's been so busy this week getting ready for the exhibition. She worked up to the last minute. And then I forgot to pick up the tickets –'

'Don't apologize, Jack. Really. You haven't missed a thing. Not a thing.'

'We heard it was a little slow in spots.'

'That's putting it kindly. Kindly! It was,' her wrists made double hoops in the air, 'it was a qualified disaster. But please don't tell anyone I said so. Especially You Know Who.'

'A qualified disaster?' Jack asked. 'What do you mean, qualified?'

'Well, you know, you can't wreck *Hamlet* completely. Something comes through. Peggy Giles was a pretty good Ophelia, especially when you think she's only nineteen. Robin was good too, but then he always is. But, ahem, Hamlet –'

'How exactly did he get the part?'

'Do you know,' she shrugged prettily, 'I'm not sure. We just sort of gave way to him. He seemed so anxious. He just wanted it so much.'

'You were mesmerized.'

'I guess so. Really, Jack, it serves us right. I guess we just thought, here is this theatre critic, he's just got to be a great Hamlet. I don't think anyone else even auditioned once they knew he wanted the role. But when you think about it, it's crazy. It's like saying *you're* an Indian because you know all about them.'

'But I don't – '

'The only lucky thing was that there were only four performances. Because he kept getting worse each time. Louder, stagier. It was almost dangerous to sit in the front row, Irv said – you could get knocked over by that swirling cloak of his. Lord! And I don't think he realized how really lousy he was either. That's the funny thing about it. But I don't know, it's not all that serious, I suppose. At least he had the nerve to try. I guess you have to give him some credit. It takes nerve to find out you can't do something, what do you think, Jack?'

'I agree. Absolutely.'

The Carpenters' glass and rosewood table was covered with plates of food. Jack helped himself to a sliver of smoked trout and winked at Bernie across the room. Bernie was lifting a wine glass to his lips and seemed to be listening with great attentiveness to a sharply gesticulating young man in a purple shirt and small black beard who was quizzing him with the sucking ferocity of a plunger. He had a damp mouth and smiled like an actor. Bernie was concentrating so hard that he didn't see Jack winking at him. Why was he winking, anyway? He never winked. It wasn't his style; it wasn't in his canon.

What he needed, he decided, was a drink.

In the kitchen the Carpenters were quarrelling. Jack found them facing each other over a tray of dirty wine glasses.

'You can still phone the bloody office and have it killed,' Janey was saying to Larry in a low voice.

'I can't do anything of the kind,' Larry said. 'Even if I were inclined to do it, it would still be too late.'

'It's not too late. I happen to know it isn't. Remember that time when they took out your review and put in the Russian ballet thing? That was right at the last minute.'

'Janey, listen. For one thing it's too late and for another thing it's unprofessional.'

'Unprofessional! You make me laugh. You're the drama critic. You're supposed to give the assignments.'

'It can't be done, and that's all there is to it.'

Jack stood awkwardly in the doorway. They turned and saw him, and Larry, for the first time since Jack had known him, seemed embarrassed.

Janey sprang forward and took Jack's arm. She was breathing rapidly and was flushed with wine. 'Jack, what do you think? Larry, why don't you ask Jack what he thinks?'

'I can come back,' Jack said. 'I was just looking for some ice.'

Janey wouldn't let go of his arm. 'Listen, Jack, Gordon Tripp – do you know Gordon Tripp? – the movie critic for Chicago *Today*? – well, he's doing a write-up of Larry's performance as Hamlet. It's supposed to be in the morning paper.'

'Forget it, Janey,' Larry said.

'Now do you think that's fair?' Janey asked Jack. 'You know they never cover amateur performances. Never. And now, just because Larry happens to be – '

'I don't think Jack's particularly interested in whether or not *Hamlet* gets a review in the paper.' Larry said this in a voice that was reasonable and good tempered, but Jack noticed that his hands were trembling in mid-air.

'You could have it killed,' Janey said, louder now. Her eyes had the mica brightness of real tears. 'You can just pick up the crummy phone and tell them at the office that you won't stand for it. That you want it out. You don't have to take that kind of crap from Gordon Tripp. You've got seniority. You can just tell him to shove it. He's no theatre critic, anyway. Who does he think he is?'

'There is no way I can stop a review, Janey, so let's just forget it.' Larry pulled open the giant door of the refrigerator. 'And now, Jack,' his voice was solemn, even though his eyes were oddly locked into dazed focuslessness, 'you were saying something about ice. Let me see if I can find some for you.'

Jack carried his drink into the living room. There were soft lamps lit all around the room, creating a white silk patrician ambience. He sat on the arm of a velvet chair and talked to a woman in a paisley blouse. He had never been able to see the point of paisley. She was an agreeable woman, however, with a dull silver chain around her throat, and she told Jack that although she wrote fashion features she would really like to do a book someday.

'Really?' And Jack told her a little about his own book.

She was fascinated by the idea of history, she said; the Indians of the southwest had been nuanced to death, but she thought the Great Lakes Indians had been neglected, especially their attitude toward property and trade. Jack sipped his drink, cheered by her observations. She was quite a bright woman, really. After a while she told Jack a long story about her graduate thesis on John Donne, which was rejected at the last minute because she refused her professor at South Carolina certain bizarre sexual favours. Jack nodded and commiserated; he didn't believe a word she was saying. Christ, Christ, Christ, Christ, Christ.

'What's the matter, Jack?' Janey asked him, smiling. She seemed to have recovered her good spirits.

'I can't find Bernie. I wonder if he went home. I've been looking everywhere for him. I just realized how late it was.'

'He's asleep,' Janey said, open-mouthed with tenderness.

'What do you mean, asleep?'

'I was upstairs a minute ago,' Janey said, 'to powder my nose. And when I peeked into the guest room, there he was. Sleeping like a baby.'

'Passed out?'

'Like a baby.' She smiled wonderfully.

'My God, how am I going to get him home?'

Larry joined them. He was rather drunk but pleasant. (Larry Carpenter is a charmer, the paisley woman had told Jack.) He gave Janey's shoulder an affectionate squeeze and said to Jack, 'Why don't you just leave him here until morning? He's okay, I think. I checked on him half an hour ago, and he was breathing like a generator.'

'It would be a dirty trick to wake him up,' Janey murmured.

'My God,' Jack said, shaking his head.

Larry spread his hands, grinning boyishly. 'Really. I mean it. Leave him. We'd love an overnight guest, wouldn't we Janey?'

'We'd love it. We've just had that room papered and we'd love – '

'If you're sure.' He longed, inexplicably, to please them.

'No problem at all, Jack, no problem at all.'

It was 4 A.M. when Jack went home, scrambling through a break in the bushes, catching a leg of his pants and muttering shit, shit, shit. In the east the city lights had turned the sky into a pale dome of hammered aluminum. The air was ringing with frost. He found the back door unlocked; he should have told the kids to lock the doors; they should have known better than to leave it open.

Inside it was quiet and dark. There were shoes on the stairs, a strong sense of habitation. He ought to check on Rob and Laurie, push open their bedroom doors, make sure they were all right, but he was already in bed before he thought of this. Medium-drunk, he was rapidly on the way to unconsciousness, but he took note of the unusual coolness of the bed sheets: Brenda was in Philadelphia; what was she doing at this moment? He pictured her in a narrow bed, weighed down by a mountain of quilts, *The Second Coming* folded on top.

The room receded dangerously. Exhausted as he was, he made an effort to take bearings: Bernie Koltz was flat out next door, and Bernie's wife Sue was sighing in the arms of her lover – somewhere in this city her sighing was contained and answered. Harriet Post was smugly sleeping the night away in a dim Rochester bedroom, her manuscript stacked and stapled and ready in a cardboard carton. His own children were asleep; children can always sleep; it was one of the compensations of childhood, the ability to transform pain overnight into the abstraction of history.

Sleep was coming to Jack, too; he stretched and let it invade his body. Words and deeds rained down silently on his dying consciousness; dreams rose, an interlacing of forms printed on the inside of his eyelids. He was suspended in snow, growing lighter and lighter, but something was asking to be remembered, something singular and plaintive – what was it? Then it came to him: his lost faith. Today, sitting at his desk, he had discovered himself to be a man without substance. The remembrance closed the day. There was a simplicity about it like the evenness of church music. Amen.

The room grew darker, but he hung on for another minute to the thought of his absent faith, holding it safe in the failing transparent vessel of his brain, partly warmed by the anguish it created, partly comforted by its decency.

Chapter Thirteen

O N SUNDAY MORNING JACK WOKE AND FOUND THAT THE void left by his shattered faith had inexplicably grown; it had spread alarmingly in all directions, a living thing, kicking and groaning, animated like a breathy conga line, involving not only himself now, but others. Perhaps it was the emptiness of the queensize bed; he wasn't used to waking and seeing Brenda's side of the bed so severely undisturbed. The quilted bedspread, with its blues and greens in overlapping spears of colour, lay in smooth contrast to his hot rumpled sheets, and this smoothness posed a question: why? Why, after twelve years, had Sue and Bernie ended their marriage? Had they lost faith, too? Faith in what? Jack didn't know. Why did people insist on making for themselves, and for others, pools of loneliness and suffering? No, suffering was too strong a word, too noisy with literary echoes, too Protestant. How had he arrived at this point of immobility, self-insulated, sealed off?

Jack pulled himself out of bed, pushing the thought of suffering aside. What he needed was hot coffee.

His pain, like a stubbed toe, had a rapid countdown; ease and forgetfulness came always; it could be depended upon.

The faith Jack had lost wasn't a religious faith. He had never been a church-goer, nor had his parents been church-goers. 'Only sinners have to go to church,' his father used to say with a waggish snort, gulping his Sunday-morning coffee. Jack's mother had fretted now and then about it, saying in her small sinus-muffled way, 'I don't know, we really should go, at least at Easter we really should go.' But they never did.

In spite of this fact, Jack had grown up in the belief that Sundays were days of particularized ritual. There was a difference in the pacing of time: a slowing of speech, a grave attention paid to newspapers, armchairs, the temperature of the living room, the view from the apartment, the quality of sunshine coming through the cloud cover. Certain things were expected; Jack's mother, who cherished regularity, attended to that. Even now, at seventy, she seemed uneasy if the day's special observations were somehow interrupted or disturbed. Her long-ago response to the invasion of Pearl Harbour had passed into family legend – 'But it's Sunday,' she had protested.

On Sundays she rose at seven, drank a cup of instant coffee and began to clean the apartment. Wednesday was her regular cleaning day, but on Sunday she 'straightened up,' beginning by shaking out the rug in the hallway of the apartment, then working her way through the living room, the small, seldom-used dining room with its ring of dark varnished furniture, and then the kitchen. After that she began on the three bedrooms, first the spare room, formerly Jack's bedroom, and then the small, dark pink bedroom at the back where she slept now. Because Jack's father liked to sleep late on Sunday – late meant nine o'clock – she did his room last, humming fitfully as she worked, sometimes talking to herself a little. She damp-mopped all the floors and dusted the table tops, reaching inside the lampshades to dust the tops of the lightbulbs – she had read somewhere that large amounts of electricity were lost because of dusty lightbulbs. In the winter she filled the pans of water on top of the radiators. She watered the wandering Jew, which sat on a low table by the front window, and then she opened the back door and put a slice of bread on the fire escape for the birds. What kind of birds were they? Jack had asked her once. Surprised, she had shaken her head; she didn't know, she'd never learned the names of birds, and except for robins and bluejays, they all looked alike to her. Jack and Brenda bought her Belding's *American Guide to City Birds* for her birthday, and she had sat down with it at once; for an hour she leafed through the more than two hundred pages, then closed the covers with a snuffling of pleasure, a smile of ease. But she'd never opened it again, though she kept it importantly on a shelf under the magazine rack. Someday, she told Jack, when she had more time, she'd study it carefully.

After she set the bread out for the birds, she took a package of sweetrolls from the freezer, opened them and arranged them on a blackened baking sheet and put them on the bottom rack of the oven. (Before arthritis attacked the joints of her fingers, she had made her own banana loaf and cinnamon rolls for Sunday morning; now they made do with Pepperidge Farm or Sara Lee.) She put on a large glass pot of perked coffee and then she set the kitchen table with plastic placemats, plates, and knives. By this time Jack's father was dressed and shaved, and the two of them sat in the kitchen, sipping coffee, watching the clock over the Frigidaire and waiting for Jack and Brenda and the children to come.

They normally arrived a little after ten.

When Brenda's mother Elsa was alive they used to bring her along with them. Jack's parents had loved Elsa; the fact that Elsa wasn't married, that she had never been married, made her especially loved. 'That poor woman,' Jack's mother used to say, 'it's not easy for a woman, a life like that.' Elsa's unmarriedness – a fact known but never referred to – gave her a certain mythic enlargement, and she had been a large woman anyway, in the literal sense, both tall and fat, with a flamboyance of style that was also out-sized; in another age she would have worn peacock feathers in her hair. Her breasts – she called them bosoms, emphasizing the plural as a kind of joke – had been huge and heavily weighted with costume jewellery; she loved copper chains and had had a number of turquoise pieces. The dresses she wore were of nylon jersey. 'I like a nice print,' she used to say, 'so the dirt doesn't show.' These dresses, size twenty-two, swung around her compacted bulk with a warm-breathing coquettish rhythm, sensuous and powdery. She loved cologne, all kinds of cologne. Her eyes were round and bright, and she had a florid face, puffed and spread out like a peony. She was always laughing.

'That Elsa's the limit,' Jack's father used to say, shaking his head, 'a carload of laughs.' Jack's mother said often that Elsa was a real goer, a humdinger, and that it was just a joy to sit and listen to her go on. Elsa's voice had been exceptionally heavy for a woman; at the same time it was very low in pitch with a light Polish accent, thin as gilt, which kept it from sounding mannish. She especially liked to argue politics with Jack's father, ancient politics from the thirties and forties, slapping the edge of the table with the flat of her hand as she talked. Roosevelt had been a goddamned saint, she claimed, one of God's own marching angels. A bastard, Jack's father pounded back, and a goddamned blight on the country. You got to be kidding,' Elsa slapped away. 'Why he was a millionaire, he didn't have to butter his own pockets like that bum Daley.' (She had a gift for mixed metaphor; Brenda was her heir.) 'You know something,'

Jack's father told her, 'it's the rich crooks like Roosevelt you got to watch out for, they want to give everyone else's money away.' 'He was a saviour,' Elsa panted, 'but the poor SOB with that ugly Eleanor of his.' Then she laughed, her dentures flashing iridescent in the sunlight – she laughed to show she didn't mean any harm.

Jack's mother always wrapped up the extra slices of banana bread in waxed paper for her to take back to the dinky little apartment in Cicero – 'for a snack later on' – and Elsa, who was a spectacularly demonstrative woman – that must have been her downfall, Jack's father once said with a wink – hugged and kissed them all, even Jack's father, whom she kissed square on the mouth – a wet smack – all the time declaring loudly. 'This sure is better than sitting in that old church listening to the priest, eh, having a good laugh, a good laugh is what keeps you greased up.' Sometimes she said, her eyes squeezed and glistening, 'My God, what would I do without youse?' (She always said youse; it was her only imperfection, her daughter Brenda maintained.)

She died four years ago September at fifty-six, from complications following a routine gall bladder operation. There was a funeral in a grey cement Catholic church in Cicero on a Monday morning. Afterwards, standing on the steps of the church, Jack had looked across at his father and saw him crying, a sight he had never seen before. His forehead appeared red and wrecked, the nose bulbous and glistening. He had wiped at his eyes with a handkerchief and in a choked voice muttered, 'Well, I'll say this, she was one hell of a good girl.' There were people standing all over the cold steps listening to him. Elsa had worked for thirty years selling men's socks and underpants at Wards, and a great many of her friends from work had come to the final mass. One of them, a girl of twenty or so, came over to where Jack's father was standing; she flung her arms around his neck, heaving with grief, causing him to utter what he believed to be a stinking lie: 'Now, now, she's happier where she's gone to, it's all for the best, you know that, don't you now?'

After Elsa died Jack's mother fell into a brief depression and her arthritis flared up so that she could hardly sleep. For a while she kept seeing women on buses and in stores who looked like Elsa. That was normal, said Brenda, who was coping with her own grief; that was what often happened after a sudden death.

'You know something else,' Jack's mother went on, her eyes pink, 'whenever I make banana bread I start to bawl.'

'You've still got us,' Jack told her. 'And the kids.'

But in the last year Rob had started staying home on Sunday mornings. He liked to sleep in, he said. If he went at all, he went grudgingly.

And so Jack was surprised on the Sunday morning after the Carpenters' party to find him up and dressed and ready to go. He stood at the back door, zipping his jacket, stamping into his boots. He didn't mention the argument of the night before, nor did Jack. The whole uproar over the Spanish rice seemed shockingly absurd, shameful, trivial, the kind of meaningless explosion that occurs between very young children, the kind of thing best forgotten, especially today on this most glittering of mornings.

It had snowed during the night, the first real snow of the year, a soft, thin, watery layer of Chicago snow, barely enough to cover the spikey backyard grass and leave a flattering loaf of whiteness on the garage roof, but it pleased Jack to see the clutter of back fences reduced and simplified by so neat a covering. The Carpenters' new cedar deck was levelled to mere surface; over the roof of his own garage Jack could see the steep Victorian angles of the Lewises' house, the way in which the damp snow clung to the sloping dormers and topped the chimney. The louvered shutters of the upstairs bedrooms were closed; they were probably still asleep. Poor Bud, Jack said to himself, cold calling all week. But his sympathy was fleeting, unfocused, dislodged from any genuine feeling. The sun, after all, was shining. This morning's snow seemed a gift, coming as it had so early in the new year and arriving with secret absolving power while he slept. 'Deep and crisp and even,' he sang to Rob and Laurie as he backed the car out of the garage.

'Ha,' Rob said, but in a friendly way.

From the backseat Laurie let out a scream. 'Daddy!'

Jack jammed on the brakes. 'Christ. What now?'

'Uncle Bernie,' she screamed. 'You forgot about Uncle Bernie.'

The engine died, Jack started it again, trying to be patient, taking it easy, remembering the choke, speaking softly to the ignition key, saying calmly, 'Bernie's still at the Carpenters'.'

'What?' Laurie shrieked, leaning over into the front seat and pounding his shoulder. 'Is the Carpenters' party still going on? Now? In broad daylight?'

The car shuddered, then slid into gear. 'He slept over there last night,' Jack said, increasing his speed, turning carefully and heading down James Madison Street.

Even Rob looked surprised at this. 'Huh? I thought he didn't even know them before last night.'

'True, true,' Jack said, his tone lightly philosophical, phony even to him. The tyres spun on the wet street; the snow was melting already.

'Why'd he sleep over there, anyway?'

'Well,' Jack paused, 'they've got all those extra beds, I guess that's why.'

'But he'll wake up and he won't know where we've gone,' Laurie said. 'He won't know where we are.'

'I left him a note. I left the back door open for him and a note saying where we are. Okay?'

'I guess so,' Laurie said.

'Weird,' Rob said. 'Weird.'

'He could've had my bed,' Laurie said.

'He could've slept on the couch,' Rob said.

'I offered my bed,' Laurie said. 'Remember? I offered it yesterday.'

'I know you did, sweetie. Now please don't yell in my ear like that. Daddy's got a headache.'

'Ha,' Rob said softly.

'What'd you say?' Jack came to a stop sign and jammed on the brakes, but the car skidded on the wet snow and travelled several feet into the intersection before coming to a stop. 'What'd you say?'

'Nothing.'

'Nothing?'

'Nothing.'

They arrived at ten-thirty, later than usual.

Chapter Fourteen

'WELL,' JACK'S FATHER SAID, EASING HIMSELF INTO HIS Lazy Boy and lighting his first cigarette of the day, 'what's new?'

He was a tall, sparely built, nervous man with standing plumes of fine white hair and large, clean, pink ears. He was sitting with his back to the window, and his ears seemed to Jack to be flamed with light. Now that he had retired from the post office he wore old white dress shirts at home, the sleeves rolled up, the collar unbuttoned. He had a thin knobbed neck, reddish in colour and a trifle distended, and small bright blue eyes that blinked behind sparkling lenses; he'd put off his first cigarette until 11:45 this morning, and – Jack found this even more unusual – he'd put off his first question until this moment.

'What's new?'

Jack loved his father and mother and knew how much they relied on him to bring them the news, whatever that meant – the news that didn't come in the morning *Trib* or winking through their TV screen, the real news. His mother was in the kitchen now, washing the breakfast dishes and listening to Laurie. He could hear Laurie describing the curried chicken rolls she helped make at the Carpenters' yesterday, and his mother was saying, 'Well, well,' in a slow, contemplative, spiral-like way that indicated her mild amazement and total rejection of such things.

'Really nothing new,' Jack said. For a moment he considered telling his father about the party last night, and then decided against it. He seldom told his father about the parties he and Brenda went to; his parents didn't go to parties; they thought parties were for small children on their birthdays. He might tell him about Bernie and Sue splitting up and how Bernie had temporarily moved in with him. His parents knew Bernie well after all these years; before Bernie's parents, Beanie and Sally, retired to their mobile home in Clearwater (Bernie called it Blearwater) they had known them, too. They knew Sue slightly.

Jack's father thought Sue was 'stuck on herself' and his mother thought she was a little 'high and mighty.' Nevertheless Jack knew that news of a separation would alarm them needlessly. Better save it for another day. What else was new? His loss of faith? Impossible. His malaise by now had formed a cool alluring surface; he felt oddly protective toward it, reluctant to see it reduced to January blues or male menopause. And he made it a point never to alarm his parents.

'You say Brenda got away okay?' his father prompted.

'No problem at all.'

'Philadelphia. Why're they having this thing in Philadelphia, anyway? City of brotherly love.'

'Search me.'

'Take Chicago. It's a helluva lot more central, if you know what I mean.'

'I suppose.'

'Chicago's a good convention town, a great convention town. Always has been. American Legion, your Shriners, Lions, and so on.'

'Hmmm.'

'Speaking of that, I was saying to Ma, I'm glad Brenda isn't staying at that hotel where they had the – what do you call it, a few years back? The Legionnaires' disease.'

'I thought they finally proved that – '

'What would she have to pay for a hotel room in Philadelphia? Per night, I mean.'

'I don't know, Dad, maybe thirty, thirty-five.'

'Whew!'

Jack knew his parents found it puzzling, the fact that Brenda had left for a week to attend a craft exhibition. A craft exhibition! They'd never been as far as Philadelphia; they'd never been east of Columbus, Ohio, where his mother's sister once lived. Nor had they ever spent a night apart except for the times when one or the other of them had to go to the hospital, the time Jack's father had his appendix out and the time his mother had the tests for arthritis. Jack suspected that they had exaggerated notions about the importance and prestige of jet travel and that they were mystified about the rites that surrounded it. A week ago, sitting at the Sunday breakfast table, his mother had solemnly passed Brenda a square white envelope. Inside was a *bon voyage* card, bluebirds flying across a sparkled sky, and inside the card was a ten-dollar bill folded in two. The card had been signed – in his father's strange rocking hand – 'love and kisses from Ma and Dad Bowman.'

'You shouldn't have done that,' Brenda had said, her eyes suddenly swimming with tears. 'They shouldn't have done that,' she told Jack again on the way home; but her tone had changed; it seemed to Jack that she sounded inexplicably defensive – even, for some reason, a little angry.

Now Jack's father was saying something else; he was saying with a wink, 'I guess you won't have any trouble getting along for a week on your own. That there Laurie's getting to be a big girl.'

'It was really my idea, Dad, Brenda going to the exhibition. She didn't see how she could get away for a whole week, but when she got the invitation I told her, why not, you only live once.'

'Listen,' his father said, leaning over and lowering his voice. 'What's got into Rob this morning?'

'Rob?' Jack glanced into the dining room where Rob was sitting at the table, reading the Sunday papers. 'Rob?'

'He sick or something?'

'I don't think so. Why?'

'Because,' he leaned closer, 'because he didn't eat a thing this morning, not a damn thing. You notice that?'

Jack shrugged. 'Kids – '

'God, the way that kid used to eat. Like a horse. Oh boy, remember the time he poked all the raisins out of his cinnamon roll and I said, what's the matter, Rob, don't you like the raisins? And he said, yeah Grandpa, I like the raisins a lot, that's why I was saving them for the last.'

'Some more coffee?' Jack asked, rising; he'd heard the cinnamon roll story before.

'Ma's making another pot, be ready in two shakes. You were going to tell me something, before we got off on the subject of Philadelphia. What was it?'

'Nothing. You asked what was new and I said nothing much.'

'What about at work? What's new at work these days? You been busy?'

'Same old thing more or less. We're setting up this new display. I told you about that last week, I think. This Pattern of

89

Settlement show. Great Lakes settlement. Kind of a statistical thing. I'm not all that involved in it.'

'You know, I was thinking about that one night this week. In the middle of the night I woke up thinking about that. What's it going to cost, an exhibition like that? I was wondering.'

Jack hedged. 'Well, this is one of the smaller exhibits, as exhibits go, not like that thing we did last March on the History of the Chicago River.'

'Well, approximately then, what's it worth?'

'Three thousand? Something like that. I'm not sure, to tell you the truth.'

'Three thousand bucks!'

'It's partly the labour. They have to install a lighting system –'

'Three thousand bucks. Whew! Anything else new?'

Jack thought hard. 'Moira Burke is leaving this week. Tuesday. Her husband's retiring. They're going to Arizona.'

'The sunbelt, eh?'

'Uhuh.'

'Who's Moira Burke?'

'You met her, Dad. Last March. At the Chicago River reception, you and Ma. She's Dr. Middleton's secretary. She's been with him twenty-five years. At least.'

'If she's the woman I'm thinking of, she's a good looker. Brunette?'

Jack nodded. 'Not so bad. They're having a farewell lunch for her on Tuesday. The whole staff, I think.'

'Hard to find a good secretary nowdays. I read an article about that. Too bad Brenda didn't keep up –'

'They've already found a replacement for Moira. They've had someone training.'

'I'm thinking of giving up smoking.'

Jack started to laugh.

'What's so funny?'

'You're smoking a cigarette. Right now. I guess it just struck me as kind of funny.'

'I've been reading this book. You seen this book here? Called *You Are Your Own Keeper*.'

'No. But I think I've heard –'

'Written by a doctor. An MD. He starts off explaining how people get hooked on things. Slavery, he calls it. Like we're all like that, slaves, pure and simple. It's not weakness though, he says, it's human nature. But he maintains no one has to be a slave. You can make a decision and break the cycle. At any minute of any day you can sit down and make a decision, this man says. He says habits are only habits if we think they're habits. You have to write it down though. He thinks that's the crux. If you don't put your decision in writing it doesn't mean a damn thing, it just evaporates like air. You've got to put your John Hancock on it. He calls it reinforcement. It makes it concrete.'

'Reinforced concrete?' Jack felt a surge of warmth toward his father.

'Something like that.'

'So you're giving up smoking?'

'Not altogether, not altogether. But what I went and did this week was write down on a piece of paper: I, John Bowman, will smoke only five cigarettes each day for the next week.'

'And?'

'Then you're supposed to take that piece of paper and hide it away. You're not supposed to discuss it with anyone. Like I'm not supposed to be sitting here talking to you about it. He sees it as a contract, see. A written contract with yourself, is what he calls it.'

'What if you break it?'

'Well, so far I haven't. This doctor maintains that by putting it in writing, you've got like a guarantee. You put a date on it and even the time of day. This here now is my first cigarette today. I've got four to go, it's part of the contract. That's how it works.'

The books Jack's father had read – all of them paperbacks – were stacked on the bottom shelf of his smoker's stand. *Take Charge of Your Life, Achieving Inner Peace and Better Health, Twenty-Two Days to Increased Effectiveness, Life Crises and How to Make Them Work for You, Living with Passion, Memory: Your Secret Weapon against Age, Imaginative Marriage and How It Operates, A Psychologist's Guide to Inner Fulfilment, Yes You Can, Goodbye to Lower Back Pain, The Undreamed-of Power of Friendship, Striking Back and Winning, The ABC's of Loving Yourself.*

Jack's attitude toward these books was basically sceptical. He clearly saw the transparencies of the self-improvement vision, the simplistic assumption that the human will can be snapped back and forth like a rubber band. It infuriated him, when he stopped to think about it, that greedy popularizers were allowed to exploit basic human insecurities. From time to time he'd tried to press other books into his father's hands: novels history, travel; but his father, at least in recent years, seemed to be interested only in these endless self-help bibles.

Occasionally Jack had glanced through his father's books, catching a glimpse of what he felt might be the well of his father's most private longings. He'd even felt himself faintly drawn in by the seductive power of the chapter headings: 'Begin Today,' 'Taking Stock,' 'Overcoming Obstacles.' The anecdotes used in these books to illustrate the various human dilemmas had sometimes caught his imagination; yes, he'd thought, I know how that feels, I've been there. He'd even felt the miniature scattered fires begin to burn, saying: yes, we can survive if we only acknowledge our own courage; yes, there is a final knitting up of meaning, a universal means to truth; brotherhood, goodness, purity, and action are more than the loose abstractions Bernie and I have reduced them to. Looking through his father's books, Jack could guess what it was that made them so popular.

What he couldn't understand was why his own father had taken to reading them. His father was sixty-eight years old, in good health, but nevertheless a year away from that well-advertised statistic on death and the American male. The shape of his life had already been drawn; he was a married man, father, grandfather, Republican, retired mail sorter. He lived in Austin, a part of Chicago that in the last ten years had become mainly black; nevertheless he refused to budge; they'll have to carry me out, he said. He was a subscriber to the Chicago *Tribune* and Chicago *Today*, an American citizen, a disbeliever, a smoker of Winstons, a payer of taxes, a lover of Schlitz, owner of a two-toned grey Pontiac in fair condition, an inactive Mason, a recipient of Social Security cheques – what was his father doing reading these books that advocated new systems of thought, new lifestyles and modes of behaviour, new freedoms and possibilities that he could not possibly achieve or even entertain at this time in his life? He was sixty-eight. Did his father – his father! – really want to find a new creativity in his marriage? Did he really give a fuck about reconciling his goals with his self-image? It was crazy, crazy; it was a new American form of masochism, the new perversion of the old American dream. For the life of him Jack couldn't understand what his father was doing reading all those books.

Nevertheless he lifted his feet onto the hassock, settled back and, calmly enough, told his father that he would be interested to hear how the five-cigarettes-a-day campaign was going. 'Sounds like an intriguing idea,' he said, at the same time reflecting to himself that he had somehow managed to become better at being a son than he was at being a father.

His mother came in then, with a pot of coffee and two mugs hooked on her finger. 'Here you go,' she said; her face was composed, almost merry. She had straight grey hair, combed back behind her ears and anchored with combs. Her earlobes were white and plumply innocent; she'd never worn earrings in all her life because she was sure they must hurt. She regarded her husband and son with love. Although she adored her daughter-in-law and thought of her as her own daughter, still Jack sensed that today her joyousness had something to do with the fact that Brenda was absent.

His mother amazed him. Once she had lived in the world, another world, marrying at seventeen a man she met at a dance, someone called Raymond R. Raymond, a shoe salesman. They lived in two rooms on North Avenue, and after a year Raymond R. Raymond lost his job and disappeared. She never heard from him again, although it was believed he went back to Upper Michigan where he came from. All this happened before Jack was born, before Jack's parents met each other. His mother, it seems, survived this blow, and went back to work in the sausage plant. Jack's father told him the whole story one afternoon, one Sunday afternoon in the park, when Jack was eleven or twelve. 'You ought to know, just in case,' he said. In case of what? Jack couldn't imagine. Just in case, his father had said, and with those words he placed a *de facto* censure on the story of his wife's first marriage; it was never again discussed. But never forgotten, either. Raymond R. Raymond – the man who broke Jack's mother's heart. No, Raymond R. Raymond didn't break it; for the extraordinary thing as far as Jack could see was the fact that his frail, nervous and shy mother had managed to absorb this short marriage and desertion and put it behind her. What courage she must have had to go back to work and to be led after a few months to still another dance, this one at the Old Windmill where she met Jack's father who had also, by chance, been taken there by friends. They had danced together twice that night and her new life had begun. His mother amazed him.

She handed him a mug of coffee. Out of the blue, Jack asked her a question. 'Ma, do you by any chance remember someone called Harriet Post?'

'Harriet Post.' She filled the second mug to the brim. 'Harriet Post? That sure rings a bell. But you know my memory for names, Jack, it never was any good. Faces, now. But Harriet Post, you say. Wasn't that your old piano teacher, Jack? Remember she used to come here Wednesdays that year you were learning piano.'

'No, no, Ma,' Jack's father said, reaching for his coffee. 'You remember Harriet Post. I know you do. We met her at that fancy do at the Institute last spring. The Chicago River thing. End of March, wasn't it? She's Dr. Middleton's secretary. Been with him twenty-five years and now she's retiring, Jack's been telling me. Going down to Arizona.' He slapped his shirt pocket for his cigarettes, tapped one out. 'Arizona, that's the place. Everyone's going down there.'

Chapter Fifteen

AFTER A WHILE ROB GREW RESTLESS AND TOOK A BUS HOME, muttering something about homework to be done, about an algebra quiz Monday morning. Laurie settled herself down with the new *Reader's Digest*. Whenever she visited her grandparent's apartment she liked to line up the couch cushions on top of the long, low radiator in the front room and stretch out there on her stomach with a book. She had been doing this for years, since she was a very small girl, three or four. Jack, eyeing her sprawled form – the whiteness of the solid legs, the roundness of rump – speculated that in another year she wouldn't be able to fit herself on the radiator anymore; even now her feet dangled off one end, one foot kicking idly at the hot water pipe.

Jack and his father decided to go for a walk through Columbus Park. They often did this on a Sunday, just the two of them. Jack's mother never came along, although Brenda was always saying to Jack that he should urge her to get out more, that it would do her good to walk a little. And it *would* do her good. Her face, especially around the eyes, was pale as plaster; there was a flakiness about her mouth and chin, a dry talcum-enriched spoilage about her throat and neck. The crisp air would undoubtedly refresh her. But Jack was reluctant to press the point; she had always been a woman relieved to be left alone indoors, where she could do what she was good at doing: straightening a scatter rug with the toe of her bedroom slipper, fluffing up a cushion, folding the newspapers in neat piles. How was she to occupy herself out in the wide freshness of the park? There was nothing but public grass and the huge simpleness of space; what was she to do? And there was her arthritis. The cold crept into her bones; even with heavy lined gloves on, the cold still got in.

Jack and his father, taking their time, their *sweet* time as Jack's father called it, walked in a long leisurely diagonal through the entire park, past the lagoon and the chilly baseball diamonds and the fountains. The water was shut off now, and the fountains were splotched with rust and mildew, and dead leaves were stuck to the rounded iron edges. After that was the area known as 'The Gardens,' and then the damp expanse of the golf course.

It was early afternoon, and at the end of the grass some people were gathering. There must have been forty or fifty of them, Jack estimated, mostly young people, students probably, even a few children. One woman had a baby strapped to her back. Some of them carried signs.

'Now what in Christ – ?' Jack's father yelped softly.

'Looks like a meeting of some kind.'

'Christ, I know what it is. I saw that in the paper this morning, that same bunch. It's those crazy hunger strikers. They won't eat. Did you read about them, what they're up to?'

'I haven't seen today's paper yet.'

'It's about those two scientists. The ones the Russians are keeping in jail. These hunger-strike people want to get them out of jail and send them to Israel or something.'

'I think I heard someone talking about that last night – ' Jack had a vague, jumbled memory, something someone had mentioned at the party, another crisis shaping up, the authorities cracking down again in Moscow.

The people with the signs were standing in a rough circle, some of them hunched over and shivering. This seemed a peaceful demonstration, unlike those Jack had witnessed in the Loop in the late sixties. Once, on a Friday, he and Bernie had come out of Roberto's and found themselves in a thicket of hurling bodies and thwacking police clubs. He had been frightened; for a minute he had thought anything could happen. Then a cool voice in his head took over, saying: here you are in the midst of a riot, here you are viewing a phenomenon of the times. But times had changed. The post-Vietnam, post-Watergate demonstrations seemed to him to have a degree of futility and bedragglement about them.

One of the demonstrators in the park was lifting his arms – a calm Old Testament gesture – and speaking. He was a large, boyish, white-haired man wearing a plaid poncho that reached to his knees. His voice was so low that it was impossible to hear what he said, but Jack could make out the lettering on some of the signs. *Freedom to Dissent – Freedom to Breathe. America Next –*

Hold Fast for Freedom. Another sign revolving, bobbing up and down, proclaimed *Americans Do Care*. Jack and his father stood watching as the circle broke abruptly and reformed into a long staggered line. Jack could hear singing – what was it? – 'The Battle Hymn of the Republic'? It seemed a quaint choice, an echo from the sixties. *Glory, glory Hallelujah* floated unevenly through the nearly empty park as the marchers filed toward the west gate and made for Austin Boulevard. Jack and his father watched until the last one was out of sight.

'A helluva lot of good it does for them to go and starve themselves,' Jack's father said. 'I mean, who the hell cares?'

'I suppose it's just a way of getting people to take notice. A tactic of sorts.'

'You'd think we didn't have plenty of problems right here, crime in the streets and what have you, inflation, bunch of small-time bums in City Hall, welfare, and these guys get all steamed up about a couple of Russians who probably can't even speak English.'

'I suppose you have to start somewhere,' Jack said with a feebleness that dismayed him.

'I say, let the bums starve if that's what the hell they want.'

They cut through the tennis courts and then through the children's playground, heading for the extreme southwest corner of the park, the dark, sober, wooded corner that Jack liked best. Except for this one corner, Columbus Park seemed to him to be exactly like the other big city parks, dusty, littered, prescribed, a facility rather than a piece of creation, all the areas designated and apportioned, utilized and maintained and knowable – all but this one corner. How had it come into being? It was a mystery. Jack could only imagine that years ago someone at City Hall had decided that what the west side of Chicago needed – what Columbus Park needed – was a micro-cosmic wilderness. A chunk of nature at the city's edge, a wilderness the size of a handkerchief. The whole area couldn't have been more than an acre in size, perhaps an acre and a half, but its minuteness had been cunningly camouflaged by thickly planted pines and spruce and by an intricate system of rustic paths weaving back and forth. Here and there the ground had been artificially elevated; there was an impression of harsh rocky out-cropping, a raw unbidden underground force. There was a stream and even a small waterfall that rested, if you

97

looked carefully, on concrete piles. The water rushed over these falls with surprising speed, crashing into a foamy pond, yellowish in colour and smelling of urine. The pond itself drained magically, steadily, into a culvert, artfully concealed by plantings. Despite the rankness of the water, the air in this part of the park had a scrubbed, Wisconsin-like scent of pine pitch and earth-rot. Jack never came here without the phrase 'sylvan glade' popping into his head.

Sylvan glade – but when he'd first discovered this place years ago, the phrase sylvan glade hadn't been part of his vocabulary; then he had called it simply 'the woods.' That was when he was ten or eleven years old, when he and Bernie Koltz came here almost every day. In those days there had been a slatted wood and wire fence around this section of the park and a stern sign warning that trespassers would be prosecuted. It hadn't stopped them, of course, since it had been ridiculously easy to lift the fence and scramble under. In those days he and Bernie brought sandwiches and apples and stayed all day long in the woods. The stream, the pond, the waterfall, the secret boreal foliage and the still, ferny undergrowth had seemed to them to comprise their own planet; Jack felt about the woods not so much a sense of possession, but a feeling of refuge, of safe enclosure – hardly anyone else was ever there, although once they had seen a tramp kneeling in the bushes, his pants down, poking at something with a stick. The sound of rushing water shut out the traffic noises from Austin Boulevard, and the tops of the red brick apartment buildings could barely be seen over the heights of the trees.

It was summer; once under the fence, they were free to be anything. He and Bernie explored the woods, climbed all the trees that were climbable. At first they built forts and dams out of branches. Later on they played other games, games that had little to do with the actual wilderness setting – the protecting woods merely offered a sanctuary in which they might act out their preposterous daydreams of adventure. Mostly these daydreams had to do with the war, with the exploits of a particular crack commando squad – The Blue Jays? – the bombing of enemy bridges, the hurling of grenades, the complicated, theatrical one-man missions in pursuit of Tojo or Mussolini or Adolf Hitler himself. Between them they shared and shifted the hero's role, accomplishing the impossible and unthinkable, crawling on their stomachs through the thorny underbrush, clawing their way into enemy foxholes, attacking with bare hands, gouging out eyes, plunging bayonets directly into warmly beating Nazi hearts. In these games recognition, gratitude, and fierce manly modesty all had a part. Some of the games were as long and as complicated as movies, requiring voice changes and shifting sets of characters; sometimes they took on the part of the enemy, sometimes the terse military commanding roles of Admiral Halsey or General MacArthur. They expertly imitated the sound of whining bullets, the rattle of machine guns, and the whistling and exploding of bombs. Their stories – dramas – turned over with spontaneity, with an easy, instant, willing adaptation; the scenes bled together, firming, fading, recurring, and reaching peaks of near tearful splendour. Wounded, they fell to the earth, released groans of agony into the leafy trees, uttered fearful tense messages moments before death came – *can you get through the lines . . . MacArthur's waiting . . . tell him I did all I could . . . . aaaaahhhh.*

At midday they stopped and ate their sandwiches by the side of the waterfall. Once they brought potatoes and made a bonfire, then quickly snuffed it out before the smoke gave them away. They took off their shoes and walked in the shallow creek water, and once Jack spotted a large toad, squat and brown, quivering on a flattened stone. He had been astonished at the sight. He couldn't believe that a toad could live and grow to such a size in the city of Chicago; it occurred to him that the brown toad might have no idea about the size of the park; probably he thought this was a jungle he was living in, immense and eternal.

Why exactly had this corner of the park been locked up during that time? Jack didn't know. He had never known. It might have been that the pond was considered dangerous for small children. He had never asked or even wondered very much about it. The encircling fence and the padlocked gate had not seemed particularly mysterious to him when he was a boy. The warning sign with its threat of prosecution – a word Jack confused with execution, imagining a mean-mouthed, squint-eyed firing squad – had seemed no more than a part of the larger universal prohibition that existed everywhere: certain things were not allowed, certain acts were not permitted, certain places were off limits; this section of Columbus Park was closed, it was as simple as that. The fact was immutable, and required no explanation – it was like the dark forbidden forests encountered in certain old folk tales, phenomena unassailable at the level of logic.

But today, entering the woods, he asked his father if he knew why the woods had once been closed.

At first Jack's father couldn't recall that the woods had ever been shut off. Then, pausing to think a minute, he remembered. Yes. This part of the park *had* been closed once, he said. Back in the forties. During a polio epidemic. Closed for a month.

'A month? Only a month? Are you sure? I'm sure it was longer than that. It *seemed* longer. More like years.'

'A month. Two months maybe, July and August it would have been. That's when the polio always was. We used to call it infantile paralysis. The infantile. Every summer here in Chicago we had the infantile. You'd be too young to remember or know what was going on – '

'I remember.'

'One year – I forget just when it was – it was real bad. Hundreds of cases. It was always in the paper every night, in the headlines. Ma and I always looked quick at the headlines for the number of new cases. They closed this part of the park then, for a month or so.'

'It was hard to believe; at last Jack felt a great reluctance to believe. His father's memory, God knows, was unreliable, especially lately, but at the same time the explanation had a simple, locked-together rationality about it. It was, he had to admit, undoubtedly true – it all fit together except for the period of time, the one or two months. It seemed impossible to Jack that what stretched so luxuriously long in his memory could be so foreshortened in reality. But on the other hand he knew – he was a reasonably observant father – that children have a way of distorting the size of events and the quality and measurement of time that surrounds them. His memory could easily have been tripped up – it wouldn't have been the first time. It may even have been a deliberate tripping up; he may, unconsciously, have wanted to remember the woods as being perpetually forbidden and dangerous, a kind of private wilderness positioned in a pure, unmarked cosmic zone of timelessness. Children did such things. He could imagine that he and Bernie might have wanted to create at the edge of Chicago, within walking distance of home, a private illusion of impossible continuing adventure. It made him smile to think of it.

Even with adults it happened, of course; all kinds of fantasies bumped along through history, half the time obliterating the facts, half the time contributing something human, a pleasing transposition of logic, a way of balancing the seeming precision of clocks and calendars. He would have to discuss that with Bernie, the place of illusion in history. The *value* of illusion. Dragons, for example, and unicorns: imagined creatures, but still a part of the human past, viable and accountable and more important in their way than real creatures like wolves and bears. How treacherous it was then, all these massed, tentative notations, illuminations, recordings; simmered down, what did it come to but mere vagaries of wishful thinking? History was no more in the end than what we wanted it to be. Like the woods in Columbus Park. The fence around the woods had been down for years, twenty-some years, yet Jack persisted in thinking of the place as being sequestered; mentally he had never really stripped away the aura of prohibition, and nowadays when he came here with his father on Sundays, although his younger self was only obscurely recalled, he still experienced a small jolt of surprise and disappointment to find he could enter freely.

The main paths of the park now led directly into the wooded area, and there seemed to be more space between the trees. The light was differently coloured, brighter. Some of the walks had been surfaced with asphalt; a certain amount of seasonal pruning took place. Despite this, it was never crowded. Today there were only three small boys, skinny, black, wearing jeans and identical blue velvety sweaters; brothers, it looked like, dangling fishing lines into the stream. 'Ha,' Jack's father said, 'they'll be lucky, getting anything live and kicking out of this sewer.'

Last night's snow had gone. All of it had melted, leaving the ground soggy underfoot. The upturned branches of the evergreens shone splendidly green, and the sky was tree-blurred and glassed over with a cover of cloud. The sun, watery, orange, fuzzed at the edges like a Nerf ball, seemed more of a moon than a sun. It's going to rain, Jack thought.

His father had already asked the question Jack knew he would ask: how was the book coming?

Every week he tensed for the moment when his father asked this question; yet, when the moment finally arrived, when the question came sailing through the air at him, he was unfailingly surprised at how easily he found the words to make a reply. And always the words were both true and not true. 'It's coming,' he'd say, or 'It's slow, but it's shaping up, I think.' He felt amazement and guilt at how easily his father's curiosity was satisfied; his father asked so little really, never questioning Jack on particulars, merely nodding, smiling widely, saying something spirited and affirmative, something fatherly. 'Slow but sure is what I always say,' or, 'Well, well, just so you keep plugging, so long as you don't get bogged down on a plateau,' or 'Rome wasn't built in a day, you know that, we all know that.'

These offerings of his father – if offerings was the word – seemed to Jack to be so innocently, willingly, delivered that he had sometimes found himself rising to the incandescence of the moment, seeking, for his father's sake, to extend its duration. He exaggerated his progress, showed unreasonable optimism. 'Should be there by spring,' he'd told his father a few months earlier, standing in this very spot next to the big feathery Norwegian spruce. 'Dr. Middleton says he has at least two publishers who've shown interest.'

'Wow!' His father received these progress reports with head-shaking pleasure. 'Boy, oh boy, that'll be something all right, a book writer in the family, I can just see it. Sort of raises your status quo, if you get what I mean.'

Today the ground at the bend of the creek was slippery. 'Watch your step, Dad,' Jack said.

'I'm fine, I'm fine.'

'It's the melted snow, it's made it muddy here.'

'I can see it, for Pete's sake, that's what I've got glasses for.'

'Just warning you – '

'Anyway, you were saying, about the book – '

'I was just saying that Chapter Six's almost finished. I'm taking it in to the office tomorrow so it can be typed up. Dr. Middleton wants a look at it.'

'How many pages would that be?' his father asked, turning to Jack, his face alight.

'Thirty or so. I'm not quite done, but I'm going to go over it again tonight.'

'Your mother's going to be real happy to hear that. Did you tell Ma?'

'No, I didn't. Of course, it's still pretty rough, lots of finishing touches, lots of work to go – '

'Let me ask you this, do you think it'll be in the library? When it's all done?'

'The public library? My book? Oh, I don't know about that, Dad. It's sort of specialized for the public library.'

'Well, for Crissakes they've got books on all kinds of strange things. Crazy damn things like collecting bottle tops and what have you. And here you are, a Chicago boy, born and bred – '

'I don't know, Dad.'

'Let me tell you what I was thinking. I woke up the other night. I don't sleep that well anymore, that's why Ma thought she'd be better off in the other room – '

'You told me that.'

' – she's better off without me waking up at night all the time and bumping around. As a matter of fact I read an article about that very thing, and you know something? It's perfectly normal, they say, at my age. The human being, when it gets older, doesn't require the same hours of sleep, it's absolutely normal. Where was I? I woke up the other night and I had this idea. I said to myself, when Jack's book's done, all finished with the cover on and everything, I'm going to go out to the store and buy a copy and give it to the Austin Library. A donation like. And, and, I thought I could stick one of those little stickers in it, you know, donated by John and Selma Bowman and – '

'Dad, I don't think they do that anymore – '

' – John and Selma Bowman, the parents of the author. Now how do you like the sound of that? This was in the middle of the night when I thought this up, so I got out of bed and wrote it down. I didn't want to forget about it. The parents of the author. Well? How do you think that sounds? Not so bad?'

A pause. Then Jack said, 'It's a long, long way from being finished. And, Dad, as a matter of fact, I may be in for some competition. It turns out that someone else has written a book on exactly the same subject.'

'Someone else?'

'This happens all the time, of course. It's nothing unusual. I found out about it the other day. Out of the blue. It's kind of a bad break, I guess you could say.'

His father had stopped walking. 'This other book, is it any good?'

'I honestly can't say, Dad.' Jack thought he saw the corners of his father's mouth tuck in. His thin whittled face seemed to shrink, a frail wedge between the wide ears.

'Well,' the voice held a tremor, 'do you *think* it's any good, Jack? The other book?'

'Actually, it's probably going to be – chances are it's going to be . . . pretty good.'

'*Going* to be?'

'It's not out yet. Not until summer.'

'Well, hell,' his father said slowly, his mouth puffed like a wreath, 'well, hell, Jack, you'll be finished before this other guy. I mean you've got the edge on him, haven't you? Spring, you said, wasn't it?'

'I'm not all that sure about spring – '

'Anyway, what the hell difference does it make? So there's two books about Indians. Everyone likes to read about the Indians.'

'It's starting to rain, Dad. Maybe we'd better head back.'

'Just a few measly drops, that's what they said on the news, scattered showers.'

'I'd better be getting back, Dad – '

'It's early, we just got here. Why don't we walk up there on the other side of the bridge?'

'I really should get home. The kids – Rob – and I've got that chapter to go over. For tomorrow.'

'Jesus, yes. I forgot about that. You've got to get that ready by tomorrow morning. Let's take the short cut, we don't want to meet up with those hungry hippies. Ha. Be home in a lamb's tail. You know something? It's going to really rain, by Christ.'

Chapter Sixteen

JACK HAD LEFT THE BACK DOOR UNLOCKED FOR BERNIE, BUT when he and Laurie got home late in the afternoon, the house was empty. Laurie dropped her coat on the floor, wandered into the living room, and switched on the TV set. On the kitchen table Jack found a note from Rob.

> Gone with Bernie K. to Charleston. Back around 7. Sue K. phoned, wants you to phone her back at hospital 366 4556. Mrs. Carpenter phoned and said Mr. Carpenter would live.
>
> Rob

He read the note twice. The words were clearly enough written in Rob's neat hand, the capital letters a trifle flamboyant, but the smaller letters tidy, economical, with finishing strokes that were definitive and strong. A good aggressive hand, Jack thought, pleased. Rob was generally efficient about taking down phone messages; all in all, Jack mused, he wasn't such a bad kid. Surly. Greedy at times. But surprisingly respectful, the way, for example, he always remembered to say *Mr.* Carpenter and *Mrs.* Carpenter. As kids go these days, he could be worse. He could be into drugs or shoplifting or flunking out of school. He was fairly reliable when it came right down to it, fairly responsible. But this note made no sense at all.

'Mr. Carpenter would live.' Jack said it out loud to the kitchen wall, testing the words for meaning: 'Mr. Carpenter would live.' Damn Rob anyway, why was he always so vague? That time he sent the post card from Cub camp when he was eight: one sentence – 'It's okay about the snake.' Now this – 'Mr. Carpenter would live' – he should know better. Perhaps it had something to do with last night's party. Maybe Larry'd really tied one on; come to think of it, he *had* looked pretty well oiled when Jack last saw him. Probably woke up with a hangover. But he *would* live – Jack supposed he was to take that ironically; he would survive his hangover; was that what this note meant?

No, too far-fetched; ridiculous. Might be a good idea to give the Carpenters a call. Just in case.

He dialled the number, listened for an answer, but there was no one at home. He counted to ten and tried again; no one.

Next, gritting his teeth, he phoned Sue at the Austin General. Dr. Koltz had gone for the day, he was told. No, she hadn't left a number. Jack put down the phone, breathed out a low whistle of relief; the last thing he felt like doing was talking to Sue Koltz.

The sense of being reprieved always came sweetly to him. He was tired. Last night's party, that swirl of faces, all that booze, how many scotches had he had? Bernie weeping, Brenda away, the damned Indians and their bloody trading practices. And Rob leaving meaningless notes on the kitchen table. Now Laurie had turned the television up full blast; the football game, the post-season special, the Bears and the Packers, already into the third quarter. Damn it, he'd meant to watch the game. His head hurt, his eyes felt sore. He'd forgotten to pick up a carton of milk. There didn't seem to be any food – he'd never seen the kitchen stove so cold and clean. Outside, the rain was pouring down.

Once again he read the note, line for line this time, word for word. What was Bernie thinking of, taking a kid Rob's age out to Charleston? Rob had never been near an institution like Charleston. Of his two children, Rob was the sensitive one. Once, years ago, Jack had seen him weeping as he watched the dispatches from Vietnam on television – children, horribly burned, wrapped in blankets by wailing mothers. Charleston would be shocking; he himself had never been to a place like Charleston. (Fortunately there had been no need. He shrank from the thought.) It was plain crazy, all of it was crazy. But the craziness, he noted with something like calm, was indecipherable, out of reach. And what could he do? He had already done what was required of him, returned the call to Sue, tried to get hold of the Carpenters, pondered Rob's presence at Charleston – he'd done what he could and, for the moment, was absolved. He could now fold this note, put it in his back pocket, push the contents outside his consciousness, and wait for the moment of enlightenment that would come, that would certainly come, to explain its meaning.

Most probably the explanation was something laughably simple; probably Rob had written this note quickly; Bernie would be anxious to get going; it was forty miles to Charleston Hospital where Bernie's daughter was, and there was always lots of traffic. In his haste Rob must have made some minor ellipsis or some curious small error of syntax, enough though to throw the whole message into question.

Jack mistrusted paper, anyway. Words, ink, paper, the limitations of language and expression, human incompetence; it was absurd, the importance that was put on mere paper. For a historian he had always had a peculiar lack of faith in the written word, and furthermore, he had never been fully persuaded that history was, by definition, what it claimed to be, a written record. More often, it seemed to him, history was exactly the reverse – what *wasn't* written down. A written text only hints, suggests, outlines, speculates. A marriage licence wasn't the history of a marriage; he had given this example to Bernie not two weeks ago. A written law, set down on a sheet of papyrus or a clay tablet, wasn't a statement of fact, but only a way of pointing to a condition that didn't exist. Everything had to be read backwards in a kind of mirror language.

Then there was the further problem about the reliability of the recorder, the one who performed the actual task of writing. Take diaries, for instance, he had said to Bernie. For every diarist there were ten thousand non-diarists. So who was to be trusted? The singular exception, with his poised compulsive quill, or the thousands of thronging cheerful non-recorders who make up the bulk of society? To record was to announce yourself as a human aberration, a kind of pointing, squealing witness who by the act of inscribing invites suspicion.

But this was only the beginning: there was an even greater fallacy, as Jack saw it: the fact that most of life fell through the mesh of what was considered to be worthy of recording. Jack had gone into this very argument with Bernie only a few weeks earlier, presenting the case of the English barmaid, a story he had invented on the spot and for which he had since developed a certain fondness. The English barmaid, he told Bernie over lunch, lived in the town of Birkenhead in the year 1740.

'Why Birkenhead?' Bernie had been alert and obliging that day. 'Why 1740?'

'Well, Birkenhead because records were less reliable in the provinces. And 1740 because that puts her fairly safely in the camp of the illiterate. To continue – '

'Okay.'

'One day this illiterate provincial barmaid was working down at the local pub. It happened that it was late afternoon, May the fifteenth, say. Business was a little slow that day, so she had a chance to polish the brasses, set up the tankards for the evening trade, give the old floor a push with the old broom – '

'Then what?'

'Then, about dusk, wham, the door opened, and in came an unemployed agricultural worker.'

'Illiterate?'

'Absolutely. To the toes. Also itinerant, a stranger to the Birkenhead region. Hailed from the south, so he said, speaking in his soft unfamiliar accent. Well, he plunked himself down on a bench, tossed a threepence on the table, and announced that he was thirsty.'

'Go on. You're taking too long.'

'It soon became apparent that he thirsted for more than brown ale. He eyed the barmaid up and down, took in her flashing black eyes and her . . . generous, country-sized proportions, her air of ease – '

'I can tell it's been a while since you've seen any English barmaids – '

'This stranger leaned over and managed to grab the wench's wrist – '

'The wench? Jesus.'

'He pulled her close. And whispered into her ear. Would you, he said, care to go for a walk when you've finished work? Down by the river, he said.'

'Is there a river in Birkenhead? What river?'

'Any river. Make it a pond then. As I said before, it was May, the month of May, the blossoms were out, there were daffodils.'

'Not by any chance a *host* of golden daffodils?'

'And, what's more important, lots of tall grass. Take note of that, tall grass is crucial to this story.'

'I can imagine,' Bernie said.

'Take my word for it. The two of them, the strapping young stranger, the lovely young lass, walked through the tall sweet grass. Eventually they decided to sit down in the tall sweet grass, rest themselves a while.'

'Ye – es.'

'The stars were starting to come out – '

'One by one.'

'And the stranger, this unemployed illiterate agricultural worker leaned over and slowly unbuttoned the barmaid's blouse. He was breathing very rapidly by this time, at least so it seemed to her.'

'This is one of your better stories, Jack.'

'After that there was a loosening of petticoats, a fumbling of knickers.'

'Aha! I think I see where this may be headed.'

'And there, under the silent stars and the blank stare of the moon, the barmaid of Birkenhead was ceremoniously deflowered.'

'Penetrated. Through and through?'

'Completely.'

'And?'

'That's it. The end.'

'The end of the story? No punchline?'

'No punchline. Well, there *is* a little postscript. Really a non-postscript since, literally, it was not written down. It's just this – that the deflowering by the river remained a secret. Each went his own way after this magic evening. But in the heart of each, this evening lived on. And on and on. Now do you see the point?'

'To tell the truth – '

'This moment was historical. It happened. But in no way did it enter into written record.'

'It might have.'

'How?'

Bernie thought a minute. 'What if she got pregnant? You could hie yourself over to England, go to the parish church of Birkenhead, look up the year 1740 in the records, and you'd find a registration of a birth, nine months after the event. Then you could call your story a historical event.'

'It so happened that on this night the stars were benevolent. Conception did not take place, there was no pregnancy and no registration of birth. But can you deny it? That this wasn't history?'

'What if the barmaid got old and forgetful and happened to mention the encounter to a passing minstrel who was really a novelist in disguise and who later wrote a book called *The Tall*

Grasses of Birkenhead? Then you might be justified in calling it history, though of a very doubtful sort.'

'But this was not the case,' Jack said. 'The barmaid converted to Methodism, quit her job, married a very up-tight shoemaker and lived the rest of her life as a god-fearing woman. She never told a soul, though doubtless her thoughts occasionally stole back to that moment of passion. But there was absolutely no written record of this event, you'll have to take my word for it. Her body is a poor, unmarked skeleton now, under the chapel floor. Even the skeleton is slowly – '

'No, it's no go, Jack. I won't buy it. You've got to write off the whole episode, picturesque as you may find it. There is no way you can possibly call this a historical event, and you know it.'

'But isn't that completely absurd when you and I both know it's true?'

'You want to go outside the definitions,' Bernie said, 'but you can't. This story of yours has no more weight than a dream would have.'

'Maybe dreams are historical happenings, too.'

'If they're recorded, yes, I'd agree to that much. Your problem is you want history to be more than it can possibly be. You want it to contain everything. All the grains of sand in the universe. Christ, you think history's a magic bulldozer, sweeping it all up as we go along. When all it is is a human invention – rather a presumptuous one, too – and, my God, it's got all the human limitations. Plus time limitations, technical limitations, the whole thing. It's never going to be more than the dimmest kind of story telling.'

Bernie was right, of course; Jack knew he was right. Even if the English barmaid had left a written record, he would never be able to bring himself to trust it. She had a soul of permafrost, despite her willing nature. If, for instance, she had somehow been taught to write in her old age – Jack pictured her bent over a rough table, a small leaded window furnishing light – what she would put down would be something altogether different from her actual experience in the tall grass; the minute her pen touched ink, a second self would begin to flow, conditioned, guarded, forgetful, ecstatic, vain, lyric, discursive, the words becoming what all recorded history becomes eventually, a false image, bannered and expository as a public freize, a mixture of the known and the unknowable. The shapely distances of the past were emblematic and no more.

Even something as brief and as nearly accidental a notation as his son Rob's message sagged under the weight of particular assumptions. Mr. Carpenter would live. Mr. Carpenter would live? The assumption would have to be – Jack turned it over in his mind as he opened a can of chicken noodle soup – the assumption would have to be that Mr. Carpenter's – Larry's – ability to live was somehow thrown into jeopardy; a calamity of some kind had overtaken Larry Carpenter. And no ordinary calamity, either; it would have to be something extraordinary and serious.

He dumped the soup into a saucepan, added water, heated it briefly over a bright flame, then poured it into two cereal bowls.

Laurie was lying on the rug in the living room, watching the last sixty seconds of the game. Green Bay was within inches of the goal line as Jack handed her a bowl of soup and slumped into a chair. He loved the Green Bay Packers, and he waited, expectantly, as the front line was whistled into motion and they let loose with their invisible ball.

It looked so simple on the tube; Green Bay was so close, only a yard away, and yet they failed. Jack leaned forward, spilling a stream of soup on the rug, but he couldn't make out exactly what was going wrong. Arms, legs, a close-up of shoulders and bullet-heads and dancing buttocks, sliding and collapsing; where was the ball? A referee stepped in, raised burly hands above his head; the game was suddenly over.

Laurie pulled herself up, stretching. Jack scooped at the last of his soup, thinking he was still hungry, then thinking that he really should phone the Carpenters again.

He could see the corner of their house from the window; there was a light burning; someone was home. He should do something. Yes, he would phone. Right away. Before he changed his mind.

Chapter Seventeen

MONDAY MORNING. JACK WAS WAITING FOR DR. MIDDLETON to arrive; he was early, it was just 10:25. For some reason he was trembling slightly; high on his left cheek, just beneath the eye, a nerve twittered. His throat rasped with dryness. Of course he'd hardly slept last night; it was midnight before things calmed down, and after three before sleep finally came – he'd dreamed, amazingly enough under the circumstances, of Brenda, a lush, burrowing, sexual dream. The alarm had gone off at seven sharp.

It was only natural, Jack reasoned, to feel a little on edge after a night like that, and his edginess was sharpened now by the sight of Dr. Middleton's desk, broad, heavy, calmed by neat piles of papers that were weighed down by small flashing specimens of Michigan ore. An antique desk lamp with an amber glass shade spread a circle of warmth on the fine-grained surface. A framed photograph of Mrs. Middleton – smiling, her Nordic lips relaxed – stood in one corner; next to her the telephone gleamed with a gentlemanly lustre. 'Dr. Middleton should be here in a sec,' Moira Burke told Jack.

She was looking jaunty on her second last day at work, almost military in a navy blazer and yellow silk scarf, thickly knotted under her chin. Twin arcs of blue eyeshadow made her look tough and quizzing.

'So,' Jack said in what he recognized as his phony good-cheer voice, the one he dredged up for hangover mornings, 'so, at last, D Day's finally arrived.'

'Ha!' Moira said.

He had more or less decided what he would say to Dr. Middleton about Chapter Six. That was one good thing about driving in from Elm Park; those early morning traffic jams provided an opportunity to get your thoughts together. Not that there should be any real difficulty, he reflected, since confrontations with Dr. Middleton required no explanation beyond the simple truth. There was about Dr. Middleton a square, straightforward frontality, unusual in a man of his particular discipline. Jack saw him as a kind of boulevard historian with an intellect both spry and elastic, and a rare willingness to deal with actuality so that there was no need for elaborate excuses or face-saving alibis. Delays, distractions, detours were all acceptable in this civilized environment. Jack could relax, take a deep breath. So he hadn't managed to get Chapter Six rounded off as promised; Dr. Middleton certainly wasn't going to fire him for that, or clap him over the head with a ruler; the worst that would happen would be a mild, sympathetic indication of disappointment, an almost imperceptible shaking of the head, a tapping of his pen upon the desk blotter, an instant's brief silence. Why then this turmoil?

Moira gestured toward a chair. 'Why don't you sit down. Might as well take a load off your feet while you're waiting.'

'Maybe I will.' There was something coarse about Moira – 'Take a load off' – a broad, snapping brassiere-strap bravado – would Mel, her replacement, be any different? Jack turned and gave Moira a companionable, low-energy smile, uttering a soft moan. 'Monday morning,' he explained, his fingers moving painfully to his temples.

'You really don't look all that perky.'

'What a weekend!'

'Oh?' She looked interested.

'Fellow next door tried to kill himself.'

Why had he said that? Why had he spoken at all? He hadn't intended to, not to Moira. Christ! At least he hadn't mentioned any names.

'Really?' A rewarding gasp.

Jack felt himself growing calm; Ah, the insidious pleasure of passing on bad news. 'Early Sunday morning, about eight. They found him just in time.'

'How – ?'

'The old garage trick, carbon monoxide. Had the car running, the door shut. But he's going to be all right, they think. No brain damage, at least nothing that can be detected at this point.'

'Old? Young?' Moira eased herself into a chair. Her brow split into a half a dozen evenly spaced furrows. Attractive.

'Middle,' Jack said. 'Thirty-something. Late thirties.'

'That can be a bad time,' Moira said. 'I remember that period. Thirty, early forties – '

Stop. Jack cringed; he didn't want to know about Moira's early forties. Or anyone's early forties. 'Another neighbour found him. Lucky, really. This other man, Bud Lewis, is a jogger. Three miles every morning before breakfast, even Sundays, if you can believe it. He does laps around Van Buren Park, thirty, forty laps every day. Well,' he paused, 'fortunately he starts his run down the alley behind us, and he was just going by the garage next door when he happened to notice some exhaust leaking out under the door. Lucky it was a cold day.'

'I'll say – '

'He broke the window and got in somehow. It was just a little window. He had to hoist himself up and then crawl through to get inside. They said at the hospital that if it had been another five minutes – '

He paused. *Five minutes*; he watched Moira absorb the implications beyond that five minutes.

'Men,' Moira remarked with energy, 'are under a lot of pressure these days. In their work. It never lets up, it's a jungle. My husband, Bradley, he's had his rough times.'

'Yes,' Jack said, 'these things happen.'

'Or family pressures, too,' Moira said. 'They can be just as bad.'

'Yes.'

'I nearly went to pieces when our daughter Sandra quit high school. She was on the honour roll and then she got in with the wrong crowd. Drugs. I know what it can be like. You get over it but it takes a toll.'

Jack nodded. He had met the daughter once. She had come with Moira and her husband to one of the exhibits, but that had been years ago. She'd been about eight then, with long beautiful brown braids. What could have happened to that little girl? Poor Moira. Poor little girl.

'Do they know *why* he did it? Like did he leave a note? They usually do.'

'No, no note. But they figure it was depression.'

'Depression can be bad.'

'It sounds crazy, to me anyway, but he was in a play, this man. A local thing, strictly an amateur deal. But someone went and did a review of it for the papers, called it a real bomb, and zeroed in on him in particular.'

'I've seen some of those play reviews. In Chicago *Today*. And in the *Trib*. They can be pretty biting. Downright cruel.'

Jack stopped, caught himself. Should he be telling Moira all this? Janey had been emphatic: she didn't want the whole world knowing about Larry, at least no one who didn't absolutely have to know. She'd even gone around, she said, to all the nurses on the floor and begged them to keep the thing quiet. Larry would die if this gets around, Janey said. 'You know what they'd say, Jack. That Larry Carpenter can dish it out, but he can't take it. That's what they'd say, I can just hear it.'

It was true the review had been rough; late last night Jack finally got around to reading it, and as he read, his heart froze. A royal hatchet job, unsparing. But at the same time it occurred to him that if he hadn't lived next door to Larry Carpenter, if he hadn't known where it would end, he might have read the same piece with a certain amount of – what? – glee? Here was a drama critic drowned in his own brand of vitriol. Rough justice. Just desserts. A chunk of irony to chew on. There was no doubt about it; Larry had on occasion been equally vituperative. He had a short, sharp way with the second-rate, although he normally muted his blows with the special Carpenter cleverness – perhaps that made the difference. Gordon Tripp – and Jack had always considered his movie reviews to be stylish and distanced – seemed out for blood; every word fell with malice. (Or did it? The year he and Bernie had discussed modern morality, Jack had argued that evil was the result of simple carelessness.) Larry must have got on the wrong side of Gordon Tripp. Either that or Larry really was the 'most pompous, self-congratulatory Hamlet, amateur or professional, ever to disgrace the Chicago stage.' (Something of an overkill, a statement like that, the kind of thing Larry himself would have avoided.) Had Larry really stood at centre stage and 'declaimed in the manner of a wet owl on the make, horny with ego, pop-eyed with importance'? Christ! Was it true he had 'scratched at his crotch behind the canvas trees'? (If he did, Janey said, it was because the polyester armour itched.) 'This too, too arrogant flesh isn't solid enough to play Mickey Mouse, let alone Hamlet,' Gordon Tripp had railed. 'Could it be that the Elm Park Little Theatre forgot about the shoes of the cobbler's children? Or were they simply bowled over by a case of downtown puffery?' (Leah Wallberg would burn at that, probably already

115

was burning.) 'At least,' the review concluded, 'theatrical history has been made. Hamlet, as played in the venerable old suburbs by Chicago's own Larry Carpenter, is no longer the tragic hero Shakespeare envisioned. He has been remodelled out of all recognition into a kind of Clark Kent unable to locate a phone booth.'

It was too bad. It was ill-natured and uncharitable. But suicide? Janey said Gordon Tripp, once a friend of Larry's, had been miffed when Larry's column was picked up for syndication and his wasn't. A case of jealousy, clear and simple. She also suggested that it hadn't been the review alone that had set Larry off. She'd told Jack and Bernie late last night, sitting in Jack's kitchen, eating chicken wings, that there had been other factors involved, *numerous* other factors. Larry had had a good deal to drink that night; certain kinds of red wine, Janey told them, were scientifically known to have a negative effect on the psyche. (Jack remembered how Larry had looked late Saturday night, strangely calmed and amicable; but according to Janey, he was sailing, by that time – fully rigged for disaster.) The play itself had worn him to a frazzle, late-night rehearsals, the demanding four-hour performances. And once, years ago, Janey confided, at Princeton, just before mid-terms, Larry had had a sort of breakdown. Nothing serious, but he'd had to drop one or two courses. He's really, Janey said, whispering, sort of a *lonely* man. So –

Janey, leaning on the kitchen table, had been close to hysteria, her green eyes glassy, feverish. She was ravenously hungry, grabbing the chicken wings out of the sauce with her fingers and stripping off the meat. Her blonde hair fell greasy and lank, the clumped strands separating over her ears. There were fearful, sodden elongations around her mouth, but her lips were soft and sensuous, with a look, Jack thought, of summer fruit. She had phoned Larry's parents in Connecticut; his father was coming on an early-morning flight and planned to go directly to the hospital.

Sitting there, the three of them, they seemed to Jack to be swimming in the heightened, ardent immediacy of other, earlier lives. Hospitals; whispers; heroism; the gorging of food; manic celebration, dangerous and cautionary and somewhat reverent. On impulse Jack had opened a bottle of wine.

Bernie tipped back his glass. The high red frizz of his hair caught the light; separate threads sprang up, bluish and electric. Tonight he looked exceptionally young; he looked twenty years old tonight. Earlier in the evening he had been fiercely apologetic about dragging Rob out to Charleston in the afternoon to visit his daughter Sarah. Rob, he said, had been sitting around the house, looking dejected, and on impulse Bernie had asked if he wanted to come along for the ride. (Rob came home from Charleston sick with shock, his stomach upset. Bernie had had to stop the car twice for him on the way.) It was all right, Jack said. He'll forget about it in a day or two, Bernie said. Of course, Jack said – weren't people always saying that kids were overprotected these days from the realities of death and deformity? He'd said it himself more than once. Well, Rob had made up for it today; he'd gone straight to bed when he got home and had fallen asleep in minutes.

'I can't get over Bud Lewis,' Janey went on, her mouth full, a bead of sauce jiggling on her lip. 'If it hadn't been for Bud jogging by at that very minute – I'll just never be able to thank him if I live a hundred years. Neither of us will.'

'It really was a – ' Bernie hesitated, and Jack hoped he wouldn't say the word blessing or, worse, miracle, 'it really was incredibly lucky.'

'And if Bernie hadn't been staying here in our guest room last night – ' Janey had inhaled sharply, gazed at Bernie with sober regard – a near brush with tragedy had cleared away her sulkiness, 'if he hadn't been in the house I don't know what I'd have done. It must have been fate. I'd have gone to pieces, probably. I was shaking like a leaf when Bud brought him in. He carried him in. Actually *carried* Larry into the house.'

'You were a lot more collected than you realize,' Bernie assured her. His tone was intimate. 'You were the one who just picked up the phone and asked for emergency. While we were arguing about who to call first.'

'And they got that oxygen unit here so fast,' Janey's voice shrilled, ecstatic. She reached across for another chicken wing. 'How long would you say, Bernie? Ten minutes?'

'No more than that. Fairly swift anyway for that hour in the morning. And they sure knew just what to do when they got here.'

Janey turned to Jack. 'I guess you heard,' she said quietly, 'what Bernie did?'

'What?' Jack said, hating himself for not knowing.

'While the ambulance was coming? That ten minutes when Larry was lying there on the couch with his eyes shut? Bernie gave him mouth-to-mouth resuscitation. While I was tearing out my hair and running around screeching, he gave him mouth-to-mouth.'

'Well, I – ' Bernie said.

'The doctor, the man in Emergency, said it probably kept the brain cells alive for that critical – '

'I took this course a couple years ago,' Bernie apologized. 'First aid.' His voice cracked.

'And he stayed with me all morning. At the hospital.'

'I hated like hell to leave you alone in the afternoon. If I hadn't had to go to Charleston – '

Jack looked at him closely. When had he last seen Bernie's face as luminously tender as it looked at this moment? He and Janey had been awake since eight; and both of them looked radiant.

And *he* had slept through it all, all of it. Bud Lewis breaking the glass on the garage window – with his bare hands, Janey said; he had had to have stitches. *He* had slept while Bud Lewis carried Larry into the house. And how exactly had this feat been accomplished? Had Bud carried him in his arms the way a child would be carried? over his shoulder? how? *He* had slept through the arrival of the ambulance and the valiant oxygen unit. Probably there had been a siren. Bernie breathing into Larry's unconscious mouth. Jack had slept through that, too. Asleep, dreaming, always asleep, that's where he had spent his life, asleep; that's where he always ended up, in a state of semi-consciousness, just outside the crowding of real events. Shut out. Cut off. As though a partition existed in the world, a heavy wall of plate glass, unassailable, where on one side people moved through immense self-generating dramas, conquests, feats of courage and knowing. Brenda was on that side; so was Larry Carpenter and Janey and Bernie and so, incredibly, was Bud Lewis. *Bud Lewis*. While he – and a few others like him, he supposed – stood immobilized on the other side; all they could do was watch it happen; there was no way through for people like him. They were condemned, something predetermined perhaps, something faulty in the genes, a primal failing, an unlucky star. He was going to be, would always be, a man who listened to the accounts of others, a man who comprehended the history of events but not the events themselves. He was a secondary-source man; he hadn't even gone to see *Hamlet*; even a simple thing like that had slipped past him. And here, at his own kitchen table, he was an incidental witness, a grotesque and fatal second step behind. Bernie and Janey seemed scarcely aware of his presence.

Nevertheless they appeared reluctant to leave. It grew later and later, but still they stayed. After a while Janey became exhausted and tearful. She began rambling, somewhat incoherently, about how she and Larry, a couple of years ago, feeling rootless, toying – she might as well come out with it, she said – toying with the idea of a divorce, had moved out here to Elm Park as a sort of last-ditch experiment. But they couldn't seem to fit in; hardly anyone ever invited them back after their parties; they couldn't understand why this was, but knew it must be, in some way, their own fault. 'And now look,' Janey was saying, 'Bud Lewis stepping in and saving Larry's life. And Hap Lewis sending over these chicken wings tonight, sweet and sour. And Bernie – even if he isn't really a neighbour – and you, Jack, phoning and asking me over here – ' Tears fell out of her eyes, spilled onto her hand. Her face melted, collapsed, reminding Jack of Laurie when she blubbered. He had wanted to put his arms around her.

'Look,' he insisted, 'you can't possibly stay in that house alone tonight. I can easily make up a bed for you here. There's Brenda's workroom – it's got this folding bed thing – '

'Bernie's offered to stay over again tonight,' Janey said. 'But, thank you, Jack, it's really wonderful of you to think of it, everyone's been so wonderful.'

'After all,' Bernie cut in, 'I've already broken in the sheets.' He spoke with resonant logic, almost merriment.

'And the hospital might call,' Janey said. 'They promised to call if anything came up, anything at all. They said I could see him first thing in the morning.'

'At least,' Jack said, 'let me drop you at the hospital in the morning.'

'Oh, I can do that,' Bernie said quickly. 'I'll be right there, it's no trouble. Actually, it's right on my way to work.'

They had left it at that. And when Jack drove off the next

morning, Bernie's car was already gone. He decided he would phone the hospital at noon to see how things were going. For the moment, there seemed little else he could do.

'Sometimes,' Moira Burke was saying into Jack's ear, 'sometimes I actually think women are stronger than men. That neighbour of yours, for instance – I don't think a woman would kill herself over a little bitty thing like that in the newspapers.'

'You could be right,' Jack said.

'Do you think so? What I've always thought is that men have more sensitive egos than women. Too sensitive for their own good. A few years ago – '

Where was Dr. Middleton? Where was he? When was he coming? It was already 10:45.

Ah, there he was. Jack could hear his soft cough, his footsteps in the corridor, the swish-swish of his black umbrella.

Chapter Eighteen

ON MONDAY MORNING ROB STAYED HOME FROM SCHOOL. He was still feeling under the weather, he said. His legs felt like water. Under the weather – one of Brenda's expressions, part of the cheerful propitiating vocabulary she attached to minor disasters and ailments. Down in the dumps. Off your mettle. On the fritz. Out of whack. She was good with the children when they were sick, positive and brisk, a swift, willing creator of eggnogs, cream soups, scrambled eggs. She had a way with a thermometer, holding it up to the level light of the window, absorbing the calm numbered reading, then shaking it down cleanly, reassuringly; when it came to disease, she had a core of optimism. Jack wondered if Rob might possibly have a fever.

At noon he phoned home from the office. Rob's voice, when he finally answered, sounded indistinct.

'Were you asleep?' Jack asked sharply.

'Sort of. Half.'

'What do you think it is? Flu?'

'I don't know. Just sick. I'll be okay tomorrow.'

'Didn't you have an algebra test today?'

'I can make it up. It was just a quiz.'

Jack could hear weariness in Rob's voice. Maybe he was just worn out, sick of school, fed up with the dark glooms of January mornings. 'I hope you fixed yourself some breakfast.'

'Yeah. I had some tea. That stuff of Mom's, the Chinese stuff.'

'Tea? That's all?'

'I'm not hungry.'

'You need some food in you.' He was sounding like Brenda, like Brenda's mother.

'Dad?'

'Yes.'

'How come there are bones all over the kitchen table?'

'They're chicken bones. We had some chicken late last night, after you were asleep. Bernie and Mrs. Carpenter came over for a while – '

'There are hundreds of bones.'

'Hardly hundreds,' Jack said. Rob had an annoying tendency to exaggerate.

'It makes me feel sick, looking at all those bones.'

'Don't look, then.'

'How can I help it? They're all over the table.'

It was true that the kitchen was in a mess; in the morning, getting breakfast, Jack had moved gingerly around the edges of the room, finally carrying his corn flakes and orange juice into the dining room. There *had* been an impressive heap of gnawed bones on the table. Nice of Hap Lewis to think of sending something over. (Jack wondered if there wasn't something rather funeral-baked-meats about it – probably not; Hap Lewis came from downstate, Danville; leaving casseroles at back doors was probably second nature to her.) He'd have to clean up the kitchen tonight when he got home. There were wine glasses standing among the bones, and two empty bottles. Paper napkins wadded into balls. Beer bottles on the counter – from Saturday? A jar of instant coffee on the windowsill, the lid lost. An empty soup can, a casserole soaking in the sink – joined now no doubt, by a shower of tea leaves. Laurie's ski jacket was on the floor; he'd almost tripped over it on his way out the back door.

Years ago, he used to phone Brenda at lunch time. The children had been babies then. It always amazed him to hear people talk about the tumult of the sixties. *His* sixties had been passed in a daydream: work at the Institute, Brenda and the children, golf on Sundays when he could afford it. In those days, to save money, he'd carried sandwiches to work to eat at his desk. When he'd spoken to her on the phone, sipping coffee from a paper cup, he liked to close his eyes and call into his mind the image of Brenda, how she must look standing in the kitchen by the wall telephone. He had been young, barely thirty. Domesticity had been more precarious and precious. Mere objects had moved him to euphoria; cans of vegetables standing in cupboards, blankets folded on a closet shelf, his socks knotted in pairs in his top drawer – the thought of these things, their arrangement and persistence, had filled him then with amazement. Brenda, in those years, still slender, had worn blue jeans around the house. (Recently she'd gone back to blue jeans after long phases of pedal pushers, plaid slacks, double knits.) Then, she used to answer the phone in a voice that was exasperated, amused, tender, put upon. The kids were driving her crazy. They were pulling over lamps and chairs, crawling into cupboards, smearing jam on the walls, fingerprints everywhere. They never spent an hour without spilling milk on the floor. They were beautiful, though, intelligent, responsive, alert, agile, inventive, self-confident. When they grew up, the world would be theirs for the asking; there would be nothing they wouldn't be able to accomplish.

Jack had joined instinctively in these dazzling visions of the future, visions that were freshened each night as he helped Brenda button their perfect, rounded, sweet-smelling bodies into pyjamas. His children, his progeny. (He loved the word progeny, loved himself in the role of progenitor.) How could he and Brenda have divined what was to happen? They had been taken in; the early vision had been false. It wasn't that the children had disappointed them, were no longer beautiful. But grace, which they'd thought was imperishable, had fallen away; the childish ease had been somehow damaged; difficulty and nightmare had crept in. Well, that was the way it was.

'Hey, Dad,' Rob said into the phone. 'Guess what? It's snowing out here. Is it snowing downtown?'

Jack looked out his office window and felt a jump of happiness. 'Hey, it *is* snowing. What do you know.'

'How long's Bernie going to stay with us?' Rob had decided to be conversational.

'I'm not sure. I'll ask him tonight what his plans are. Actually, he's sort of staying next door at the Carpenters'.'

'I know. Weird.'

'Well – ' Jack began, hovering on the brink of some kind of explanation, then deciding against it. What was there to be explained, anyway?

'Maybe he'll get back together with Sue,' Rob said, filling in a silence.

'Maybe.'

'She phoned this morning. She wants you to phone her at the hospital.'

'Shit.'

'What?'

'Nothing. It's just that I've got so much to do. Okay, I'll phone her later.'

'What's up with Mr. Carpenter? How's he doing?'

'No real news.'

'He's going to be okay though?'

'They think so. I just phoned the hospital a few minutes ago, but all I got was the switchboard. He's stable, she said. In a stable condition.'

'I guess that means he's going to be okay.'

'Probably. It's hard to tell. Apparently it takes forty-eight hours until they can really tell.'

'Is he nuts or what? Why'd he do it?'

Jack hesitated. With Rob he had to be careful to weigh his words – Rob tended to dramatize things. 'I think,' Jack said cautiously, 'that he just hit a low moment. Depression.'

'Was it that thing in the paper? About the play being such a bummer?'

'Partly. They – Mrs. Carpenter thinks that that's what might have triggered it off. But these things,' he hesitated again, 'are usually more complex than they seem.'

'Why would a guy like that want to do himself in? A guy with a car like that.'

Jack decided to ignore the mention of the car; Rob wasn't that simple; he was just fishing for something else. 'Everyone gets depressed now and then,' Jack told him. 'Everyone.'

' Yeah.'

'Now listen, let's get back to you for a minute. I phoned to see how you were feeling.'

'I already told you, not too bad.'

'What exactly does that mean?'

'Huh?' Rob sounded belligerent.

'What I mean is, when did you start feeling sick? Was it yesterday morning or was it later, in the afternoon?'

'Both. I don't know, all day I guess.'

'You didn't mention feeling sick in the morning. Remember? You were okay when we went over to Grandma's and Grandpa's.'

'Uhuh.'

'Was it when you got out to Charleston?'

'I don't know. I can't remember.'

'Well, try to remember. Because if you've got something,

124

some bug, I can phone the doctor and get you on to some medication.'

'Let's drop it, okay? I'm fine. I'll be fine tomorrow. I already feel better.'

'What I'm trying to say is, you've never been to Charleston before. Or any place remotely like it. For that matter, I haven't either. It would be only natural if you – '

'You mean you want to know if I'm really sick or is it just psychosomatic.'

'Well,' Jack hedged, 'yes, I guess that is more or less what I was wondering.'

'I dunno. Maybe. Sort of.'

'You can't be a little more specific than that?'

'Well, it was kind of – '

'Upsetting?'

'Weird. Creepy, unreal. There was this one guy – Bernie said he was eighteen. With webbed feet and no nose. He just sat there on the floor in this big room and made these sounds. He . . . he had to wear diapers.'

'I know,' Jack said, not knowing.

'We had to walk through this long room full of these creeps to get to the room where Sarah was.'

Jack waited.

'She was in a bed. A crib, with sides on it. She didn't look like five years old. She looked like a baby. She weighs thirty pounds, that's all. She didn't even look like a girl. She didn't have any hair, not very much anyway. You could see the bones through her head, right through, the skin was so thin. She was sort of grey-looking and her eyes were shut and she's got these tubes in her nose.'

'Rob – '

'Even if she opened her eyes she wouldn't be able to see anything. And Bernie – '

'What?'

'He goes out there every Sunday. I guess Sue does, too, most of the time. They just go out there and stare at it. Just stand by the bed, I guess, and stare at it.'

'I know these things must seem tragic – '

'Then, before we left, do you know what he did, what Bernie did?'

'What?'

'He leaned over and kissed her. On the face. Just above where the tube went in, on the bone part. I guess that's when I started to feel – '

'Sick?'

There was no reply.

'You still there?' Jack asked.

'I better go, Dad. I'm going back to bed, I think.'

'Good idea. I'll see you around six. Okay?'

Jack put the phone back. He sat at his desk for a few minutes and watched the snow come down, large wet flakes drifting past his window and falling out of sight into the invisible street below. He felt panic, a shortness of breath, a sharp pain that was not his but that belonged to his son. Couldn't he, with a doubling of will, keep Rob safe a little longer? Spare him terrible sights? Deter him from absurd sacrifices? There must be a way, if only he had the imagination to find it.

As an emergency distraction he browsed through the new *Journal*, and as a self-imposed piece of torture read once again the announcement of Harriet Post's book. There was a clean cutting edge to the pain it brought today, not entirely disagreeable. He opened his briefcase and got out the manuscript for Chapter Six. He should have gone out for lunch; or ordered a sandwich; he felt hollowed out. There was a push of pressure in his chest.

Everyone else on the floor was out for lunch. When had the place ever been this quiet? For once even the noise of the traffic seemed muffled and distant. All the sky was filling with whiteness. Amazing how the corrupt, old downtown sky could be so quickly transformed and widened.

126

Chapter Nineteen

FROM A MACHINE IN THE CORRIDOR HE BOUGHT HIMSELF a cup of coffee and something called a Leisure-Snak, made of pressed sesame seeds and honey, which he chewed while he browsed through the newspaper. He lingered over it, feeling obscurely that he owed himself half an hour's escape. There was a new play at the Apollo and a review of it by Gordon Tripp. Jack skimmed it quickly, taking in the mildness of tone, the straining toward fairness, a certain surprising humility: 'This young playwright has things to teach all of us.' Of course, Gordon Tripp must know about Larry by now – some sort of chastening must have taken place. At the bottom of the review was a brief note in italics from the editor: *Our regular reviewer, Larry Carpenter, is on vacation.*

On vacation! So much for history. So much for the reliability of the printed word. Wait until Bernie sees this.

And what was this on the back page? A newsphoto of the hunger marchers in Columbus Park. Jack recognized the man with the poncho and the white hair. The picture was over-exposed and crudely flecked with white, but he could make out the placards and, yes, there was the woman with the baby on her back. He and his father had been standing just off to the left. If the photo had been half an inch wider, they would have landed in Chicago *Today* – his father would have liked that. Perhaps they *had* been in the picture; these pictures were always being cropped to make them fit on the page; it could be that he and his father ended up in a wastebasket at the Chicago *Today* office. The caption read: *Hunger strikers demonstrate on behalf of Russian dissidents Sunday in Humboldt Park.*

Humboldt Park!

But this was Columbus Park. He'd been there, And besides, he recognized the corner of the wrought-iron fence. Someone – the photographer? the person who wrote the captions? – someone had made a mistake.

A mistake, and yet hardly anyone in the whole city of

Chicago would know a mistake had been made. The people in the photo would know, of course. And he and his father. But no one would bother writing to the newspaper asking for a correction. Why should they? It was too trivial: Columbus Park, Humboldt Park, it was all the same.

Nevertheless – and Jack felt perversely pleased by the fact, almost triumphant – it represented a false recording, similar in a way to Larry Carpenter's 'vacation.' It was this false form which would undoubtedly survive; this moment of history would have taken place in Humboldt Park. The picture would be filed away forever, and what was written underneath would become the truth.

The historical knot is hard to untie; unlocking one moment of history can be a life's work. So said Dr. Gerald Middleton, appearing as Guest Lecturer at Northwestern a year or so ago. A particular kind of persistence is required, he said. A temperament that is rigid but at the same time capable of settling for less than perfection. There must be a willingness to stop and rest from time to time on certain boggy suppositions. Hardness and brilliance were desired but seldom attained. The task was heartbreaking. The men who choose to be witnesses and recorders of the historical process must partially remove themselves from society. What was needed was a steady but disinterested hand, groping and feeling its way – no wonder, he said, historians were generally considered to be dullards (appreciative laughter). There must exist, he went on, an instinct for melding particular but seemingly unrelated facts, and this instinct, which required a leap of imagination, was accessible only to those fortunate few – he eyed his audience warmly – who possess that vital element, a historical sense.

A historical sense; a sense of history, a relatively rare thing. Brenda, for instance, had no sense of history. It had taken Jack years and years, first to discover this, and second, to comprehend the fact that she was able to function in the world without it.

She had no father, either, had never had a father; this and the missing historical sense seemed to Jack to be inextricably linked.

'But you must have had a father once,' Jack remembered saying to her the first time they met. She had been working then as a junior typist at the Institute, and Jack, beginning his

128

research project on LaSalle, had stopped in at the Institute library to look at some old maps. She had been helpful in an awkward way. And remarkably friendly. He'd asked her out for lunch, inviting her around the corner to Roberto's. They sat in a corner booth and talked about where they'd grown up, the schools they'd gone to, their families, and that was how Brenda happened to tell him she had no father.

'Well, of course there was *someone*.' She'd smiled beguilingly at him over her bowl of vegetable soup. Her teeth were good. 'A biological father, but that's all.'

Why was she telling him this? They'd just met. 'But you're so off-hand about it,' he told her.

'You'd have to meet my mother,' she said to Jack, laughing, 'to understand.'

You'd have to meet my mother – the words, lightly uttered – carried carloads of predetermination – yes, he would have to meet this girl's mother. He *would* meet her mother. For once he grasped the fact that something was happening.

'But didn't you mind?' he asked her, 'not having a father?'

'Isn't it funny, everyone asks me that. I just say it's like being born with one toe missing. You never miss it if you've never had it.'

'But surely you had to explain it somehow. Wasn't it hard, when you had to fill out forms, at school for instance, asking for your father's name, date of birth, occupation and all that?'

'I just left a blank. That's how I always think of him, as a matter of fact. A blank. Like one of those metal slugs people put in juke boxes. Origin unknown.'

'You mean you really don't know? You never asked?'

'No.' The smile again. Teeth on the small side. 'Not really.'

'But you must have been curious – '

'No. You'd think so, but I've liked the old blank. I'm used to it. I just sort of inherited it, so to speak.' She shrugged, a gesture which would bind him to her forever, a miniature lifting of the shoulders, a sway of breasts under her soft sweater.

'Most people would want to know,' Jack said. 'The circumstances, anyway.'

'Probably,' Brenda said. 'But I'm lucky. I guess I just don't have much curiosity or something.'

She's sublimating, thought Jack at the time; he had taken the required course in basic psychology.

But when he knew her better, when he'd been married to her for several years, he realized she had been truthful. She was not curious. She lacked all sense of historical curiosity.

Her imagination, it seemed to Jack, was confined to a thin slice of present time. Confinement, in fact, was the word that came to mind when he tried to picture Brenda's concept of time. 'Tell me what comes into your head,' he'd asked her once, 'when I say George Washington, the Battle of Tippicanoe, Dunkirk, and, let's see, the Magna Carta.'

They had been lying in bed, a weekend morning in the Elm Park house. 'Just tell me,' he said, 'what kind of image comes to you?'

She lay back, her eyes shut. 'Coloured slides,' she said at last. 'A handful of coloured slides.'

'But are they in any particular order?' he'd persisted. 'Are some further back than others?'

She'd taken her time answering, cushioning him, no doubt, from possible disappointment. 'No special order,' she said. 'They're just, you know, lying in the same old box.'

He couldn't believe it.

'Well, maybe some are further back than others,' she'd said. 'I mean, I know perfectly well there's an order to it all. Magna Carta first, then George, but as far as I'm concerned, it's all back there together.'

He was amazed. What she had revealed, it seemed to him, was a kind of spacial blindness; she could see backward in time, but not with the perspective and shading that Jack had long taken for granted. And she didn't *care*. He would have pitied her if pity hadn't seemed so ludicrous.

He *had* taken it for granted, his vision of time, assuming that everyone perceived events as he did, through a multiple lens, a dense superimposed image composed of layers and layers of time. The image was always with him. Driving home from work, he was never entirely unconscious of the fact that he and the Aspen were skimming across the surface of a great alluvial basin; under the concrete of the expressway, just at the rim of consciousness, was the old glacial lake, Lake Chicago. For him the lake was still there, would always be there, a sub-image that a thousand layers of concrete couldn't obliterate. He could, if he wanted to, keep going, driving straight through Elm Park, out into the country, past small country towns and the sad rural frosts of the Illinois farmland, following the path of the old glacier to its westernmost limit, populating the spaces as he went with overlapping generations. Place names along the way would call into being events and genealogies, chanting soberly in an off-stage colloquy, all of it profiled and indexed on an inner landscape, enough room for everything, everything in its turn.

The time line in his head curved and circled – each century with a colour, an aura, of its own – a complex grillwork placed over the transparency of the past, winking with patterns and riddles and curious, random, heroic happenings. He couldn't remember a time when it hadn't existed. Except for this one luminous structure, his head seemed to him to be no more than a ragbag stuffed with half-truths, faulty resolutions, phoniness, evasions. But when he scratched for authenticity he never failed to find, securely in place, the wide-screen full-colour panorama of time. Once, when he was about fifteen, he and his father had taken the El downtown. General MacArthur, discharged by President Truman, was making a triumphal tour of the country. There was a motorcade down State Street, and through the crowd Jack had glimpsed the blurred redness that was General MacArthur's face. An abstraction made suddenly, vividly real. The time line had touched him them, connecting him directly to all possible events and creatures. Past and present flowed together. At the time he had supposed it must be the same for everyone.

It wasn't only Brenda; he'd talked to other people, felt them out. And was finally convinced that he had *it*, what Dr. Middleton called a sense of history. It was more rare than he had thought, and its rarity made him doubt, in his case, its truth. Perhaps it was an affectation, an intellectual adornment; no, he tested it, imagined living without it, and watched the structures on his mental horizon collapse. It was his!

That *it* was overly expanded and lacking in details, he admitted; he was, in a sense, no scholar, but only someone who was able to feel out the surfaces of time. Trade practices, the whole Indian thing – his interest in these things was simulated, not even, in fact, part of his area of specialization, belonging more truly to anthropologists, sociologists, economists. But it had been open, available, as Dr. Middleton explained. No real work had been done in the area. There was no point in going on with

131

LaSalle; LaSalle had been done down to the last hangnail; it was time for Jack to move into a new and potentially rewarding area. He might lack expertise in this new area; there were certain books he would have to look at, theses to consult, but it was virgin territory. It was his if he wanted it, and he did have what mattered most, the feeling for history.

How simple, how accessible the world must look to Brenda – but how flat, how lacking in colour. She would probably shrug and compare it to the missing of a toe – you didn't miss what you never had. This though, he knew, must be a larger loss, a leg gone or an eye put out.

She had been wearing an angora sweater the first day he met her and took her for lunch. Some shade of blue. After the soup she had had a toasted cheese sandwich and coffee. She only had an hour for lunch, she said; she had to get back.

'Couldn't you, just this once, be late?' he had pleaded.

'I just started working there a month ago,' she told him. 'I wouldn't have the nerve.'

'We could order a bottle of wine,' he said, feeling daring.

She was already pulling her coat on. It was late March, a cold spring day. 'Wine for lunch isn't my cup of tea,' she'd said without a trace of irony, and he had felt a small expansion of joy.

'Please?'

'I'd love to but I've got to get back. Honestly.'

He'd walked her down Keeley Avenue to the Institute. The sidewalks were covered with a gauze-like frost. At the entrance she turned and shook hands with him. She was wearing mittens; it must have been the fashion then. The mittened hand in his, the soft wool touch of it, sprang a lever of love in his heart, a flare of happiness that left him dazed for weeks.

All that winter he'd been going out with Harriet Post, a professor's daughter from Madison, Wisconsin, whom he'd met in his American Civilization seminar. Harriet of the springy nylon sweaters and straight A's. The first time he took her out they'd gone to a movie called *Wages of Fear*. He'd walked her home to the apartment where she was living, and kissed her chapped lips in the shadow of the front door. She had reached down, unzipped his pants and slipped her hands inside – an event that had filled him with astonishment and joy, but that for sheer power was equalled by the weight of Brenda's mittened hand in his.

He would have to choose.

And he had chosen the prized and possible safety of his desire for Brenda. The ease of it had made it seem right. All around him, flickering at the edge of his vision, were storms of passion, strife, risks, and dangerous and unproductive longings, but he had made his choice.

The historical underpinnings of that choice had occasionally tormented him. Had it been a choice conditioned by the tenor of the times, those curious mid-fifties, the sunny optionless Eisenhower days? Had he, slumbering in the faint radiance of Hollywood – June Allyson, good teeth – made the cliché American choice, purity over corruption? No. He hadn't chosen Brenda for any of those reasons. She, for reasons that he had never fully understood, had chosen him.

Chapter Twenty

'THIS IS THE LOUSIEST MOVIE I EVER SAW,' ROB WAS SAYING, an arc of wonder in his voice.

'There's nothing else on,' Laurie said happily.

'Shh,' from Jack.

It was eight o'clock, still snowing. Tonight it had taken Jack two hours to drive home; for the first time that he could remember, the Expressway had been closed to traffic. Now the three of them were watching an old Betty Grable movie on television. They were eating the hamburgers and french fries he'd brought home – except for Rob, who was gulping China tea and looking pale.

'Can I have yours?' Laurie asked him.

'I don't care.'

'I'll split it with you,' Laurie offered.

'Take it all.'

They were sprawled in the living room, at peace with each other, relaxed. A slice of pickle slid out of Laurie's hamburger and landed in her lap; she retrieved it distractedly, eyes on the screen, glued to Betty Grable's face. 'She *is sort* of good looking,' she said, 'except for that hair. And the way her eyes kind of pop.'

'And that weird hat.'

'That's what they wore,' Jack said.

Betty was playing a sweet young thing kicking her way to stardom. A place in the chorus line was more than she'd ever dreamed of. But she knew she had to be tough if she was going to make it to the top.

'Is this for real?' Rob asked. He was looking somewhat brighter, Jack thought; at least he's not moping in bed. Maybe Bernie's right – kids forget quickly.

Now Betty was dancing on the sidewalk in front of the theatre. She had just seen her name up in lights, and happiness had overtaken her. Passers-by were stopping to watch her. They began to tap their umbrellas on the pavement. Then they

134

too started to dance. They hoisted Betty up on top of a mailbox, where she tapped and sang with insane, open-mouthed joy. Her arms sliced crazy, brave windmills over her head, and her legs stretched out, inhumanly long.

'Hilarious,' Laurie said, chewing.

Then Betty was back in her dressing room, sombre now, rebuffed, injured, baffled. Her voice was stiff and courageous. She couldn't help being decent, she said. That was the way she was.

Jack put his feet up on the coffee table. He had hours of work to do for Tuesday, all of Chapter Six promised – again – for the next morning. But first he owed himself a little relaxation, a little time with his children.

He regarded them with love; what had he and Brenda done to deserve these two good, intelligent children? The innocent, rapt attention with which they gave themselves to this improbable and dreadful movie touched him. Tonight, watching Betty's sequin-splashed resilience, he felt his despair resting lightly on him. He would like this moment to stretch out forever, an eternity of Betty, her hair ribbons bobbing on blonde curls, her short pleated patriotic skirt flashing red, white, blue. Beautiful.

And then the sweet spot of the evening: when Laurie, watching Betty hook up her diamond-mesh stockings, cried out, 'Look, Daddy, she's wearing those one-legged stockings.' Even Rob laughed.

It seemed that Larry Carpenter was making good progress.

Tonight news of him came from all quarters. First Hap Lewis phoned to tell Jack that she had got through the hospital switchboard at last and had actually spoken to the floor nurse, the bitch. 'She isn't allowed to give reports on patients,' Hap said, 'but she did say that there's absolutely no cause for concern.'

'Well,' said Jack, 'that's certainly good news.'

'Who would ever have thought it,' Hap said. 'Larry Carpenter. Of all people. It makes you wonder.'

'You're right,' Jack said, wishing Hap would say goodbye and let him get down to work. But she hung on; she seemed to be waiting for something. Then it came to him – of course.

'You must be proud of Bud,' he told her. 'If it hadn't been for Bud –'

'I know,' was all Hap said, but she said it with immense solemnity. And Jack had a sudden flashing image of a future in which both Bud and Hap would be transformed into other, nobler people. Bud would emerge from his lean, shadowy stillness, shed some of his easy dexterity. Hap would move by imperceptible degrees toward a new softening, a kindly, embracing awe for life's darker complexities. It seemed to Jack that he could hear the beginnings in her duskily withheld voice tonight. 'I know,' she said once again.

Bernie himself brought news from the hospital. He had dropped by there earlier in the evening to see if he could do anything. He looked burly and cold in his snow-covered windbreaker, the very image of the loyal family friend standing by in the moment of crisis. Larry was allowed no visitors, Bernie said, except for Janey and his father. (The father had arrived in the morning, had seen Larry briefly, conferred with the doctor, and had taken the afternoon plane east – just missing the storm; his short visit was a sure sign, Bernie said, that everything was going well.) Larry would have to be under observation for a week. He'd be seeing a psychiatrist, of course. Janey was calm. Bernie had arranged to pick her up later at the hospital and bring her home. He should be on his way now, he told Jack; he only came back to let Cronkite and Brinkley out for a run. Janey would be waiting. And what about tonight: where would he stay? Bernie didn't say. Jack didn't ask.

Sue Koltz phoned. 'Don't panic now,' she told Jack briskly, 'I'm not after Bernie. I'm after you.'

'Oh?' Jack could tell she was calling from the hospital; she was using her doctor voice, crisp, acerbic; he pictured the cropped colourless hair above the white coat, the slight red blotchiness of her neck.

'I know he's there, all right. At least I'm pretty darn sure he is.'

'Actually –'

'But to tell the truth I'd prefer not to see him at the moment. Not until I've settled a few things. Thought a few things through. You might just mention that to him, that I don't want him hounding me.'

'Hounding?'

'I saw him tonight, in the waiting room here at the hospital. I just managed to duck out of sight in time. I don't,' she spoke with icy deliberation, 'like being spied on.'

'I'll tell him.'

'Well, is he or not? Staying with you and Brenda?'

'Look, Sue, I don't really think it's my place – '

'I know he hasn't been back to the apartment. I was there this afternoon picking up some things and feeding the cat. God, all this snow, we're getting buried. And Bernie doesn't have his overcoat with him. I saw it hanging in the closet.'

'I imagine he'll survive.'

'Or his boots.'

'I'll lend him mine.'

'Actually, Jack, I've called you a number of times. Then it gradually sank through my thick skull that you weren't going to phone me back. That you had no intention of phoning me back.'

'I have tried. A couple of times, but you're never – '

'I can understand you might be reluctant to get involved – '

'Sue. It isn't a question of reluctance, exactly. I've been up to my ears with other things, swamped. And I've got hours of work ahead of me tonight. So – '

'By the way, one of your neighbours has been admitted to my floor, not that I'm supposed to mention this kind of thing. Carpenter. Larry Carpenter. Did you know?'

'Yes, I know.'

'I had a look at him this morning. He's in pretty good shape, considering.'

'That's good news,' Jack said.

'He's lucky to be alive,' Sue said. And added, with surprising kindness, 'the poor bastard.'

Poor bastard, poor Larry Carpenter. For the first time Jack thought about Larry. A shadowy double image came to him: Larry's hands shaky as he reached for ice cubes; and his eyes fixed in space.

Amazingly enough he had hardly thought of him at all, only of the blare of circumstances, the Saturday-night party and the tense, triumphant Sunday-morning rescue. He had not thought at all about the actual moment when Larry entered the dark garage, shut the door, got into the car, and turned on the engine.

Someone whom he and Brenda knew – not well, but moderately well, as well as they know many people – decided to terminate his life, and almost succeeded.

And then later at the hospital – Jack tried to picture how it must have been: Larry surfacing to consciousness in a strange bed surrounded by screens and the unglinting whiteness of faces and walls. Movements of air and sounds. The clinking of hospital apparatus, footsteps, the stirred breath of voices, all of it testifying to failure. Would this knowledge of failure come to Larry gradually as in a dream or would he open his eyes and immediately perceive what had happened? And would he come back to life with anger or gratitude? All suicides are victims of the moment – where had he heard that? One of his father's books, probably. Those who survived were supposed to welcome their reclaimed lives and be thankful to those who intervened. Really?

And then what? How was the new post-suicidal life to be lived? Everything back to normal, clickity-click? All the old routines taken up again? Hi-ya, Larry, how you doing? Larry backing his car out of the drive, setting off to work. Would the day come when he would again invite people to his house for parties, press introductions upon them, uncork bottles of burgundy – Jack could not imagine any of these things happening. Nor could he imagine what he would say to Larry when they met – as they surely would – over the shrubbery. Sorry to hear you've been sick. Sick, ha! Hope you're feeling your old self again. What old self, for crissake? Sorry about what? Welcome back to the land of the living, you poor bastard.

Should he send flowers? No. A note? Brenda would know. A short note, something sympathetic and encouraging. Why were people so afraid of words these days?

He rummaged in a drawer for writing paper; he should send it tomorrow – hadn't Bernie said he'd be in the hospital only a week? He found Brenda's notepaper. 'Hasty Notes' it said on the box, and on each sheet a picture of a deer, Bambi-style, nibbling grass. No! There was always his typing paper, ordinary bond, fair quality. Dear Larry, he might write, all best wishes for a speedy recovery. That sounded fairly neutral, but more the kind of thing for after an operation. Dear Larry, my thoughts are with you? Too social, too dishonest, although true in a way. Dear Larry, so you couldn't take it when the chips were down, eh? Dear Larry, I know how you feel. I know exactly how you must feel. I can understand . . . .

By midnight Jack had made the decision not to send a note, but to send a plant instead. Cut flowers, nice at this time of year, would be overly suggestive of celebration. Or severance. A small green plant with broad healthy leaves; he didn't know the name of the plant he had in mind, but he could visualize perfectly its shape and colour. He could phone the florist near the hospital in the morning and have it delivered. And tell them to include one of those tiny florist's cards. *From the Bowmans*; that would do it. The decision spread a tent of calm over him.

The house was quiet. Both Rob and Laurie slept well. Rob, in fact, had gone to bed before ten; maybe, Jack thought, he did have some kind of bug. If he's not better tomorrow, well, we'll face that when it comes.

It was too late to phone Brenda in Philadelphia, although the thought had come to him earlier in the evening. What would Brenda be doing? a banquet? the mayor's reception? She would be phoning anyway on Tuesday, she said – tomorrow night. And it was too late, too, to phone Harriet Post, but he would, he decided, try to reach her tomorrow. The thought of speaking to Harriet over the telephone – an alarming thought earlier in the day – now seemed ripely possible and even rational. He should have phoned days ago, when he'd first seen the announcement of her book. (Had he feared she might answer his call with a puzzled, irritated 'Jack who?')

It was Dr. Middleton's idea that he contact Harriet. Dr. Middleton had received the news of Harriet's book with gravity and alarm, more alarm than Jack had been prepared for. 'This is most worrying,' he had said, his hands travelling across the width of his chin. 'This bears looking into.'

On the other hand, Dr. Middleton had never heard of Harriet Post. 'De Paul graduate, you say?' She was certainly not a recognized scholar in the field; her name was not in the least familiar to him. At the same time, he went on, areas of expertise were changing all the time. Lately amateurs – he pronounced the word with some harshness – had started crowding in, some of them not easily dismissed or despised. The best policy, Dr. Middleton felt, was cautious inquiry. And since Jack was acquainted with Miss Post – *Miss Post* – it would be relatively simple and quite professional to approach her and attempt to ascertain the scope of her monograph. If it turned out that too many similarities existed – these things did happen from time to time – it was sometimes wiser to cut one's losses, to shift the focus perhaps, or even – here Dr. Middleton hesitated – even to abandon the project if absolutely necessary. Meanwhile, he looked forward to seeing Chapter Six on Tuesday morning. Ten o'clock. He had been surprisingly firm about Chapter Six.

In the empty kitchen Jack made himself a cup of instant coffee and a slice of toast, which he spread with raspberry jam. He kept his eyes averted from the chicken bones still heaped on the kitchen table. And from the kitchen sink, which appeared to be clogged with tea leaves. The den was bitterly cold, and for a minute he considered carrying the typewriter into the living room. But the coffee table was covered with debris from dinner. And soup bowls? Of course, he and Laurie had had soup last night. Tomorrow he would have to organize the kids and clean the house up. He was running out of rooms. For tonight, there was no choice but to put up with the cold den. On the living-room floor he found a blanket – could this be the same blanket he covered Bernie with last – when was it? – last Saturday afternoon? He wrapped the blanket around his shoulders and settled into his desk chair. The old gooseneck lamp ground its harsh oval of light onto the typewriter. He tapped out a sentence.

The patterning of trading goods in the lower Great Lakes Region suggests a number of ways of interpreting the relationships and communication level between various tribal communities.

In the middle of the word 'communities' the typewriter ribbon jammed, rucking up between the little steel teeth that held it in place. He attempted, gently at first, to pull it down. It refused to slip back. He pulled harder. The ribbon, an old one, tore in two. Oh, fuck it, shit.

By extraordinary good fortune there was a new ribbon in the desk drawer. He pulled it out, hardly able to believe his luck; Brenda must have bought it, ah Brenda. He took it from its box and examined it, his elation dying. He had no idea how to put it into the typewriter.

Brenda had always changed the ribbons for him: Lesson One at Katherine Gibbs. Besides, she was good with her hands, while he – how had he reached this age, forty-three, without knowing how to change a typewriter ribbon? Fuck. He'd watched Brenda do it dozens of times; she did it in a trice, in a wink of the eye, whipping it out of its box, snapping it in place, trying it out by typing a few words on a scrap of paper. She was always leaving these little scraps of paper in the typewriter for him: 'The lazy brown Brenda jumped over the quick foxy Jack' or 'Now is the time for all good Jacks to come to the side of their Brendas.' And once, in their first apartment, a winter night like this, 'I love you love you love you love you.'

Between 12:30 and one o'clock he tried to insert the new ribbon. What he couldn't understand was what made it so difficult. It couldn't be as complicated as this – thousands of ribbons, exactly like this one, were changed every day all over Chicago, all over America. Why were there no instructions on the box? What was the matter with him? His fingers were black from inked ribbon. His coffee was cold in the cup and he had started to sweat. The clock ticked maddeningly; the house seemed lurid and frightening and his stomach contracted; he would never get the cock-sucking thing in.

Then, like a spark catching in his brain, he thought of Laurie asleep upstairs. Laurie: she had inherited something of Brenda's knack for mechanical things. Once, when he'd taken the lawnmower apart, it had been Laurie who had managed to get it back together – he had put a nut on backwards. She knew some surprising facts, such as how to turn off the water main that time they'd had the broken pipe in the bathroom. Once, when the windshield wiper was sticking, she had freed it by bending the blade a fraction of an inch.

He tiptoed up to her bedroom and pushed the door open.

The room was filled with reflected whiteness. Behind the swags of white net curtains, snow was falling. A streetlight held the snow in a lacework suspension; snow was falling on Elm Park roofs, windowledges, hedges, every object made double-edged and newly created, transformed under its load of brightness.

Laurie, asleep on her back, lay with her hands flung open, looking braver now than she did awake. Her breathing came evenly and with exquisite calm. Jack sat for a minute on the edge of the bed, regarding her.

'Laurie,' he whispered.

'Yes.' Her answering voice was husky.

'Sweetie, open your eyes.'

The eyes opened at once, stared at him blankly.

'Laurie, listen. Do you know how to change the typewriter ribbon?'

'Yes.' Her eyes shut again; she was drifting back to sleep.

'Laurie. Dear? Daddy wants you to get up. For five minutes, okay? Just to put the ribbon in. Can you do that for me?'

She was on her feet, lurching toward the lighted hall, hitching up her pyjamas as she went. At the stairs he took her elbow so she wouldn't fall, but she glided steadily now, with a sleepwalker's numb radar. Downstairs in the den she stood, swaying slightly, in front of the desk, and Jack placed the ribbon into the palm of her hand. It took her ten seconds to put it in. He could hear it snap into position. She had done it, it seemed to Jack, with her eyes shut.

'Okay, baby. Go back to sleep.' Then, 'You're a doll.'

She started back up the stairs; her hands stretched ahead of her, feeling the way, and Jack rushed to her, swooped her up in his arms and carried her up to her bed. She was amazingly heavy; he couldn't remember when he had last picked her up. Would she remember in the morning, being carried upstairs in his arms and tucked into bed? Probably not. She was asleep already.

He was so grateful. His gratitude was extreme, absurd. Already he was seeing this moment with the gauzy brightness of nostalgia; the night it snowed, the night his daughter came to his rescue. Laurie.

Chapter Twenty-One

WHEN HE WOKE IT WAS NOT TO THE GREY DULLNESS OF a January dawn, but to sunlight entering the bedroom as a long rod of translucence lying across the top edge of the curtain. Morning? Something was wrong; this sun was wrong; he must have slept in. The clock on the bedside table said eight-thirty.

Impossible. Unless he had forgotten to set the alarm. And the appointment with Dr. Middleton was at ten o'clock. The spectre of Dr. Middleton sprang into view, a Torquemadian fury. No, that was unlikely, impossible in fact, completely out of character – yet, when Jack pictured Dr. Middleton as he really was, full of calm, reliable expectancy, he felt a surge of rage.

And no time this morning for a shower; he chafed at the sacrifice – he was not the same man without the daily galvanizing thrust of hot water thumping between his shoulder blades; the stickiness of genital flesh and night sweat slowed him down, reduced his powers. Well, it couldn't be helped. He dressed quickly, T-shirt, boxer shorts. The new suit – it was Moira Burke's farewell lunch; a certain formality was in order – with the faint pinstripes, cream on chocolate. The pinstripes had been Brenda's idea; pinstripes were back, she said; everyone was wearing pinstripes this year. Nevertheless Jack felt uneasy in the new suit – there was something period and flashy about it.

At least the children were up, their rooms empty, Rob's room a dust jumble of heaped clothes, coffee mugs, magazines, and records, but in the centre his bed stood, neatly, quaintly made up, topped by one of Brenda's early quilts, a blocky bright collage of navy sailboats, spritely green sea waves, and a primitive orange-coloured sun with long arms of light travelling all the way to the scalloped borders. It had been meant for a younger boy, a different kind of boy.

Laurie's room, neater, paler, was ablaze with sun, and from her window Jack surveyed the brilliant new Siberian landscape. Franklin Boulevard was buried. This was *real* snow; he hadn't seen snow like this for years. Well over a foot it looked like, and the drifted peaks around the sides of the houses and trees had the Dream Whip perfection of snow that he remembered, probably falsely, from childhood. Forts, tunnels, towers, miracles of possibility. Once in Columbus Park by the fountain, in the the light of the moon, he and Bernie had made a snowman with a thrusting torso and an immense icy erection; the next day the penis had been knocked off; the following day the whole snowman had melted to a soft lump; Chicago snow had no keeping power. Even a full day's deluge like this would be gone in a matter of days.

Laurie stood at the kitchen counter crumbling Shredded Wheat into a bowl. 'You're going to be late,' she said, her mouth full; her eyes watchful.

'You don't say.' Why did this child of his always seem to have her mouth full? 'You could have called me,' he said in a somewhat kinder voice.

'I'm late too. Rob got me up. Did you see the snow?'

'Where is Rob, anyway?'

'School.' That jarring cheerful tone! At this hour of the morning!

'He's feeling better then?'

'I dunno.' Why didn't she know?

'Did he eat breakfast?'

'I dunno.' Again? 'But he made some coffee. A whole pot. You want some, Dad?'

He brightened. 'Real coffee?'

It was good coffee. Perfect, in fact, fresh and dark as chocolate. He would have liked a second cup, a third; he wanted – he longed – to linger over the papers this morning, to huddle in a corner of the dining room with his coffee cup and paper, burying himself in the steamy fumes and the stern crises of inflation and unemployment and hunger strikes. The decisions of the auto industry, the arrests of murderers, the marriages of movie stars – it kept him sane and safe to read that the world was going forward despite the complicated meddling of human beings. What had Carter said about the Russian dissidents? What was happening to the ceasefire in Lebanon? He knew Carter would say something cautionary and self-serving: Americans stood for individual freedom but would not, ahem, interfere; he knew too that one Middle-East ceasefire would blend inevitably with another, and all so far away; the world would endure as long as the *Trib* was able to boil columns of print from human catastrophe. It was comforting and preserving, a pleasing drug to feel one's self at times of little consequence. But today he was already running late. Christ, it was nine o'clock. Laurie streaked past him to the front door, shrieking, 'I'm late, I'm going to be late.' A cry of anguish.

His briefcase stood ready by the kitchen table. He had placed it there last night, early this morning really, at 4 A.M., after tapping out the concluding sentence of Chapter Six.

Thus it can be seen from the foregoing that the extent of ritual exchange between the different families and communal groups was less pronounced than previous evidence has led us to believe.

Firm but speculative, the right touch, or so he had thought at 4 A.M.. He really should look it over again.

He put on his overcoat and a pair of warm gloves. In the back of the hall closet, behind the vacuum cleaner, he found his old rubber boots, shiny and floppy, with cheap looking buckles, ten years old if they were a day. These boots seemed at least two sizes too large, incredible.

Stepping onto the back porch he found himself suddenly up to his knees in snow. It was deeper than he'd thought, fifteen inches at least and twice that where it had drifted. The sun sparkled on its wet surface; the temperature must be exactly at the freezing point. He should have turned on the weather report. From the back steps the whole world – acres of it, it seemed – looked deserted. Where was everyone?

The width of snow beckoned. With enormous difficulty, holding his briefcase high in the air, Jack waded through the yard to the garage. A ring of numbness instantly gripped his calves; the snow had fallen inside his boots, wet caked chunks of it plugging the flapping boot tops. Already the neat hems of his pinstriped pants were soaked through. Goodbye, knife-edged press, goodbye, trim, tailored hem. Christ!

Behind the garage the back alley, normally a narrow and scraggly-edged passage, had become a newly created meadow, filled from end to end with glittering, sun-topped snow. Jack saw at once that he would have to give up the idea of driving downtown. It was ludicrous, taking a car out in this weather. It would take him hours to shovel his way out to the street.

Impossible even to open the garage doors. He must have been crazy to think he could drive; it was absurd. Thank God for the El.

It was just eight short blocks to the station, a four-minute walk usually, but today he was walking through fresh heavy snow. He was aware suddenly of the weight and sloshiness of his socks; the snow with its wet, collapsing, counterfeit solidity was breaking under his feet to instant iced greyness, a level sherbet of slush. It had been a mistake to take the alley; he would have made better time going down the street. Luckily, though, someone had gone before him, and he took pains to walk carefully, easing his boots into the deep regular holes of footprints; in and out, in and out. Whose footprints? Rob maybe on his way to school? Or Bud Lewis? Where was everyone? he wondered.

As he ploughed along, the bottom of his woollen overcoat collected a weighty border of crusted snow; he shifted the briefcase high under his arm, pinching it in place with his elbow, and hoisted his coat tails as high as he could. Immediately a coat button snapped off, sprang into the snow and disappeared. At the same instant the briefcase slid sideways from under his arm, landing upside down in a drift. God! He tore off his muffler and mopped at it furiously, hoping the zippered closing was waterproof. A chill struck the back of his neck; his teeth were suddenly chattering.

Twenty-five feet and he'd be out of the alley. He lifted the briefcase, balanced it with one hand on top of his head, and with the other hand gathered his coat, skirtlike, womanlike, in front of him. It must be 9:30. It had taken him half an hour to get to the end of the alley; this was insanity.

Once in the street, walking became somewhat easier. He kept to the middle of the road, stepping carefully along a tyre track. There was little traffic to be seen – Elm Park was a desert. Even the station was close to being deserted – just three people on the platform. He set down his briefcase with relief, feeling light-headed and slightly sick.

'Don't know if the trains are running,' said a woman with a shopping bag and a voice like a door buzzer. 'I've been waiting twenty minutes already.'

'I've been here for twenty-five,' a slim girl in a knitted hat said.

146

'They're running all right,' counselled a grey-headed, square-nosed man in a yellow ski jacket. 'I heard it on the radio. They're slow, but they're getting through.'

'I've got to be downtown by ten,' Jack told them all.

'Fat chance,' cheered the slim girl.

'No way you're gonna make that,' the man in the parka said. Smartass!

And at that moment, the train, almost silent in the sparkling air, pulled into the station. A quarter to ten. Jack felt a kick of joy. He could still –with luck – make it.

The city flashed past, familiar but strange under its quiet village-like covering. Chicago seemed innocent, intact, becalmed. The man in the yellow parka, rank with whisky-breath, wanted to talk weather records – the ice storm of 1949, the blizzard of '53, but Jack kept his eyes on the window. The Merchandise Mart, immense and antique, the quick one-second leap across the white band of river and into the Loop. Ten o'clock. He was late. But nearly there.

He ran the eight blocks to the Institute. The downtown streets, deserted, seemed nevertheless miraculously cleared of snow, an empty, almost nuclear blank. There was scarcely a car on Keeley Boulevard; Jack skittered down the middle of the street, his black boots flopping. At the corner of Keeley and Archer the stop light had gone blind. A power failure? He stopped for a second or two in the centre of the intersection and whirled around in the white glare; the streets stretched wide and empty, a circumference of stripped light, opening to clean-liness and a clear sky. He felt like yelling.

The elevator at the Institute was dead, too. He pounded up the stairs, down the corridor. It was 10:30. He was half an hour late. The tiled floor was slippery underfoot. His breath was coming hard. Outside Dr. Middleton's door, he knocked. No answer. He banged. Nothing. He took off his boots and shoes and, sighing, padded down the hall to his own office.

Why this jubilance? He couldn't imagine where it had come from. He peeled off his coat and hung it on a hanger, letting it drip on the closet floor. He spread his soaked gloves on the heating duct, turned his boots upside down in a corner, removed his socks. And then, kicking the door shut, he took off his drenched pants. Poor old pinstripes – they'd never recover from this. He squeezed as much water as he could from the legs, wringing them out over his philodendron, then pressed the material flat on his desk with the heel of his hand. There was an extra hanger in the little closet, and Jack hung up the pants carefully, running his hand along where the crease had once been.

An extraordinary surge of energy seized him. He considered doing push-ups on the office floor. Knee-bends? Too bad he didn't have a chinning bar in the office like Brian Petrie. Smiling foolishly to himself, he sank into his desk chair and clutched at his hair. His bare legs were beginning to warm up; his thighs tingled. He had made it, he had beat Dr. Middleton to the office. He had, in fact, beat everyone. He was the only one here.

No. Someone was knocking on his door. 'Come in,' he bellowed happily.

It was Moira Burke. She was wearing a soft blue skirt, velvet. And a silk blouse with large loose sleeves. Her hair had been done in a new way, something vaguely Grecian, Jack thought, the way it looped grandly over her ears. Her smile was crooked, perplexed, tentative, hard.

'Moira! You made it through the snow.' He was shouting.

She answered shortly. 'I took a taxi. All the way from Evergreen Park. Fourteen bucks.'

'What about Dr. Middleton? We had an appointment for ten.'

'Ha! He phoned. Can't get in, he says. All the roads in Highland Park are closed.'

'Christ. I stayed up half the night finishing Chapter Six.'

'Hmmm.'

'Moira! Your lunch. What about the farewell lunch?'

'Cancelled.'

'What?' He whirled his chair around.

'Cancelled.'

'You mean postponed. They'll reschedule it. Tomorrow or something.'

'Tomorrow. Don't make me laugh. Tomorrow I'll be in Arizona.'

'Oh, Moira.' He stood up abruptly. Moira's tense locked eyes reminded Jack sharply of Larry Carpenter standing in his kitchen. He opened his mouth to speak.

She crashed against his chest, beating on his shoulder with her fist, wailing.

Chapter Twenty-Two

'THESE THINGS HAPPEN,' JACK WAS SAYING TO MOIRA.
'You're telling me,' she said.

They were eating spaghetti at Roberto's. The mood was one of emergency celebration. Back at the Institute Moira had produced from her desk drawer a small plastic hair dryer that she applied first to Jack's pants and then to his socks and boots. In an hour the pants had dried stiff as construction paper, and their heat against his calves had been unexpectedly pleasurable, the flushed sensual pleasure he remembered feeling on rainy days when he was at school, baking by the radiator after recess.

At Roberto's he and Moira were the only customers. And for some reason the spaghetti was passable today, the sauce plentiful and spicy. There were no waiters in sight; instead the meal was served by the cook, a short man with a heavy neck and shadowless slits for eyes. His jowls danced, dark and friendly. 'I just about stayed in the sack this morning,' he told them, coming out of the kitchen. 'At first I thought, what's the use, no one'll turn up for lunch on a lousy day like this anyways. Then I thought, hell, I better see what's what, check the refrigerator, what with the electricity conking out all over the place. You know something, I've never closed this place down yet, except for Christmas Day and New Year's. That's a record, twenty-five years, and all that time I've never closed, rain or shine. Not a bad record, so today I said to myself, what's a little snow?'

Jack straightened. 'Then are you,' he paused 'the owner?'

'Right on. Owner, proprietor, founder, and cook.'

'I've been coming here twenty years,' Jack said.

'Is that right? Waddya know.'

'And I've never seen you.'

'I keep to the back. I like to keep an eye on things.'

Jack had to know: 'Are you Roberto?'

'You guessed it. Hey, you folks want some wine to warm you up?'

'Absolutely,' Jack said, taken aback by the hideous ring of zeal in his voice.

'Tell you what, the wine's on me today. You and the wife want the cheap stuff or the good stuff? Have the good stuff. I've got a double bottle here, a magnum, they call it. Bet you didn't know I had some good stuff around. It's not on the menu on account of the kind of clientele we get here, they don't know wine from bananas, present company excluded. Only I can't drink the crap we serve, so I keep a few bottles locked up. I gotta lock up everything, or you know what'll happen. That's why I make it my business to stick to the back. Keep my mouth shut and my eyes open. Wide open. Well, enjoy your meal, folks.'

Jack, his feet warm under the table, gratified by the glow of the soft red wine, tried to divert Moira. He spoke rapidly, almost compulsively, filled with a sombre excitement, wanting to commit for her a pure act of kindness, to fill the emptiness of her disappointment with his own misery; the whole world was plagued with disappointment, he wanted to say, a series of disappointments. She was not alone, she was in good company, no one had a monopoly on suffering, we all have setbacks. In his case – he leaned forward on his elbows – in his case it was Harriet Post; after all these years of work, he told Moira, he was going to be stomped upon by a woman in Rochester, New York, called Harriet Post.

'Lord,' Moira said. 'Of all the rotten breaks.' She shook her head sadly, making Jack feel, guiltily, that he had earned her sentiment falsely; something lavish and accidental about Moira's face made it shine with too-easy a sympathy.

Tonight, Jack told her, he was going to phone Harriet Post and find out the scope and nature of her book. But regardless of what she said, he had decided, almost definitely, that he would abandon the book. What was the use? 'As Dr. Middleton says –'

'That old eunuch,' Moira muttered under her breath.

'It's better sometimes,' he drew a sharp breath, 'to cut your losses.'

'Hmmm.'

'These things happen,' he told Moira, astonished at the firmness in his voice.

It seemed to him that he'd been hearing that phrase a lot lately – *these things happen*. Wasn't that what someone said about Larry Carpenter's suicide attempt? He'd said it himself to Rob when they were talking about the visit to Charleston – *these things happen*. The words had a seductive ring of magic about them – say them fast enough and they expelled blame and responsibility. They had the power to defuse all kinds and shades of disappointment. You have to acknowledge the realities, roll with them, et cetera. Men and women do conceive monstrous children, do dissolve their marriages, do commit suicide; they win a few, lose a few, they suffer absurd humiliations. His own children, despite the fact that they lived in a century characterized by alienation and in a city famed for violence, would undoubtedly survive. The world wouldn't end because Harriet Post had cut him out – what was the use crying over spilt milk, as Brenda would have said.

'You really don't mind, then?' Moira said, her eyes, to Jack's surprise, brimming with tears, 'after all the work you've put into it?'

'What can I do?' He shrugged. And wondered if he should confess to her that the thought – the mere thought – of abandoning the book had come as a release. Since Dr. Middleton first implanted the idea in his head – 'these things happen, Jack' – he had at last, this week, found space to breathe. It was true. The small spark of possibility had burst into flame – he could, he saw, with a measure of dignity, walk away; he could put away his notes forever.

'Uhuh,' Moira nodded. She had always appeared a heavy-featured woman to Jack; today her lips had a frilled swelling, a wobbly near-tearfulness that was oddly attractive, reminding Jack of his curious demi-excitement as he stood in the office and experienced the pressure of Moira's thighs through the thin material of his undershorts. He reached across the table and refilled her wine glass.

He grew boisterous and told Moira that he never should have started the Indian thing. It wasn't his kind of research; he did better on short papers, on specific problems. Some people liked long, in-depth studies, but for him the Indians and their trade practices – so abstruse and difficult to document – had been frustrating and wearing. A bore. One long nightmare.

Why was he telling Moira this? It must be the wine going to his head. She was nodding now, smiling at the floor, looking revived. She let loose a bark of harsh public laughter that Jack found cheering.

151

'The trouble is,' he told her, 'everyone keeps asking me how the book is coming along. My parents, they can't wait to see me in print. *Their son*. It's what they've lived for. Even my kids ask me when the book's finally going to be done. *The book*. And this guy next door – '

'The one who tried to kill himself? In the garage?'

'That's the one. He invites me to parties – he's always having parties, the kind of parties you don't get invited to unless you do something, and he introduces me to people as this guy next door who's an expert on Indian trade practices.'

'You could tell them all to fuck off.'

Jack regarded her over the empty plates. Her face was flushed. The wine bottle was empty. Empty! And Moira was drunk.

'Would you like some coffee?' he said. He heard his voice, buoyant and chivalrous; his stomach turned. The checks on the tablecloth hurt his eyes. 'We could order a pot of – '

'Would you like to make love to me?' Moira asked.

'I'm sorry, I didn't mean – '

She said it again, easily, as though the nozzle of her hair dryer aimed up his wet pant-leg had given her the right to say anything. 'Would you like to make love to me this afternoon?'

'I really think we should have some coffee,' Jack said.

'No, that isn't what – '

'Wouldn't you rather – '

'I'm going home,' she said, suddenly demure. 'I'm going to get a taxi.' One of her silk sleeves shot crazily into the air. 'What's another fourteen bucks? Tomorrow I'll be free. Broiling in the good old sun.'

'I'm sorry if – '

'Would you mind,' she spoke with deliberation, 'calling me a taxi?'

He moved to his feet. There was a pay phone by the door, and Jack staggered over. The inside of his head had loosened to plaster, a buzzing whiteness, long, lined chalky arches stretching as far as he could see, Catholic-looking and pure. He wanted to tiptoe through them lighting candles as he went. Salvador Dali. He managed to dial a taxi.

'Ah,' he said to Moira, coming back to the table. 'You're the lucky one. Arizona, lots of years ahead – '

'I love you.' She was speaking quietly and with a quavering

152

unevenness of tone. 'I'll never see you again after today so I can say what I want for a change. I love you. You don't know anything about me. All the time I've been at the Institute. How do you think I've stood it, typing all those reports on glacial remains and fur traders with French names – I had to put in the goddamned French accents by hand, did you know that? Not the most thrilling job in the world, let me tell you. And Dr. Middleton oozing all that Old World stuff, begging my pardon six times a day, it hasn't been a bed of roses. I had to keep myself going somehow. I had to keep sane. Sexual fantasies, it's called. And you – you're my partner, my steady, so to speak. Bet you never suspected a thing.'

'Moira – '

'When it first started, me thinking up these fantasies, I thought for sure I was going nuts. Oh, Moira, I said, you're ready for the nut house. The men in the white coats. Ha. Then I read a couple books from the library, by this New York lady, who writes about sexual fantasies and who says even people who are normal and love their husbands and so on, even people like that have these weird ideas at times. Like with men they work with, you know.'

'I think – ' He gave his awful laugh.

'The things I've done to you. Oh. The things you've done to me.'

'Christ, Moira.'

'Don't be embarrassed. It's not something to be embarrassed about, its normal. You should read this book. And you'll never see me again, so why be embarrassed? What does it matter? I'm not crazy. I hope you don't think I'm crazy.'

'Of course not – '

'Sometimes you tie me to the bed with my pantyhose. Sometimes I suck your fingers, one by one. You nuzzle the backs of my knees – '

'Don't you think – '

'This morning? When you stood up in the office? with those boxer shorts on? To tell you the truth, I'd always thought you'd be the type to wear jockey shorts. That's how I've always pictured you, all this time – '

'I'm sorry if – ' He held his mouth stiff.

'Sorry? Don't be sorry for crying out loud, it doesn't matter to me. Underwear, what's underwear? It's what's underneath in a person that matters to me.'

'I'm glad if – '

'I could have picked someone else. Brian Petrie. I tried him for a while. But the thing about you that really got me was, now don't laugh, was those little hairs on the tops of your hands. Even on the fingers. You don't see that too often, the hair growing that far down on a man's hands, all the way to the nails, almost. I noticed it the first time Dr. Middleton introduced you. Way back when. Happy to meet you, you said, and I was thinking, my God, those beautiful hairs standing like that on the backs of his hands.'

Jack couldn't speak, although he wanted to. Moira's hands lay on the table, palms up – *I've told you everything*, she seemed to be saying. And he, in return, had told her nothing, nothing that mattered. Nor would he ever. A sudden perception of human secretiveness came to him, the depth of it, the useless-ness of it, the waste.

Unburdened, Moira seemed to grow sober. She seemed younger now, in a state of repose. 'You did come,' she said with this new calm voice. 'You were the only one to come through the snow today. That says something, doesn't it?'

He wanted to say yes, but feared the entrapment of words; instead he covered her hand with his; it was soft as a young girl's. What had he expected? Roberto called from the kitchen, 'Hey, there's a cab sitting out front. You call a cab?'

'Yes.' Moira spoke distinctly.

Jack helped her into her coat.

'Don't you ever have fantasies?' she said, clutching the bone buttons.

'Yes. Of course. Everyone does.'

'I'm drunk. God, am I ever soused.'

'So am I.'

'I love you.' She bumped against him on her way out the door. 'I love you, too,' he called after her. What did he mean by this? He didn't know. He hoped she wouldn't turn around and ask.

Chapter Twenty-Three

FOR A NUMBER OF REASONS, NONE OF THEM VERY CLEAR, Jack decided to walk home to Elm Park. Moira's outburst had left him giddy; a shaky euphoria filled his head; his teeth were chattering; he felt overwhelmed and dizzy. He needed to think, to descend. There was no use going back to the Institute – today was plainly going to be an unofficial holiday. And it appeared from the look of the vacant snow-blasted downtown streets that there were no buses running. He supposed he could get the train, but what was the rush? It was only two o'clock; he had all afternoon to walk home.

It was something he'd never done, although now that he thought about it, he couldn't imagine why not. Ten miles wasn't considered such a spectacular distance, nowadays; for a marathon runner, for a jogger like Bud Lewis even, ten miles might be thought of as little more than a warm- up. It would do him good to walk ten miles, it would sober him up, it would use up the afternoon – for the afternoon suddenly yawned before him, a maw of time that he must somehow fill. A long solitary walk was what he needed. He could even say later, should people ask him, or even if they didn't, that on the day after the big storm he had walked from the Loop out to Elm Park. 'Is it true you walked all the way from . . . ?' 'Are you the guy who actually . . . ?' (He often wished he could shut them off, these buzzing thoughts – why was it he could never do anything, never even think of doing something, without playing at doing it; there was something despicable in his small rehearsals and considered responses; was he the only one in the world who suffered these echoes?)

Strange that he could have lived in Chicago all his life without ever once entertaining the idea of such a walk. Why was that? No, it wasn't the distance itself; there was something prohibiting about this particular distance, the sprawl of it, the seeming impermeability and unyieldingness of its layers, its tough urban clutter. It stretched, a wide alien terrain, a dry basin, which could be safely traversed only from within a closed vehicle.

And walking ten miles out in the country was one thing, but walking one's way out of the hub of a large city was plainly eccentric, cheaply romantic in fact, troubadourish. And furthermore, there was no easy way out to the west side, no channel of softened parkland to scurry along. Just the whole harsh, seedy nexus of city blocks and masonry and traffic – and now all this buried in snow. And danger of course: gangs on corners, knives, strange tongues and taunts, hucksters, pickpockets, drunks, pimps. Today, though, it was easier to believe that these dangers might be quelled. The snow was less a hindrance than a form of mitigation. It was whiteness that made the idea of walking home seem possible. Snow and purity: a symbolism effortlessly grasped; snow was capable of making strange instant conversions, offering as it did a casual coat of simplicity atop Chicago's jumble-heap. One snow-plugged city block would look like all the others; one trafficless city street like the next; neighbourhoods would meld together, one after another, a blurring of postal districts, precincts, schools. It pleased Jack, and made him feel oddly safe, to think of this new namelessness, and the way in which the snow had obliterated geographical boundaries, stretching even beyond the city limits to bind this rusty downtown sprawl to the stillness of forest preserves, small farms, villages, lakes. He breathed deeply. The wine was wearing off, replaced now by a quirky mushrooming of faith in his own feet and in the huge white light of the sky. He decided to take Washington Boulevard all the way.

He had a liking for Washington; in the summer its surface was smooth and bland with asphalt; it seemed to him the most civilized of the east-west streets, straight as an arrow, but with certain continental softenings here and there; further out there would be Garfield Park, the golden dome of the Conservatory, trees and apartment buildings whose substantial brown facades glowed in good weather like trustworthy faces. Even downtown Washington purred with a different, richer tune. There was something better-behaved about it, something cooler, more mannerly. The snowploughs had partially cleared the road, leaving long mounds of snow on either side. He walked in the middle of the street, facing the white glare. A few drivers on the roads, seeing him plod along, slowed so as not to splash him with the rapidly accumulating slush.

One car pulled up beside him, a small rusted Ford with a melting crust of snow on its roof. A man leaned out the window and offered Jack a lift. 'Hop in if you're going west.' He had a crazy mop of hair, student hair, and a fine face.

'I'm out for a walk,' Jack said, then called after him, 'but thanks anyway.' It had been years since he'd been offered a ride by anyone.

By the time he reached Halsted the flapping of his boot tops had become intolerable. He noticed a cigar store near the corner and went in and asked if he could buy a ball of string. 'String?' A short, stout, immensely wrinkled old woman in a grey cardigan sat on a stool by the cash register, looking as though she had never heard of string. Her voice was purest Chicago growl. 'We don't handle string here. We don't get much call for string.'

'I just need a couple feet. To tie the tops of my boots. The snow – '

'Well, if that's all you need – ' The mouth smacked shut; was this thick, moist drawing back of lips a kind of smile? 'I guess I could let you have some of our own string.'

She cut a length, divided it in two and handed it to Jack. Her earrings clacked against humped shoulders. 'Here,' she said. 'You can sit down over there and tie up your galoshes.' A command.

He sat on a wooden box and laced the string through the boot buckles, then wound it twice around each leg, stuffing the bottoms of his pants down inside so that they formed a fairly comfortable cushion between his ankles and the sliding rubber. Then he stood up; ah, much better, much more secure; he felt he could walk miles now.

'Thank you so much,' he said. God, he sounded elegant – awful. A gentleman out of a costume romance.

She was reading a newspaper, but looked up. 'Holy Jesus, what's a little string on a day like this.'

'I'm surprised you've stayed open on a day like this.' Jack lingered by the door; only at Halsted and already dying for conversation.

'Yeah, well,' she shrugged, 'the choice we got is do we open or do we leave the dump wide open for looters. Kids out looking for cigarettes, up to no good – '

Realities, Jack thought, walking between Halsted and Damen toward the dark shape of Chicago Stadium, the continual facing up to realities; was that any way to live a life? – always on the lookout for muggers, looters, loiterers, always assuming the worst would happen if you let down your guard for a minute? Did it ever let up for the people who run cigar stores? Did it, for that matter, ever let up for anyone, this daily dealing with actualities? This cautious daily round, this sameness? Something unexpected had to happen to break the cycle; a special set of circumstances was required.

In the last hour a man had offered him a lift; a woman had given him a piece of string. It wasn't enough. Ah, but a woman had told him she loved him. She had loved him for years. It was incredible. The more he thought about it the more incredible it seemed. He felt dizzy, but fortified; a muscle twitched in his face. And what else? It was January and Chicago was buried in snow. It had to be a record of some kind. And here he was, walking down Washington Boulevard at three o'clock on a Tuesday afternoon. Surely that was enough to blow the whistle on ordinariness. Or at least call a temporary suspension. Another thing: no one in the world knew where he was. He could not be reached. Nothing at this moment was demanded of him; he could not be held accountable. He had, right in his two hands, a whole afternoon, wide open. It might be an illusion – it *was* an illusion – but for the next three hours, which was what he estimated it would take him to get from Damen to Elm Park Avenue, he was, temporarily, set free, an invisible man gliding down a ghosted street in an unfamiliar city.

A few cars passed. Willa Cather School sat darkly vacant; a few children played in the snow outside – the schools must be closed – and threw snowballs. He felt himself impervious to danger and catastrophe. The lunch with Moira had left him curiously anaesthetized, but at the same time liberated. Certain answers had been given him, but the questions themselves were mysteries that couldn't be named. Washington Boulevard was a country road and he was walking into the dull, metal-coloured sun toward a not unpleasant net of connections and possibilities. Tonight he would phone Harriet Post. Tonight Brenda would be phoning home from Philadelphia, the clear lightness of her voice breaking through the receiver. His children would be waiting at home. He would speak to them wisely. He would talk to Bernie, sit down with him, ask him what he intended to do, and offer, if asked, advice or consolation. Order could yet be made of his life.

He passed a locked store that had a hand-printed sign in the window: Catfish. An intense sobriety overcame him. He should reach out, dispense his calm awareness to others. If some poor guy came along asking him for a buck, he would give him ten. If he got mugged, he would say, take my wallet, take my hat and gloves, take everything. He was a man, a historian, walking home; a certain seriousness had been called into his life today, a levelness of vision, considered and selfless. Discontent, he reflected, was caused only by a reluctance to look at life soberly – we cannot always be escaping into easy exits.

'Of course,' he had told Moira Burke, standing drunkenly in the open door of Roberto's, 'of course, I've had sexual fantasies.'

But what he had withheld from her was the fact that his fantasies invariably circled around Brenda, his wife; and always they were played out in the safety of familiar surroundings, the house in Elm Park, the blue and white bedroom with the pictures of the children on the dresser. Moira would have been astonished and possibly saddened to hear this, after the books she'd read. Even he was somewhat astonished and saddened; either he had no imagination or he was possessed of a dull nature, doggedly monogamous and domestic. (Someone he'd met at a party recently, a psychologist with the school board, had told him that the average male thinks of sex once every twenty minutes – he had wondered, and doubted, how average he was.)

The sweet swelling of Brenda's hips – Jack could not imagine a time, although he knew human flesh inevitably sagged and aged, when he would not be stirred by the sensation of his open hand resting on Brenda's hip. Or her fingertips, easy and familiar, brushing the side of his face.

Twenty years ago Harriet Post had invited him up to her one-room apartment and had, with a single gesture, elbows over-head, whipped off her sweater. She had yanked open the studio couch with a thump that banged thrillingly on his heart, and said, 'Well?'

The first time she had had to help him, but he learned fast. Winter evenings, lying on the black corduroy cover of Harriet's studio couch, he practised the intricacies of timing and intensity, feeling his slow body coming to life. Beneath him Harriet moaned and gasped realistically; her thin pelvis had the weight of wood framing securely nailed. He swam over her body, almost drowning, almost melting into her, but called back always by something dry and careful at the back of his head, a shameful prickling speaking to him in a voice oddly akin to radio static, saying, 'But what is this for? What is this for?'

After he married Brenda the voice went away. It disappeared without a trace. He hadn't thought of it for years. Nor had he ever told Brenda about it; he wouldn't know how to tell her. He was merely grateful to be rid of it. And amazed. He had, he sensed, just narrowly escaped, although from what he wasn't sure.

On Washington Boulevard it was growing cooler. Crossing Kedzie, the string around his left boot snapped. Shit, just when he was starting to make good time. Next to a liquor store, locked and chained, was a café, miraculously open, 'Margie's Lunch,' and he stopped to buy coffee and to retie his boots. The place was deserted. He sank onto a counter stool and felt the jarring weariness of back and legs; he flexed his knees, testing the alternate shocks of pain and relief, and it occurred to him for the first time that he might not be able to make it after all. Kedzie was less than half way home – Christ. He eased off his boots and through his sock he could feel, on his right foot, a small blister starting on the top of one toe.

'Ya wanna doughnut with that coffee?' The boy behind the counter looked about Rob's age. White teeth in a black face, tentative and sick with melancholy.

'Just coffee. Black. You wouldn't have a piece of string by any chance? For my boot?'

'Naw. We don't have string.'

'I guess maybe I could tie this back together, only it's a bit short.'

'Jeez, where'd you get those boots, man?'

'I've had them for a while.'

'You're kiddin' me. How you move around in boots like that, man?'

'If I just had a little piece of string – '

'Hey, gimme that. Lemme see that.'

Jack handed the pieces of string over the counter and

watched as the boy grasped them, whirled them between pinkish-brown fingers, made a thick-looking knot that he tested with a sharp tug and a meow of satisfaction. 'Hey, man, that oughta do.'

'Well thanks.'

'If I was you, I'd get me some new boots.' He looked at the ceiling and gave a sharp, mysterious cackle.

'Yes, that feels a lot better,' Jack said. The coffee had warmed him through, and he felt ready to go again. 'Well, so long.' He smiled hard across the counter, trying to force this young boy to smile back; he had laughed – why couldn't he smile?

The sun was going down as Jack crossed Garfield Park and arrived at Pulaski. The buildings on the corner – a grill, a gas station, the Temple of Deliverance – seemed to catch fire. A good Chicago name, Pulaski, Brenda's maiden name. You know, 'Pulaski, like the street,' Brenda had told him when she had introduced herself. And afterwards, whenever he saw a sign with the word Pulaski on it, he was able to recall exactly the way she had said it: lightly, but with a meaningful intensity, as though it were a very old joke, but with some juice left in it. She had held her head slightly to one side, her lips parted, the start of a smile.

How easily he was able to retrieve these images. It was as though he carried a film strip around with him, a whole history of Brenda Pulaski Bowman that was altogether separate and different from her history of herself. No doubt she had a film strip on him, too – he could not imagine what it would consist of, but its details would be puzzling and foreign. Certainly he had never dreamed that he had lived another life all these years inside Moira Burke's head. (He thought of tying her up with pantyhose and felt a painful piercing pressure rise at the back of his throat, a hillock of pleasure – should he laugh or weep?) The number of histories one person might have locked in his head was infinite. The most sophisticated tracking device in the world couldn't collect them all and consolidate them (something he must discuss with Bernie on Friday). Some source would be forgotten or some fact left unexamined.

He remembered one night years ago telling his mother he was bringing home a girl called Brenda Pulaski. 'A polack girl?' his mother had asked, alerted. 'Polish,' Jack had corrected her pompously. His mother would never remember now that she had uttered those words – 'a polack girl' – and would never recall the variety of expectations that word aroused. Once, only once, he had brought Harriet Post home. A Sunday; his mother had fixed a pork roast; and now she couldn't even remember who Harriet was.

In all probability, Jack thought, Harriet had forgotten his mother too, forgotten the pork roast and apple sauce, possibly even forgotten about him and their long nights of groping on the narrow studio couch. When he phoned her tonight, he would have to start from the assumption that she had forgotten; he'd have to work his way back slowly. 'Hello? Harriet? This (ahem) is a voice from the past, I don't suppose you remember me, but . . .' Or boldly, 'This is Jack Bowman, Harriet. From Chicago? 1956?'

Cicero Avenue. At last. A furniture store on the corner advertised a four-room special. A medical clinic sat in gloomy darkness. It got dark fast this time of year. At least Washington Boulevard was fairly well lit. If he saw a taxi he might give in and ride the rest of the way. The blister on his toe was getting worse, and he was starting to feel shaky with cold. It was five o'clock.

He passed a florist's shop, 'Flower City,' and was surprised to see that a shop selling such nonessentials was open. A tidy balanced arrangement of gladioli filled the window, and there was a sign: *Sale. Today Only* – which struck Jack as hilarious. Who would rush out to buy sale flowers on a day like this? Was today someone's wedding day? Or funeral? Then the idea came to him that *he* ought to buy some flowers. He should – and the idea lit him up with happiness – he should send Moira Burke a bouquet of flowers.

Here he was, outside a lighted flower shop. And Moira Burke was at home, packing her suitcase, sobering up, arriving, no doubt, at dread realizations. His heart flared with genuine warmth. He would send her some flowers. But not gladioli. What would a lover send? Roses. 'Do you have any roses?' he asked the woman behind the counter. She looked at him suspiciously. She had her coat on, her keys in her hand, and seemed anxious to lock up.

'We've got anything you want,' she told him. 'In the back.'
'A dozen roses?'
'You want to take them with you or send them?'

162

'Send them. Evergreen Park. Do you deliver out there?'

'I can arrange it, but it'll cost plenty.'

'Can you guarantee them for tonight?'

'I don't know. With all this snow? Maybe. I can try.'

'It has to get there tonight.'

'What d'you want on the card?'

'What card?'

'The card that says who the flowers are from.' She was faintly mocking, tapping her pencil.

'No card,' Jack decided. 'Just the flowers.'

'Suit yourself.' She gave him a level look.

'Can you take a cheque?' he asked.

'Hmmm. I don't usually.'

'Please.'

He pulled off his gloves and reached for his cheque-book, and under the bright lights the hair on the back of his hand danced. He spread his fingers, observing the play of light; he was a man who was sending roses to a woman who said she loved the hair on his hands. He shook his head, dazed, happy. What was to be done with knowledge like this?

'Thank you, Mr. Bowman. If you'll just sign here – ' The way she said Mr. Bowman, the way she handed him the pen, told him he was getting close to home. Another hour, if he walked fast.

It was actually a little more than an hour before he stood by his front door. The sky overhead looked matted and close, and the snow in Elm Park was thicker and firmer than the city snow, banked everywhere around the lighted houses, beautiful. Small shrubs swayed with the weight of it; his own house was delicately lined with narrow shelves of blue-whiteness. No one had bothered to close the curtains, and light poured out the living-room windows, sending golden squares across the front yard. He pushed open the front door and inhaled warmth and the smell of meat cooking. Laurie met him with a ferocious, head-on embrace. 'Bernie's here. He's fixing us steak. T-bones.'

Rob appeared in the doorway to the kitchen, dreamy-eyed, looking surprisingly tall. 'Mom just phoned from Philly. Ten minutes ago.'

'Five minutes ago,' Laurie corrected him.

'She's called?' Jack felt dizzy with fatigue. 'Already?'

'We all talked to her.'

'What did she say?' He should take off his coat, sit down, get out of these boots.

'Just that she's having a great time.'

'A great time?'

'*The Second Coming* got honourable mention,' Laurie said.

'What else?'

'Besides the honourable mention?'

'Did she say anything else? Any messages?'

'She said to give you her love,' Rob said.

'Is that all?' Jack said. He was so tired he thought he might faint. 'Is that all?'

Chapter Twenty-Four

BERNIE, WHISTLING, STOMPING, SERVED THE STEAKS AT THE kitchen table, plunking them onto plates with a meat fork. There was something bewildering in this domestic scene – Bernie performing kitchen duty like a lodger who had been pressed into service – but Jack, who was sick with hunger, felt too grateful to ponder the point. Looking around he saw, too, that the kitchen had been cleaned up. The dishes had been put in the dishwasher. A large green garbage bag, neatly tied, waited by the back door. Even the floor looked as though it had been swept.

Bernie, chomping into red meat, was cheerful but agitated; his amber bush of hair rose steeply off his forehead, and there were ridges of whiteness over his eyes. Jack would have liked to have told him about going to Roberto's today, not about Moira Burke, but about coming face to face with the real-life Roberto, but Bernie was preoccupied with other things; tonight he was going to the Austin General to visit Larry Carpenter. He glanced at his watch; visiting hours started at eight.

Larry was feeling much better, Bernie reported, at least that was the latest news according to Janey, who had spent all day at the hospital. He was feeling ready to have visitors, Janey said, and the psychiatrist thought that it was probably a good idea. One at a time of course. Janey had asked him to go with her tonight for an hour. 'Oh, and by the way, Janey says to thank Laurie for feeding the dogs.'

'I meant to send a plant,' Jack said.

'Larry's actually cheerful, Janey says. It's amazing. Anxious to get home, get back to the paper and all that.'

'So soon?'

'She says he might even be able to come home tomorrow. Of course he'll have to be on tranquillizers for a while.'

'I suppose.'

Bernie jumped up, grabbed for his jacket. 'Sorry to eat and run like this, but I'd better get going.'

165

Silence. Then Rob, eyeing Bernie's windbreaker, said, 'You want to borrow my ski jacket?'

'This'll be fine. It's not that cold.'

'What about boots?' Jack asked.

Bernie shrugged, a dipping vaudeville shrug, and a strange neighing laugh came out of his mouth. 'My shoes are already soaked, so why worry now . . . .'

'About tonight – ' Jack began.

'Don't worry about me,' Bernie smiled, giving off an almost bridegroom aura, 'I'll just bunk in next door.'

He left by the back door; they could hear the slipping of his shoes as he stepped onto the wooden porch. Under the kitchen light Rob and Laurie sat silent as statues; without looking up, Jack could feel their eyes on him, accusing. Damn it, why on him? Laurie sawed at her steak and said, 'I still don't understand why.'

'Why what?'

'Why you didn't come home on the El instead of walking.'

'Why?' This quizzing wasn't what he had expected. Not that he expected congratulations or a round of applause for something that now seemed whimsical as well as foolhardy; but on the other hand, he hadn't anticipated this kind of challenge, either. 'I don't know,' he told her.

'You never did it before.' She was genuinely puzzled – Jack recognized the tone. It was the puzzlement of a very young child threatened by change. Twelve is not very old, he thought.

'Maybe that's why I did it,' Jack said. 'Just because I'd never done it before.'

'That doesn't sound like a very good reason – '

But Rob cut in. 'You don't have to have a reason for everything you do, stupid.' There was a clink of comradeship in the way he pronounced the word 'stupid' that took the edge off.

Jack regarded him across the table, solemnly approving.

Rob was on his third cup of tea. He wasn't in the mood for steak tonight, he said. No one was surprised at this; no one even questioned him. He'd been like this for days now.

But his loss of appetite had yet to assume the weight of fact. Jack had not begun to worry about it. Or even, for that matter, to acknowledge it. On the other hand, it had been noticed. And absorbed. And for the moment, at least, accepted.

166

The long-distance operator was wonderfully kind. 'I'm really, really sorry about this,' she said.

'What are my chances if I try again in an hour?'

'I don't know.' She was letting him down gently. 'They tell us we won't be able to get through to Rochester tonight, or Buffalo either, for that matter.'

'Are you sure?' He had already rehearsed exactly what he would say to Harriet. 'What I mean is, it doesn't seem possible that Bell Telephone can't – '

'It *is* unusual, but they tell us,' – who were they? – 'that our storm has moved that way.'

Jack loved the way she said 'our storm.' He pictured her as a slightly older, slightly greyer version of Moira Burke, and was reluctant to hang up. 'We received a long-distance call from Philadelphia this evening,' he told her. 'If you can get through from Philadelphia, wouldn't it make sense that you could get through to Rochester?'

'What time was this Philadelphia call, sir?' Why did she have to spoil it by calling him 'sir'?

'About six, I think it was.'

'Well, all I can tell you is that things have got a lot worse since then. Apparently there are lots of lines down, and we've been told that the east is getting hit a lot harder than Chicago.'

'Incredible,' Jack said sociably. 'Hard to believe that anything could be worse than what we had.'

'Isn't it,' she commiserated. 'It's been unbelievable.'

'It looks as though I'll have to try tomorrow night.'

'You shouldn't have any trouble tomorrow night. I'm sure the lines will be in order by then. I can practically guarantee it.'

'Who were you trying to phone?' Laurie asked as he hung up. The three of them were sitting in the living room, reading.

'A woman who lives in Rochester.' *A woman who lives in Rochester* – as though she were someone mythical, the Lady of the Lake.

'Who?' Laurie asked directly.

'Her name is Harriet Post.'

'Harriet Post?' Rob came out from behind the newspaper. For an hour he'd been reading news stories about the storm. 'Who's Harriet Post?'

Jack sat back, sipping at his coffee, happy to have an audience tonight. 'As a matter of fact, Harriet Post is someone I used to know back when I was a student.'

'So why are you phoning her?' Laurie seemed more than usually intent.

'Well, I just discovered that she's written a book. And it so happens that it's the same kind of book I've been working on.'

'Indians you mean?' From Rob.

'You mean you've both written the exact same book?'

'Well, more or less. What happened was she didn't know I was writing it, and I didn't know she was writing it. It's not unusual, this kind of thing. These things happen.' Useful phrase.

'So why're you phoning her?'

'Well,' Jack paused, 'I have to find out exactly what material her book covers. What I have to do, at this point, is decide whether it's worth finishing my book or not.'

Rob put the paper down. 'You mean you might not finish it?'

'Well, it would be a bit absurd to have two books on the same subject. Coming out in the same year. If you see what I mean.'

'Yeah,' Laurie said, 'that would be dumb.'

'That's for sure,' Rob said, going back to his newspaper.

Jack listened to the wind rattling on the storm window. He felt peace drifting over him; he could fall asleep right in this chair.

At midnight the telephone rang.

'Hello,' he said in a daze.

'It's me, Jack. Dad.'

'Dad. For Christ's sake, what's wrong?'

'Nothing wrong. Nothing at all. You sound as though you were asleep.'

'Just dozing. Not really asleep.'

'Just thought I'd phone.'

'Is Ma all right?'

'She's fine, just fine. Been sound asleep for hours.'

'And you're okay? Weathering the storm?'

'Fine, fine, no problem for us. No sidewalks to shovel here.'

'Dad?'

'Yes.'

'Why are you phoning? You never phone in the middle of the night. Something's got to be the matter.'

'Nothing, Jack, nothing – '

'You can't sleep. Is that it?'

'Well, that's nothing new with me.'

'Then do you mind telling me – '

'Well, I bought this new book the other day. I've been reading it all day.'

'What book?'

'It's called *Living Adventurously*.'

'Go on.'

'It's by this California real estate man. Or at least he used to be a real estate man. A smart man, it sounds like to me. At least he's got a lot of good ideas.'

'Such as – '

'On how to put adventure into your life. You know what I mean, Jack. Getting out of the old rut.'

'Uhuh.'

'Like all kinds of things you can do without rocking the boat completely.'

'Such as?'

'Well, this is just an example, you can eat your dessert before your dinner. That's one thing, he says.'

'Oh yeah? Did you try that?'

'Tomorrow. Another thing he says is write someone a thank-you letter, like some cousin maybe or your congressman. Out of the blue, you know.'

'Did you do that?'

'I'm thinking about it.'

'What else?'

'Well he says, phone someone up in the middle of the night. On impulse, like.'

'And you did.'

'He says if you're going to put adventure into your life you've got to start with something small. So I start thinking, why not?'

'Great, Dad.'

'Glad you weren't in bed. I'd have hated to wake you up.'

'I'm just going now.'

'Well, then, I'll say goodnight.'

'I'll see you tomorrow, Dad.'

'Tomorrow? Tomorrow's Wednesday.'
'I thought I'd stop by on my way home from work.'
'Are you sure? On a Wednesday.'
'I'm sure.'
'Well – '
'Goodnight, Dad.'
'Goodnight, Jack. Sleep well.'

Chapter Twenty-Five

ON WEDNESDAY MORNING JACK'S DAUGHTER LAURIE WAS going to be killed. Or so she said.

She was going to be killed, slaughtered, by her seventh grade Home Economics teacher because she hadn't bought the pattern and material for the skirt she was supposed to be making. 'Don't be silly,' Jack told her. 'It's not the end of the world, not having a pattern.'

'It is, it is,' she wailed miserably. Her head rolled back and forth with the rhythm of suffering, and her fists thrashed at the air.

'You'll just have to bring it tomorrow,' Jack said firmly.

She began to cry wildly, not bothering to cover her face with her hands. Laurie's tears, so different from Brenda's rare slow tears, boiled out in steamy sheets. 'She'll kill me. You don't know her.'

It was eight o'clock. He had been sipping a cup of coffee quietly when Laurie had come howling into the kitchen. 'Why didn't you mention all this yesterday?'

She let loose a long cry of grief. 'I forgot.' Her face was swelling before his eyes; the amoeba softness of her body always moved him to pity.

'You've probably had weeks to get it.'

'Mom was going to get it for me last week.' She was holding on to the back of a chair, blubbering more quietly now.

'Your mother was busy last week.' Here he was, making excuses for Brenda – he felt a spurt of anger, *Damn it, Brenda, what's going to become of this kid, with you* – the phrase *gallivanting across the country* occurred to him, but he rejected it as unfair.

'Okay, okay, Laurie, what time do you have Home Ec?'

She slammed her fists into her eyes and stopped crying. 'At 9:30. Right after Home Room.'

'Look, honey, I can't promise. I've got an appointment with Dr. Middleton for ten. But I'll try, okay?'

'Oh, Daddy!' The force of her gratitude was annihilating; her soft face shone wonderfully.

'Just write down exactly what you need and I'll try to drop it off at school. I'll have to leave it at the main office. Do you know what you need?'

'I've got the pattern number right here. It's Butterick. They've got it at Zimmerman's.'

'And the cloth?'

'It has to be part polyester. But not plain. It's got to be a print.'

'A print? Okay.'

'But Daddy, it's got to be a small print, okay? Mrs. Frost said a large print would just make me look like an elephant.'

'Did she, sweetie?'

'And a dark colour. She said I have to have a dark colour. It would be more flattering, she said.'

'Whose skirt is this, anyway? You can have what you want, for Pete's sake.'

'I'd better get what she says to or she'll kill me. Oh, and Dad, a zipper. A seven-inch zipper, okay?' She grabbed his hand, kneaded it violently.

'God, Laurie!'

'Do you really think you can get it there by 9:30?'

'Sure,' he told her. 'We'll give it the old try, anyway.'

Rob, waking late, yawning, gathering his books together, putting on his snow boots, was – in contrast – infuriatingly calm. Almost in a trance. 'Hey, Dad, do you think you can drop me at school? I slept through my alarm.'

'I've got to pick up something for Laurie. Can you be ready in five minutes?'

'I'm ready now.'

'What about breakfast?'

'I had some coffee.'

'How about some toast or something?'

'I'm not all that hungry.'

'Why not?'

'What do you mean, why not?'

'Okay, Rob. That's enough beating around the bush. What's going on with you?'

'Me?'

172

'As far as I can make out, you haven't eaten anything since last Saturday.'

'I don't know what you're talking about.'

'Oh yes you do.'

'So?' he said 'So I'm not hungry. Is that supposed to be some kind of crime?'

'It happens to be Wednesday. Saturday to Wednesday – figure it out. That's a fairly long time for someone who's supposed to be healthy.'

Rob examined the backs of his hands, brooding.

'Just tell me this much, Rob,' Jack sucked for breath. 'Are you ever planning to eat again?'

'Sure.'

'When?'

'Saturday.'

'Saturday? Why Saturday?'

Rob made a face at the floor. 'That makes seven days.'

'I see,' Jack said. Amazingly, he did see. There was no explosion of light inside his head; instead the truth struck him with a clear, approaching ringing noise, rather like a bicycle bell. 'This is a kind of starvation thing you're on, then? A fast?'

'Sort of, yeah.'

'I see.' Couldn't he think of anything better to say to this boy than *I see*! 'Well, look, do you mind telling me if there's any particular reason?'

'No reason, not exactly. I just want to see if I can do it.'

'You're not doing penance for anything?'

'No.'

'And it doesn't have anything to do with going out to Charleston last week?'

'No. It's not that, I'm over that. In fact I told Bernie I'd go out with him again on Sunday.'

'To see if you can do it.'

'Sort of.'

'I see. I think I see.'

'It probably sounds crazy.'

'No. Well, it may sound crazy but it's probably not.'

'Now that really does sound crazy.' From Rob's throat came a dry croaking sound.

'Look, Rob, we'd better get going. I don't even know if I'll be able to get the car out of the garage.'

'A lot of snow's melted. And Bernie shovelled out most of the alleyway yesterday. De Paul was closed so he was here all day.'

'Good old Bernie. He cooks us steaks and shovels our alley. What did we ever do without him?'

'About Bernie,' Rob began, 'do you think, I mean does it seem sort of odd to you, Bernie staying next door?'

'Sort of.'

'I was wondering if they . . . do you think they? . . . Bernie and Mrs. Carpenter . . . do you think they, well – '

'Probably. Yes. Chances are good. Human nature being what it is.' Jack searched through his coat pockets for his car keys. How calm he sounded, how surprisingly moderate and detached.

Rob rubbed at his chin with the back of his glove. 'Well, doesn't that seem kind of . . . I mean, here's Mr. Carpenter in the hospital. I mean the guy tried to do himself in. And Bernie's, well, you know, screwing around . . . with his wife.'

'Have you seen my car keys?'

'On the hall table.'

'Thanks. Lots of things probably don't make a whole lot of sense. Sometimes people don't react the way we think they're going to.' He waved his arms in the air. 'Like when Grandma Elsa died. The funeral was on a Monday, remember? You were only, lets see, ten – '

'I remember the funeral.'

'Well, do you remember after the funeral? What we did?'

'Not exactly.'

'We went back to Grandma's and Grandpa's apartment and played canasta all afternoon.'

'Canasta?'

'I know it's not the same thing, but what I'm saying is – '

'I know what you're saying.'

'I'm sure when Mr. Carpenter gets home everything will be back to normal.'

'Have you ever – ? I mean after you married Mom did you ever . . . you know . . . with someone else?'

'Never.' The force of declaration in his voice almost took his breath away; so many small dishonesties in his life, so much false posing and faithlessness, but now and then an exhilarating chance to tell the truth. 'Never. I can't tell you why. But to

174

make a long story short, I never wanted to. It's too complicated, but never.'

'We better go.'

'What's the first thing you're going to have when you break your fast?'

'A kingburger. With the works. And a double order of fries and either a banana milkshake or a large root beer. I haven't decided for sure yet, but probably it'll be the root beer.'

Chapter Twenty-Six

THE OFFICE WASN'T THE SAME ON WEDNESDAY WITHOUT Moira.

Calvin White, Geology, who had the office next to Jack's, leaned against the coffee machine just after lunch, lamenting the fact that now that Moira had left and been replaced by the golden-haired Melvin Zaddo, the Institute had become an all-male bastion. 'Moira kept us on our toes,' Calvin said, somewhat ambiguously, swirling coffee in a styrofoam cup.

Brian Petrie, Cultural Anthropology, agreed. Moira Burke was going to be sorely missed around here. 'The hours that woman put in! *Unpaid* hours. It was Moira, if you remember, who put up the Christmas decorations in the board room. Year after year, for crying out loud.'

'Mel Zaddo looks like a loser,' Milton McInnis, Restoration, said. 'And he can't spell.'

'Poor Mel – can't spell. Ha!'

'His typing's not too bad,' Calvin White said with a squeezing frown. 'Amazingly good, in fact.'

'He's got that look of temperament,' Brian Petrie said. 'The way he slinks around. Up one day, down the next.'

'He did all right condensing those minutes,' Jack said. 'A surprisingly good job, to tell the truth.'

'I've a feeling he won't be around all that long.'

'The amazing thing is that Dr. Middleton ever – '

'Bizarre's the word.'

'It's going to be interesting to see how long he manages to hang on to that hair of his – '

'Just so he gets the cataloguing done – '

'And mans the phone the way Moira used to – '

'That cologne,' Brian Petrie said, 'or whatever it is he wears, is getting to my allergies.'

'Moody as a rooster, but – '

'Time will tell.'

'Apparently; he's already negotiating for one of those new typewriters. With the ball?'

'Christ, those have been around for years.'

'Not here, they haven't.'

'Here he comes, speak of the devil. My God, purple pants.'

'Hi, Mel, how's it going?'

'Not bad.'

'Well, you're on your own, starting today.'

'Yeah, it looks that way.'

'Coffee?' Jack asked.

'No, thanks. I just wanted to tell you, Mr. Bowman, that there's someone waiting for you in your office.'

'For me?'

'She says her name's Dr. Koltz.'

'Dr. Koltz?'

'So she says.'

'Well, well.'

'Hello, Jack.'

'Sue.'

'Surprised?'

'A little. Sit down. Let me take your coat.'

'You know, I've never been here. To your office.' Her tone was peremptory, but sensuous too.

'It isn't much. Sit down. Please.'

'Look, I don't want to keep you.'

'Don't worry. I'm not all that busy this afternoon.'

'You sure?'

'Sure. Sit down, really. You're looking . . . very well.'

'Thanks. It's the hair.'

'Nice.'

'They call me Fuzzball at the hospital.' She smiled abruptly, shyly grateful, pleased with herself. 'Dr. Fuzzball.'

'I like it,' he told her truthfully. Sue's cheeks, with short fringes of hair against them, had always seemed aggressively bony to him. Like sinuses turned inside out. The curls were an improvement. Her face looked out, intelligent and lively; he could imagine that such a face might excite ardour.

'So how's the great book coming?' she said, sinking into a chair.

'Not so great, as a matter of act. It seems' – here I go again, he

177

thought – 'it seems someone else is coming out with a similar book. Dr. Middleton – maybe you remember meeting Dr. Middleton at our place once – '

'How could I forget.'

'We had a long talk this morning, and he thinks . . . he agrees with me that maybe I'm flogging a dead horse.'

'The book you mean?'

'I haven't decided definitely, but it looks as though I might dump it.'

Sue's small eyes blinked once. 'Dump it?'

'Chuck it. Give it up.'

She filled her cheeks with air and let it out with a pop. 'Well, sometimes, Jack, I think maybe there are too damn many books in the world. I ask myself sometimes, who's going to read all those books?'

'That's the question, all right.'

'Jack, listen to me.' Her voice plunged an octave, going suddenly splintery. 'I know Bernie's at your house. I mean, he's got to be there. Right? It's the only place he could be. You know how I know? Because you're the only real friend he's got. So I brought a few things I thought he might need. His overcoat and some sweaters and socks and stuff like that. I thought I'd drop them off here and maybe you'd see that he gets them.'

'Sure. I'd be glad to.'

'And the apartment keys. My set.'

'You don't need them?'

'I moved my stuff out this morning. My clothes I mean. And the cat. I left everything else. Maybe you could tell him that, okay? Would you do that?'

'Okay.'

'You sound kind of dubious, Jack.'

'No. I was just thinking – of course it isn't my business – '

'*Tell* me what you're thinking, Jack.' She put her small elbows on his desk; her bare elbows reminded Jack of new potatoes, brown and cunning. 'You never say what you think. You never have. At least not to me. I suppose when you and Bernie get together, it's different.'

This struck Jack as an accusation. 'I was just thinking that this seems a little final. The handing over of the keys and all.'

'I know. Final and sad. Don't think I don't feel it, too.'

'It's just that I can't help thinking that, here you are – you've packed up Bernie's overcoat and lugged it way over to the Institute, up the elevator, into my office, just because you thought he might be cold. Doesn't that sort of suggest, well – what I mean is – doesn't that say something? That you must still love him a little.'

'Don't – '

'Doesn't it – ?'

'But I don't.' Tears filled her eyes. Her mouth was faintly blue. 'I don't want him to be cold, I don't want him to catch cold and get pneumonia. But I don't – love him anymore.'

'How can you be so sure of a thing like – '

'About a year ago Bernie and I went to a movie.' She took a breath. 'Woody Allen. One of the old ones. You know, we never go to movies. Hardly ever. In the middle of this movie I turned and looked at Bernie. He was eating popcorn. I looked at the side of his face, and I knew I didn't love him anymore.'

'Just like that.'

'More or less. I wish it wasn't like this, believe me. But it's gone. Part of it was Sarah, of course, but it's gone.'

'And you don't think it could come back?'

'No. It's all history now, as you and Bernie would probably say, something metaphysical like that. Isn't history your topic this year?'

'Yes,' Jack said, feeling obscurely foolish.

'Twenty years you've been at it, you and Bernie. Every Friday! Amazing.'

'Yes.' Jack couldn't tell whether she was taunting him or not. 'Not all that amazing – '

'I suppose you'll go on forever.'

'It's hard to say – ' He felt a flutter of panic.

'You'll be grey-haired, the two of you. Or bald. It'll be interesting to see if you become more abstract or less.'

'I'd think – '

'I'll put my money on less.'

'I'll let you know.'

'I'd appreciate that. Seriously, I would.' Her head swayed, willow-like. 'I suppose I'll worry about Bernie for quite a while. Do you think he'll be okay, Jack? Or not?'

Jack paused. Happiness was only a useful abstraction, Bernie had said to him once, the year they did Kierkegaard, 1972.

'Well, Jack, what do you think?'

'I think he'll be fine. Really. Of course I have to admit we haven't really talked about – '

'Of course not.' She was only slightly mocking.

'But, who knows, maybe our next topic will be – '

'Love? Now that would be interesting. I wouldn't mind eavesdropping on that.'

Jack smiled, and said nothing.

'You and Brenda,' Sue went on, 'you've been lucky. You've got a kind of context or something with the kids. How are the kids, anyway? I haven't seen them for ages.'

'Not bad. Growing up. Half the time they drive us crazy but – they're okay.'

'Great.' A chilly smile, determinedly bright. The question had been merely a polite inquiry.

'At the moment Rob's on a kind of strange kick. Maybe . . . well . . . maybe I should ask your advice. It's a sort of medical question.'

'Masturbation?'

'He's not eating.'

'Really. Why not?'

'He's fasting. For a week he says.'

Her face softened. 'Part of the hunger strike group?'

'No. He's on his own. A solitary fast.'

'Testing himself,' she nodded. Jack had never seen her so solicitous. 'Lots of kids do that. I wish I could do it. I've gained ten pounds this last year.'

'It suits you.'

'Thanks. Anyway, a week shouldn't hurt him.'

'He won't collapse or anything?'

'As long as he drinks plenty of fluids he could go for weeks. They even say it's good for people in small doses. Makes them feel like they've got control of their lives.'

'Maybe I'll go on a fast.' He was only half joking.

'You, Jack?' Her mouth pulled sideways. 'You make me laugh.'

'Really? Do I really?'

Chapter Twenty-Seven

'YOU SOUND LIKE YOU'RE SERIOUS, JACK,' HIS FATHER SAID. 'I can tell.'

'Yes.'

'But you haven't completely one hundred per cent made up your mind?'

'Not a hundred per cent. But almost.'

His father drummed on the table, thinking hard. His mother nodded in a kind of agreement, or was it sympathy? Jack could see the familiar pink spot at the top of her scalp where the hair parted. She worked her jaw soundlessly; her face was long and narrow. They were sitting solemnly around the kitchen table, the three of them, drinking coffee.

Jack had stopped by on his way from the Institute, something he seldom did. He had arrived at 5:30 to a strange scene.

'The door's unlocked,' his mother's voice had quavered, and he had come in to find his mother and father sitting side by side on the old red couch. His parents' living room was in semi-darkness; there was only a small table lamp on in one corner and the purplish flicker of light from the television. It took Jack a minute to make out what it was they were doing.

His mother's hand lay on his father's lap atop a white hand towel. His father held in his hand a small pair of scissors, manicure scissors, and with it he was cutting her fingernails. 'You want to turn down that volume, Jack?' his father directed.

'Sit down,' his mother sang, 'We're almost done here.'

Jack sat and watched. His father finished with the cutting, and then he filed her nails with an emery board, grasping each of her fingers in turn. And last, finally, he painted each nail with a coat of clear polish. The air in the small room filled briefly with varnish fumes; speechless, Jack watched his father holding the delicate Cutex brush and making deft feminine little strokes. It took him less than a minute – he must have been doing this for years, Jack thought – and then he screwed the top back on and set the tiny bottle on the coffee table, offering no explanation at all.

And why should he? Jack asked himself. His mother had suffered arthritis in her hands for several years now. It had been a long time since she'd been able to knit or even hold a pen in her hand. It stood to reason that she could not look after her own nails, although, oddly, this was something that had never occurred to him.

Later, in the kitchen, Jack explained about the book, and his parents listened silently.

'I can sure see what the problem is, Jack,' his father said. 'I certainly see what you're driving at.'

'It's not so much the work,' Jack explained. 'It's a question of needless duplication. And is it worth it in the end?'

'It's not like you *have* to finish it,' his mother said, pouring more coffee. 'Like there's no rule that says you have to.'

'That's for sure,' his father said. 'After all, you've got a good job, book or no book.'

'And, as you said, Jack, these things sometimes – '

'So what's to worry about?'

'I guess I was just afraid the two of you might be disappointed.'

'Jesus, Jack, you can always write a book later on. Pick some other subject, what the hell.'

'Plenty of time for that,' his mother said. 'You're still young.'

'Not that young.'

'The important thing,' she said, 'is to do what you want to do.'

'How d'you like this coffee your mother bought?' His father's face had a steamed, exuberant look of contentment.

'Good,' Jack said. 'Nice and strong.'

'Turkish coffee. Ever had Turkish coffee? Your ma bought it today at the deli. Remember that book I told you about? *Living Adventurously*? Try Turkish coffee, he says. For a change. Just one of his many ideas.'

'Have some more, Jack. I made lots.'

'Sure, help yourself, it'll put hair on your chest, as the saying goes.'

He hadn't thought them capable of this – this kind of diversion and easy forgiveness; and their concern for that crazy thing, that illogical and shapeless thing – his happiness.

He listened to their voices; first his father, then his mother, back and forth, back and forth, a kind of weaving. His mother's polished nails caught the light; she saw it too, held up her hands, spread her fingers, appraised them with mild approval.

Jack watched them; between them, it seemed, they'd made and kept countless bargains. And he had imagined them powerless in his absence.

Chapter Twenty-Eight

Historians, Jack thought, tend to see time architecturally, as something structured and measurable, something precise and non-transferable. A hundred years is a hundred years. Five days is five days is one hundred and twenty hours. The fact that five days can be sometimes short and sometimes long is immaterial and romantic. Which had always seemed to Jack to be one of the failings of the historical perspective. There was, he knew, such a thing as slow time and fast time. History was a double-souled art, a yardstick and a telescope.

It seemed to him by ten o'clock on Wednesday night, after Rob and Laurie had both gone upstairs to bed, that Brenda had been away for a hundred years, not five days. He remembered what she looked like, but he couldn't remember the sort of thing they talked about on midweek evenings like this. Public affairs? No, seldom anyway. His day? Her day? Children? Odds and ends? Gossip and resolution? Weather? What?

A little after ten there came tapping at the front door. It was Bernie, shivering with cold; Jack had wondered what had become of him.

'Here,' Bernie said, coming in, 'with my apologies.'

'What's this?'

'Your vest. Remember? You lent it to me last Saturday.'

'What's it doing all wrapped up?'

'Dry cleaners. Somehow – it must have been toward the end of the evening – I seem to have dumped about a gallon of wine on it. Red wine. Anyway, I think they got it all out.'

'I've got something for you, too. Here, in the closet.'

'My coat! How'd you get that?'

'Sue brought it to my office this afternoon.'

'Sue?'

'She thought you'd be cold.'

'She was always big on gestures.'

'And,' Jack paused, blinked, 'she sent the apartment keys, too.'

'Keys?'

'Her keys. She said it was all yours. The apartment, that is.'

'I figured it would work out that way.'

'I'm sorry, Bernie – '

'Don't be. It was inevitable.'

'Would you like a drink or something?'

'No. I'm heading back to the apartment tonight. Might as well start in on the new life.'

'Why don't you stay here tonight? You can have the sofa. There's no rush.'

'I think I'd rather get back. And actually I appreciate your letting me hang around here all week.'

'Why don't you stay just – '

Bernie sank into a chair. 'I've got something to tell you.'

'What?'

'Larry Carpenter came home today.'

'You said he might. Last night you said – '

'The story they're giving out is this. That last Saturday night he had too much to drink. After everyone went home he decided he'd drive down to the lake and see the sunrise, but passed out in the car, right after he turned on the engine.'

'Before he opened the door?'

'Right. You've got it.'

'What did I tell you about history, Bernie? You can't trust second-hand accounts.'

'We all need our fantasies, I suppose.'

'How did it go last night? When you saw him at the hospital?'

'That's what I'm working up to, Jack.'

'What do you mean?'

'Sit down, Jack. I can't talk when you're jumping around like that.'

'Okay. Is this better?'

'Yes.'

'Go ahead.'

'This is very difficult for me.'

'Shoot.'

'I've done something fairly rash. And stupid. I don't know how it happened, to tell the truth. I guess the whole disruption of this week sort of got to me.'

'Come on, Bernie. What are you trying to say?'

'I got – I guess you could say – carried away. If you know what I mean.'

'I think so, yes.'

'I'd do anything to undo this thing. But I can't think of a way. And it's you I really feel bad about, Jack.'

'Me?'

'I feel I've sold out on you.'

'What in hell do I have to do with it?'

'I'm trying to tell you – '

'Well, tell me then.'

'Me and my big mouth.'

'Come on, Bernie, spill it.'

'When I was talking to Larry last night – in the hospital room? Janey was sitting right there, of course.'

'Of course.'

'She was so anxious just for him to have a little company. She's been wonderful, really. She just wanted him to have some conversation. That's what she said earlier when we were driving over there. She wanted me to try and get his mind on something interesting.'

'Go on.'

'It was a little awkward at first. Until we started talking about you. I mean, you're our common link. If it hadn't been for you I never would have met this guy and been sitting there in a hospital room on a Tuesday night – '

'Get to the point.'

'So I told him I'd known you since we were kids.'

'Yes?'

'And that we'd gone to school together, all that, right through college. And that now we have lunch together every Friday.'

'And so?'

'Well, I told him what we talk about, some of the topics we've covered over the years. I could tell it was really getting his mind off his problems, listening to some of the things. He was really interested in entropy, he said, at one time. And he's read all of Kierkegaard.'

'What happened then?'

'Well, he was really responding. Asking questions and looking lively and so on. He kept saying how he thought it was really remarkable that we've kept this up all these years. Twenty years. Actually, Jack, you know, it is rather remarkable.'

'I know.'

'The thing was, he *kept saying* how remarkable it was. And how important it was to have that kind of – well, I forget the term he used – that kind of bond. Or something like that.'

'And?'

'And the next thing that happened was I opened my mouth and said maybe he'd like to join us this Friday.'

'Larry? You asked Larry Carpenter to come for lunch?'

'Don't ask me why. I did it, I just did it. Maybe it's a little more complicated than that but – '

'And he's coming?'

'I hate to say it, but yes. He was – I can only say he was elated at the idea.'

'Of going to Roberto's? Christ, wait until he gets there and sees the place.'

'Jack, I could cut my throat. One minute after I suggested it, I could cheerfully have cut my tongue out.'

'But it was too late.'

'But, look, it's only for one Friday. I mean, we're not committed to this guy forever, you know. I didn't say to come and join the club or anything like that.'

'We can sort of try him out, then?'

'It was just that – I'm not making excuses – but if you'd been there – '

'I would have done the same thing?'

'I don't know. Maybe not. I know you're not all that crazy about the guy. Anyway, I did it and I'm really sorry. I feel first cousin to Benedict Arnold, to tell the truth.'

'It's okay, Bernie. Maybe we need a little fresh blood after all this time. Maybe we're into a new era or something – '

'It was an act of charity. Well, maybe that's not quite the word.'

'Expiation?'

'That's closer.'

'You're sure you don't want a drink?'

'No.' Bernie stood up, stretched. 'I'm going home. You've probably got some work to do on the book.'

'I'm thinking of maybe bowing out to Harriet.'

'Why?'

187

'Oh, I don't know.' Jack tried for a light tone. 'I'd like to say it was an act of charity.'

'Charity?'

'Or maybe I just want out.'

'Well, if that's what you want – '

'I think it is. I think – '

'Sleep on it.'

'That's the first advice you've ever given me, Bernie, you know that?'

'Really? Is it really?'

'Good night, Bernie.'

'Good night, old friend. See you – Friday I guess.'

'Right. See you then.'

Chapter Twenty-Nine

A T ONE MINUTE AFTER ELEVEN JACK PHONED ROCHESTER.
The call went straight through. No cozy chats with Bell
operators tonight; the world was back to normal.

'Go ahead,' the operator said.

'Harriet?' Was that his voice, that craven squeak?

'You wanted to speak to Harriet?' A man's voice, solid,
educated, wonderfully baritone; Jack pictured a cask of a chest,
plentiful hair.

'Yes. May I speak to Harriet please?' Ah, that was better.

'I'm afraid Harriet's out of town.'

'Out of town?'

'She won't be back for another three days, I'm afraid. She's
out of the country actually. Is this long distance?'

'Yes. Chicago.'

'Perhaps' – the voice was polite, warm, solicitous, something
British about it – 'perhaps if you left your number Harriet could
ring you back when she gets in.'

'Three days, you said?'

'Yes. She's in Calcutta, but she's flying to Bombay tomorrow
and directly home from there.'

'Calcutta?'

'May I tell her who called?' Yes, definitely British.

'A colleague of hers.' An old colleague – the word colleague
came as an inspiration. Much better than old friend or fellow
student or –

'I see. Well, Harriet dashed off to check a few sources and so
on for her new book – '

'The book on Indian trade practices?'

'Yes.' A rising tone of wonderment. 'You know about the
book, then?'

'Yes, well, I saw the announcement. In the *Historical Journal.*'

'Good lord, has it been announced already? Her publishers
don't miss a trick.'

'Calcutta, you said? Bombay?'

'New Delhi, too, but that was just a bit of a holiday.'

'I see.'

'You in the same general field, then?'

'Not exactly. No. Not at all, in fact. I just phoned to offer my congratulations.'

'I'll have her ring you back.'

'Perhaps you could just convey my heartfelt – '

'Certainly, I'd be delighted to. Harriet will be pleased you thought of her.'

'If you could just tell her – '

'I'm afraid I missed your name.'

'Jack Bowman.'

'Wonderful, Jack. So thoughtful of you to call.'

'Not at all.' Not at all.

Chapter Thirty

BRENDA'S PLANE GOT IN EARLY THURSDAY EVENING. JACK drove to O'Hare straight from the Institute and arrived half an hour early.

Much of the snow in the city had melted. Brenda would never believe how bad it had been. How could such a weight of snow melt and run so quickly into the earth? The downtown streets were almost bare, returned overnight to their state of dry grittiness. The roofs of houses and factories under the warm, humid-looking moon were losing their loads of whiteness. All flights from the east, he was told, were on schedule.

When he had phoned home, Laurie had answered in a voice that was close to hysteria. 'I'm trying to get the living room cleaned up,' she shrilled. 'Can you hear that vacuuming in the background? That's Rob.'

'Don't worry too much about cleaning up.'

'But it's such a mess.'

'No one expects perfection.'

'I cut out my skirt today, Dad. In Home Ec.'

'Good.'

'Mrs. Frost likes the material you picked out. It suits me, she says.'

'That's great, sweetie.'

He waited for the plane, thinking how, early this morning, he had pushed open the door to Brenda's workroom. The air in the room had been settled and chilly; the door must have been shut since Brenda had left. This morning this room had seemed to him to be the only orderly place left in the house. The frame, the box of quilts, the flash and splutter of sun through the plants at the window, the confused cleanliness of tangled thread and cut cloth; a kind of slow-moving music rose from the stillness, each note spoon-shaped and perfect. Laid out on two chairs was Brenda's newest quilt-in-progress.

It was a whirl of colour, mostly yellows with a few slashes of violent green. The yellows churned from a boiling centre. He had never realized that there were so many shades of yellow. The shapes meant nothing to him. There was no recognizable image here, as there had been in Brenda's earlier quilts. This was a simple – no, not simple – a strange and complex explosion of light. Brenda is so *open*, everyone was always telling Jack, but this whirlpool had been laid down in cipher. What, he wondered, did Brenda think about as she sat in this room, hour after hour, sewing? Those hours existed and must mean something. He ran his fingers over the stitching. A thought slipped into his head, a silverfish, in and out, too quick to grasp. This kind of quilting, Brenda had told him, was called meandering, the meander stitch. It wandered across the fabric, following and reflecting the pattern, a dancing adhesive, plucking and gathering at the coloured shapes. But meander seemed the wrong word for it, for this stitching was purposeful and relentless, suggesting something contradictory and ironic that interested him; he would like to ask her about it. But he wouldn't. She wouldn't know what his question meant; he wouldn't understand what she said in reply.

He jumped as a light flashed on the ARRIVALS board overhead. Brenda's plane was down. She would be coming through the gate in a few minutes.

She had often met him at this same gate. From here it was a half-hour drive home; it always took longer than they thought because of the traffic. 'What's the best thing that happened to you when you were away?' she always asked. And then, 'What was the worst?'

It was a formula she had, a way of defusing the strangeness of reunion. First the good news and then the bad news. Or was it the other way round? He couldn't remember.

He had often noticed that these revelations in the car only skated toward truth, that the real best and worst news was inevitably saved until they got safely home. What they settled for on the way was something in between, some mild and humorous representation, the kind of anecdote that told well in the car, that eased them back on their first step toward familiarity.

The best news, he would tell her, was that Laurie might be on her way to thinness. She had told him over the phone tonight that she had decided to fast for a week. She planned to start on